TRUE COMPANIONS

RESIDENTS OF ASHWICK HALL BOOK 2

A REGENCY ROMANCE

JENNY HAMBLY

Copyright © 2024 by Jennifer Hambly
All rights reserved.
No part of this book may be reproduced in any form or by any electronic or mechanical means, including information storage and retrieval systems, without written permission from the author, except for the use of brief quotations in a book review.

The moral right of Jenny Hambly has been asserted.

www.jennyhambly.com

This book is a work of fiction. Names, characters, places and events, other than those clearly in the public domain, are either the product of the author's imagination, or are used fictitiously. Any resemblance to actual people, living or dead, are purely coincidental.

Many men and women have claimed to be descended from those who accompanied and fought beside William the Conqueror on his invasion of England. Only twenty men have been established as the Companions of the Conquerer, however. Of those, only fifteen have proven descendants. My characters are purely fictional and their names will not be found in connection to The Companions.

Ashton Manor was inspired by Haddon Hall. It is an amazing property situated close to Bakewell in Derbyshire, and well worth a visit if you are ever in the area. My house is not an accurate reflection of Haddon Hall, although there are several similarities.

CHAPTER 1

ASHWICK HALL, SEPTEMBER 1818

To the world at large, Ashwick Hall was an orphanage owned and run by Lady Westcliffe. Wealthy families frequently applied to her when they were in need of servants, as did small business owners who required apprentices. It was not generally known, however, that her philanthropy also extended to a few genteel ladies who had suffered some extraordinary circumstance.

One of these ladies, a young woman with midnight hair and eyes only a shade lighter, sat by the fireplace in the kitchen, examining a disreputable-looking cat. It had an angry cut on its nose, and several patches of inflamed skin where its fur had been pulled out.

"You really must stop fighting, Titan," she said, gently patting a damp cloth against his injuries.

The feline rubbed its head against her arm, purring.

"I don't know how you do it, Miss Lucy," the cook said. "He's generally a bad-tempered critter who won't let anyone touch him. If he weren't so good a mouser, I'd not have him in the kitchen."

Lucy began to spread some salve on his wounds. "Poor, Titan. You don't mean to be so disobliging, do you?"

The cook stirred a pot, giving a crack of laughter. "Try telling that to the new scullery maid. She tried to pick him up and got scratched for her pains."

"That is unfortunate," Lucy said. "But she should not have attempted to do so before she made friends with him."

She sighed, put down the cat, and washed her hands. "I am expected in the ladies' parlour, but I would much rather stay here. I'd like to try my hand at making the gingerbread cakes the children are so fond of."

"That's mighty kind of you, miss, and I'll admit I enjoy your visits, but if you don't mind me saying so, it's the ladies' parlour where you belong."

Lucy brushed the cat hairs from her dress. "I am not at all sure I belong anywhere, Mrs Lally."

She left the room on the words. As she passed the servants' stairs, she heard giggles and glancing up saw two small girls round the bend in the staircase. She knew them well as she often took them to the home farm to see the chickens and pigs. The latter were a particular draw for the five-year-olds as there were two litters of piglets recently born.

"Ruth, Lottie, you know you are not allowed to wander about unsupervised. What are you doing here?"

They looked at each other in dismay and shifted from foot to foot.

"If it is gingerbread you are after, I can tell you that cook has not made any, and even if she had, you must wait your turn like all the other children. If Mrs Cricks discovers what you are about, you will most likely go without the next time a batch is sent up."

The girls gasped. Ruth, who was the bolder of the two and undoubtedly the instigator of the plot, recovered first. "Oh, Miss Lucy, you won't tell her, will you?"

She repressed a smile. "Not if you promise not to sneak down to the kitchen again."

"We promise," they said in unison.

"Very well, off you go."

They turned and fled back up the stairs. Lucy chuckled and continued on her way. The girls were twins, and in some ways, they reminded her of herself and her sister as children. Abby had always been much braver than Lucy and had cajoled or bullied her into several escapades she would not have attempted on her own. She hesitated before the parlour door as she recalled the time they had tiptoed down to the kitchen not long before midnight. Lucy had quaked with every step, terrified the stairs would creak and they would be discovered.

Their father had paid one of his rare visits the day before, and within their hearing had complained about their appearance to their governess, Mrs Wardle.

"They are sallow of face and thick of limb, madam, and both have spots. Restrict their diet and exercise them more."

They had each had one spot on their chins and may well have been sallow as they were rarely allowed outside, Mrs Wardle not enjoying exercise. If their limbs had been a little rounded, they had certainly not been fat, however.

They had been relieved when he had left that morning, the day of their thirteenth birthday. They had not expected it to be marked, but cook had surprised them that afternoon by bringing a plum cake to the schoolroom.

"I know as how you don't approve of the young ladies eating sweetmeats as a rule, Mrs Wardle, but I thought we might make an exception on this occasion."

Mrs Wardle had allowed them the smallest sliver whilst helping herself to a generous portion.

"It is our cake," Abby had protested, eyeing it with longing. "And we will enjoy it."

"What you will do, Abigail," Mrs Wardle had said, her eyes frosty, "is go to your room and ponder the fate of impertinent girls who have neither manners nor looks to recommend them."

As Abby remained unrepentant, she had been denied her dinner, hence the bolt to the kitchen. The plum cake had been in plain view and a knife laid beside it as if it had been purposefully left for them. Abby cut them each a generous slice. It had been dense, a little sticky, and bursting with fruit, each mouthful requiring several chews. They had eaten barely half a slice when they had heard footsteps.

"Into the scullery, quick," Abby hissed, pulling Lucy towards a door.

She had barely pushed her in when Mrs Wardle arrived. Abby had had the presence of mind to pull the door almost closed before turning to face her.

"So, Abigail, you have decided to defy me once again. I thought you might."

"It was made for us, and I was hungry," she said sullenly.

"Well, that will never do," Mrs Wardle had replied, her tone unusually kind. "Please, finish your cake."

Lucy had let out the breath she had been holding as quietly as she could. There was silence for what must have been only a few minutes but seemed much longer to Lucy, and then her sister spoke again.

"Thank you, Mrs Wardle. I have finished now."

"You have not," came the steely reply. "I said finish your cake, and I meant it. You will eat the whole of it."

Cook had come into the scullery from the door at the other end of the room, put a finger to her lips, and gestured for Lucy to follow her, thus she had been spared the sound of her sister being violently sick some time later.

She sighed. Abby may have got her into scrapes, but she had always hauled her out of them again. Her hand tightened on the door handle. Apart from on one occasion, the most important occasion of all. Pushing the thought away, she entered the room, murmured a greeting, and sat near the other two ladies present. She picked up her sewing and began to ply her needle.

"Those stitches are crooked," the eldest occupant of the room said in a blighting tone.

Lucy raised her fine eyebrows. "I think your eyesight must have deteriorated, Flora."

A muscle twitched in the old woman's creased

cheek. "And what have you done with your hair? You look as if you have been pulled through a hedge."

Lucy yawned. "I believe it is the latest fashion."

A glint came into Flora's keen, blue eyes. "And you should not slump in your chair. Straighten your shoulders, girl."

Lucy smiled sweetly. "So that my assets might be shown to advantage?"

Flora harrumphed. "Indeed, what few you have."

Lucy shrugged. "If I have so poor a figure, there is little point."

The third occupant of the room, an attractive lady in her late twenties, laughed softly. "Very good, Lucy."

She smiled. "Thank you, Anne."

"Now, go to the pianoforte, if you will," that lady continued, "and play the Haydn sonata I requested you learn."

The assumed air of bored languor left Lucy, and she promptly stood and crossed the room. She settled herself on the seat, took a breath, and arranged her fingers over the keys. Ignoring the sheet of music in front of her, she closed her eyes and began to play from memory.

Flora and Anne exchanged a satisfied glance as Lucy delivered a faultless performance. A small smile hovered about her lips as she played the final notes. Her eyes remained shut after they had died away as if she still heard them. Flora nudged Anne gently. She sighed but nodded.

"That was adequate, I suppose. With a little more practice, I daresay you might become competent on the instrument."

Lucy's eyes opened, dismay hovering in them for a

brief instant before she smiled. "Thank you, Anne. I hope you will not be disappointed. I have heard, however, that a pupil can only become as accomplished as her teacher."

A low laugh came from the doorway. A tall lady with an abundance of raven hair and slate-grey eyes entered the room.

"A masterful put-down, my dear, if a little impertinent."

Lucy blushed. "But it is not real, Lady Westcliffe, only play-acting. It is not really me saying those things."

"Is it not?" Lady Westcliffe said. "No one has told you what to say, after all."

"That is true, but I would never have the nerve to utter such things anywhere but here."

Flora chuckled. "That is perhaps just as well, for you are undoubtedly an impertinent chit."

Lucy smiled ruefully. "I simply imagine what my sister would say." Her eyes dropped. "I am not like her, however."

"You are not and neither need you be," Lady Westcliffe said. "You need only be able to hold your own in her or anyone else's company. Now, I would like you and Flora to come to my study. There is someone I would like you both to meet." She glanced at Anne. "Thank you for playing your part in this morning's performance, my dear."

Anne nodded, rose to her feet, and smiled at Lucy. "Your playing was certainly not play-acting, my dear, and your words were patently untrue. I am a competent player, but you have a feel for the music that I, alas, will never possess."

A flush of pleasure warmed Lucy's cheeks. "Thank you."

"There is no need for thanks," Anne said gently. "I merely stated a fact. I agree with Lady Westcliffe that your ripostes to the various criticisms aimed at you this morning did come from some part of yourself. That your sister would utter them and you would not is to your credit." A humorous twinkle came into the lady's grey-blue eyes. "We all think things we should not utter, my dear. We resist because we do not wish to offend, be impolite, or appear unladylike. There are more subtle ways to establish our opinions, as there are times when only the truth will do. You have come a long way, Lucy. I saw that my criticism wounded you for a moment, but you overcame your sensitivity and gave me my own again."

"Yes," she said softly, "but I knew you did not really mean it."

Anne smiled. "Many people do not mean the cutting things they say for they know they are untrue. They are driven by some fault in their own character such as jealousy, spite, a need to make themselves feel important, or some other flaw. Remember that, for once you understand a person's weaknesses, you are both armed and shielded from their malice."

"Wise words, Anne," Lady Westcliffe said. "We must have a discussion about your future very soon."

Anne brushed a tendril of red-blonde hair from her brow. "Yes, I suppose we must. I have trespassed on your kindness long enough."

"Not at all. You know you are welcome to stay as long as you wish, but your talents are wasted in our schoolroom. We prepare our girls for the working world not to grace polite society, after all. I have a proposition to put to you that I think you might find interesting. It will keep for another day, however." Lady Westcliffe turned and went to the door. "Come along, Flora and Lucy, the lady who awaits us is not known for her patience."

Flora raised her pencil-thin brows as Lucy glanced anxiously at her. "Do not be ridiculous, child. There is no one more impatient than I, after all, and you are not afraid of me, are you?"

Lucy's lips tilted. "No, not anymore. You remind me of someone I knew as a child. She had a razor tongue but a kind heart."

She glanced over her shoulder, met Anne's encouraging gaze, touched the middle stone of the topaz necklace she wore, and followed Flora from the room. The grey-haired lady gestured for her to go ahead.

"Go on, child. Lady Westcliffe would not introduce you to anyone she thought you should not meet."

"No, of course not," Lucy said, pushing her natural shyness aside.

She could not imagine who would wish to meet her. Perhaps it was the latest lady their kind benefactress had rescued from some unfortunate situation, or perhaps Lady Westcliffe wished to test her, to see if she would shrink from a formidable person she was unacquainted with, as she had when she had first met Flora.

Her shoulders went back and her chin lifted a fraction. If so, she would not disappoint Lady Westcliffe or any of her fellow residents. For the past several months, they had all encouraged her to be less timid in forming and offering her opinions.

You are too milky by far, sister. Lucy drew in a deep breath, banishing her sister's voice. It intruded into her thoughts less and less as time passed. She would not ape Abby's words or mannerisms for this encounter. She would just be herself. Giving a little nod, she entered the study calmly, her mouth curving gently and an expression of polite enquiry in her eyes. They went first to Lady Westcliffe, who stood by her desk, a smile flickering on her lips.

"Drucilla! There you are, at last. I might be forgiven for thinking you were in no hurry to see me after all this time!"

Lucy's head snapped sideways, her heart beginning to thud painfully in her chest. A woman stood in front of the fireplace, her once-dark hair streaked with grey. Her twig-thin form suggested a fragility at variance with her strong chin and bright eyes.

"Lady Frampton!" Lucy gasped, the tears gathering at the back of her eyes and throat turning her voice hoarse.

Lady Frampton's rather hard features softened. "You have become as beautiful as your mother was. But why such formality? When last we met you called me aunt."

That was true, although Lady Frampton was not her relation. But it had been so long since she had last seen her that she had hesitated to use so familiar a term. She and Abby had just turned twelve when Lady Frampton had come to Talbot Hall to help care for her mama in the final month of her long illness. It had been a strange time. Her father, unable to bear the stink of death he said pervaded the house, had removed to London. The sadness of seeing their mother fading away had been leavened by the happiness that both she and Abby had felt when they had been frequently liberated from the schoolroom and permitted to spend their days in her and Lady Frampton's company. She had only seen her on two other occasions, the last on her fourteenth birthday when Lady Frampton had given her the pendant.

"Oh, Godmother, how glad I am to see you!"

She flew across the room and wrapped her arms about the lady. She was clasped in a bony grip for a moment before being lowered into a chair. A handkerchief was thrust into her hand.

"Mop your eyes, child."

"Honora!" Flora said. "I had no idea you were Lucy's godmother."

Lady Frampton glanced at her. "That is hardly surprising. Although we have been acquainted for many years, we did not become friends until we were widowed, and our circumstances outweighed the clashing of our characters. I, on the other hand, knew you were here, and it was the knowledge that you would watch over Drucilla when Lady Westcliffe could not that persuaded me to put off my return until I was fully well. Thank you."

"Are you sure you are well?" Flora said. "There is nothing to you. I thought Lucy would knock you down when she embraced you so fiercely."

Lady Frampton smiled wryly. "You underestimate me, and I think your memory is playing tricks on you. I have always been slender. You, on the other hand, have grown shockingly stout." Her eyes dropped to the vibrant pink gown embellished with an abundance of green ribbon and lace that Flora wore. "I see your taste is still questionable, and I think I may have overestimated your abilities. I was led to believe that you had stiffened my goddaughter's spine somewhat."

Flora bristled. "Give Lucy a chance—"

"Her name is and always has been Drucilla. I abominate the shortening of names. Even if I did not, surely Cilla would be more appropriate."

Lucy was, at first, a little overwhelmed by this exchange, but she suddenly realised that in a strange way both ladies were enjoying it. She gave a watery chuckle, mopped her eyes, and rose to her feet.

"Perhaps, Lady Frampton, but I have never liked my name, you know. I never felt like a Drucilla."

Her godmother regarded her in some surprise. "I am not sure that statement makes the remotest sense, but it is an opinion, at least."

Lucy smiled. "It makes sense to me, and perhaps that is all that matters. I much prefer Lucy; it is who I have become, and I would very much like for you to refer to me thus."

Lady Frampton's eyes returned to Flora, a twinkle of appreciation lightening them. "Perhaps I did not overestimate you, after all. However, although I might be able to bring myself to address my goddaughter as Lucy, nothing will induce me to call you Flora! I had, for a short time, a gin-swilling housekeeper who bore the name."

Flora gave a dry laugh. "I remember her well, particularly the occasion she fell over and landed face first in the cherry cake. Where do you think I drew the inspiration from?"

Lady Westcliffe had thus far merely observed the proceedings, but at this, she cleared her throat.

"That is, of course, up to you, Lady Frampton. I would ask, however, that you do not refer to Flora as anything else."

That lady gave a bark of laughter. "I cannot possibly refer to her as 'anything else'."

Lucy stifled a laugh.

"I think I may have done my job too well," Flora said dryly.

"Forgive me," Lucy said unsteadily.

"Flora," Lady Westcliffe said, "perhaps you would instruct one of the maids to pack Lucy's trunk, and it might be better if you supervised her."

"You may be sure I will," Flora said gruffly.

"Thank you, and then please return and take tea with Lady Frampton. I am sure there is much you wish to say to each other."

"You may be sure there is," Lady Frampton said. "Such as how long you intend to—"

Lady Westcliffe again cleared her throat.

"Ah, yes... well, that can wait until we are quite alone."

"Indeed," Flora agreed. "But I hope you have your purse with you. I believe I have won our wager."

"Flora," Lady Westcliffe said warningly, her eyes going to Lucy.

She need not have worried. Much of the interchange had escaped her notice. The moment Lady Westcliffe had asked Flora to oversee the packing of her trunk, Lucy had sunk once more onto her chair. She sat very straight, her eyes large in her pale face, and her fingers kneading the handkerchief her godmother had given her.

"I do not know if I am ready," she murmured.

"You have nothing to fear," Lady Frampton said quietly. "Your father has been dead for a little over a year now, and I will hear no nonsense about it being your fault. It was no one's fault but his own. Talbot's temper once roused was always ungovernable. He should have mastered it long before you and your sister grew to womanhood. What your poor mother suffered with him as a husband, I can only imagine for she never complained."

Lucy sighed. "Poor Mama. Papa used to berate her for providing him with two daughters rather than another son."

"Undoubtedly in your presence," Lady Frampton said dryly.

Lucy nodded. "When he sent us away after Mama died, I thought it was because he had no use for mere daughters." She gulped. "It was true enough when we were young… if I had known what he intended…." She trailed off, unwilling to revisit the events that had resulted in her flight from Talbot Hall.

"Talbot was an idiot and his behaviour, disgraceful. I have not seen your brother above twice in my life, but I do not believe he is cast in your father's mould, despite Talbot's best efforts. He arranged for you to come to me, after all, and although I would not generally approve of you travelling on the mail coach, I concede the case was pressing and it would not have done for you to put up on the road alone. Another thing in his favour, is that he has not insisted on putting your father's plans for you and your sister into practice."

Lucy's eyes rose, anguish in their chocolate depths. "Perhaps you are right. I hardly know him. What must he think of me?" Her lips twisted. "And how can I face my sister?" A half sob escaped her. "I have missed her so much, but I do not know if I can forgive her for what she did or ever trust her again."

Lady Westcliffe moved to her side. "Lucy. The upbringing you had was unreasonable and difficult for both of you. You are naturally quiet and shy, and it only made you more so. Your sister is a very different character. From what you have told me, she is bold, perhaps recklessly so, and the isolation you endured must have been torture for her. She did, however, try her best to protect you when you were children."

Lucy nodded. "Yes, it is true. It is why her betrayal was so devastating."

"I understand that, but you do not yet know what drove her to behave as she did. Things are often not what they seem. I brought you here because I knew you needed time to recover from your ordeal, and because I understood how distressing it would be for you to return home. I also feared that if you did not strengthen your character and learn to be yourself you would be forever in Abigail's shadow and vulnerable to the manipulation of anyone who sought to take advantage of you. I have kept you here so long because Lady Frampton's ill health kept her in France, but you are in no danger that I am aware of, and it is time for you to move on with your life."

Lucy blew her nose and summoned a wan smile. "You have been very kind, Lady Westcliffe, as has everyone here. It is true I never craved parties or gaiety as Abby did. I like the country, and if Mrs Wardle had not been more jailor than governess and had been kinder, I believe I would have been happy at Glasbury Heights, as I have learned to be here."

"That is because you have known little else. Your sister aside, you do not know what it is to have friends of your own age," Lady Frampton said. "Even I was not allowed to visit you above two times at Glasbury. I had every intention of taking you and your sister under my wing when you came out, however." Her lips thinned. "I should have known that you were not destined to have a season. If I had not had word shortly before your eighteenth birthday that my daughter was dangerously ill with typhoid fever, I would never have left the country, and if I had not also become so very ill, I would have returned long ago. It is a shame that the disease left me weak and prey to a host of other ailments."

"It was unfortunate that I missed you by only a few days," Lucy said. "For if I had come with you, I could have helped nurse you. I am so happy that you are well again."

"It is as well you did not, for you too might have become ill. Many in the nearby village did, and several died. Besides, although Guillaume's estate was returned to him, the chateau had suffered much neglect not to mention wanton vandalism, and only half of it is, as yet, in a fit state to inhabit." Her glance fell to the necklace Lucy wore and her voice softened. "You still have it then."

Lucy touched the pendant. "It is my lucky charm. I was wearing it when Lady Westcliffe found me on the steps of your house." Her fingers shook at the memory. "I had no idea what to do, for it was shut up and even if I had possessed enough money to return home, I could not have borne it." She gulped. "Is what my father said of my mother true? Is that why he was so unkind to her?"

Lady Frampton sighed. "It was most certainly untrue, as I told Talbot, but he would not listen."

Lucy nodded. "He said that we must be kept separate from the world to protect our innocence, that our sex was weak…" She broke off, unwilling to voice all the vile things he had said.

Lady Westcliffe sighed. "You must know that is untrue, my dear. Most gentlemen wish to protect their wives, sisters, or daughters from insult or danger because they know the weaknesses of their own sex and understand the world can be a perilous place. They do not generally do so, however, by allowing them no freedom and completely disregarding their need for society and friendship."

"Lucy," Lady Frampton said. "You know nothing of the world, and you cannot take your father as an exemplar of how gentlemen behave. You must form your own opinions on many things. The only way you can do so is to step into it. I will be by your side. Your brother has agreed that you may continue to reside with me for the present. We are to return to London, and you will reunite with your sister and brother under my roof. They are both very eager to see you."

CHAPTER 2

Mr Frederick Ashton did not possess a title, nor would he ever do so, although he had the honour of being related in one degree or another to several families who were so privileged. He had not made a noticeable mark on the world, having neither the capability nor desire to strive for greatness in any field. He had not excelled at school, finding himself unable to concentrate for any length of time, and this trait had followed him into adulthood.

He was fondly regarded by his friends and the more benevolent members of the *ton* as a harmless, good-natured soul, and by those of a less tolerant disposition as a buffoon.

If he had been a noted whip, a fine shot, or a neck-or-nothing rider to hounds, his critics might have looked upon him with a more forgiving eye. But he was no Corinthian, nor did he profess himself to be one. He cheerfully accepted his shortcomings and if, as occasionally happened, a gentleman displayed his irritation at his lack of understanding or perhaps accepted a wager and attempted to prick his good temper, they soon gave up. If they called him a nodcock, numbskull, addlepate or any similar insult, he would merely agree that he had no brains and take himself off.

It was universally agreed, however, that he was a gentleman. Unfailingly polite and possessed of a comfortable fortune, he was accepted everywhere. Indeed, he was a favourite with society's hostesses as he was amiable to all and could be relied on to dance with the wallflowers with the best will in the world.

His curly blond hair, guileless blue eyes, and slightly chubby figure had, to his chagrin, earned him the nickname Cherub, although few addressed him thus to his face. To his closest friends and family, he was simply Freddie.

It was a mystery to many that some scheming, matchmaking mama had not yet managed to secure so amiable a man for their daughter. It was clearly not any acuteness of intellect that had thus far protected him from any underhand machinations. Freddie was fast approaching thirty, however, and remained unwed.

His aunt, Lady Wirksworth, found Freddie's unshackled state no mystery at all. She had armed him against such situations merely by ensuring he understood precisely how a lady should and should not be treated and in what circumstances. If truth be told, it had not been any extraordinary prescience that had initially prompted her to instil these lessons in Freddie's head from a young age. She possessed firm opinions on the subject, believing that men often treated women with less respect than was their due, and she had been determined that her nephew would not be one of their number.

Her respect for her own sex, however, had forced her to acknowledge that in the unequal world in which they lived, a female might be forced to use underhand tactics to secure her future. She had no fault to find with this as long as it was not Freddie who was the object of their wiles. This had not worried her overmuch when the time had come for him to take his place in society, for she had the satisfaction of knowing that his upbringing would protect her rather naïve nephew from being lured alone from the ballroom to a secret alcove or a moonlit terrace.

Many had attempted it, believing it would be a simple task, but all had been thwarted. Mr Ashton merely opened wide his innocent blue eyes and shook his head, his response always a variation on the same theme.

"I hate to disoblige a lady, am honoured by your trust in me, but it is not at all the thing, you know. I am the last man to risk staining a lady's reputation. If you are suffering from a headache, I will fetch your mother, at once."

If their excuse was that they needed a breath of air, he would simply ensure that he gathered up a few others to join them on the terrace. One particularly foolish lady, a Miss Appleton, who was known to be in desperate need of a wealthy husband, had been driven to attempt fainting gracefully into his arms. Freddie had, at that moment, been leaning against a pillar and had just closed his eyes, becoming overcome by a sudden wave of tiredness, and she had landed in a very ungraceful heap on the floor at his feet. This had jerked him out of his semi-comatose state, and he had, of course, helped her to her feet, informed her that he was sorry she was not feeling quite the thing, and sent a footman to fetch her a glass of lemonade.

If this unfortunate damsel had had the sense to look at him pitifully and thank him prettily, his tender heart may very well have been wrung, but fortunately for Freddie, the ignominy of her situation had overcome her, and her shrewish nature had been revealed, not only to him but to everyone else present at the ball. Such an entertaining on dit had, of course, spread like wildfire, and as Miss Appleton, despite her pretty face, had failed to attract a suitor since this unfortunate event, many mamas had had the good sense to use the incident as a cautionary tale for their daughters. No young lady had ever tried to entrap Freddie in such a way again.

It was entirely possible, of course, that he might have been tempted to stray from the honourable principles so thoroughly instilled in him if he had ever developed a tendre for a particular lady, but as he had not, his fortitude had never been tested, and his honour and bachelor status remained firmly intact.

His two closest friends had married, however. Viscount Robert Kirkby had wed Freddie's younger sister, Lucinda, and Mr Oliver Carne had riveted himself to Winifred, the daughter of a wealthy merchant. He was fond of both ladies and had spent the last several months meandering between their homes, although Carne's estate in Cornwall was a long way from his and Kirkby's, which were in Yorkshire. Freddie did not mind the inconvenience in the least. He found the sway of a carriage soporific and discovered that he slept much better there than in his own bed.

He had just enjoyed an extended visit with the Carnes, only the letter he had received from his aunt, Lady Wirksworth, complaining that he seemed to have abandoned her, had prompted him to leave. He thought his sister might also thank him for returning and escorting his aunt back to Wirksworth Hall. Although she had begged him to bring their aunt to her, the nausea that had plagued her for months showing little sign of abating, he had an inkling that Lucinda might have become exasperated with the disruption to her household, and if she had not, Robert certainly would have.

As his departure coincided with Winifred Carne's younger brother's return to Harrow, he offered to escort him there before breaking his journey in Town. It was no hardship. He liked Adrian Emmit. The boy had been far too serious when he had first met him, but an idyllic summer in Cornwall fishing, swimming, and hacking over the countryside, seemed to have revived his spirits.

Freddie's eyes flickered open as he felt a hand on his arm. "Sorry, Adrian," he said with a wry smile. "I did not mean to drop off again."

A pair of dark eyes regarded him with amusement. "I haven't spent the last two months in your company without knowing that you never mean to do it. You can fall asleep anywhere. What I haven't yet worked out is why you do it. I don't know how you manage to sleep at night."

"That is the trouble," Freddie explained. "I wake up several times and have trouble dropping off again.

It has been the case since I was a small child. I cannot explain it, and neither can the dozens of doctors who have examined me. I have tried hot baths and milk before retiring, sleeping on my front, side, and even with my head at the foot of the bed, turning the bed in another direction, various herbal potions, and several other things. One doctor requested my nurse wake me every time I nodded off in the day so that I would go to bed exhausted, but even that did not work. That only left laudanum, but my aunt would not hear of dosing me with it."

"I am surprised it does not make you ill," Adrian said. "Or at least testy, but you are always so cheerful."

Freddie chuckled. "Why shouldn't I be? I get enough sleep, just not all at the same time."

Adrian glanced out of the window as they ascended a steep hill. "We're nearly there. Thank you for accompanying me."

Freddie thought the boy looked pale. It was hardly surprising that he was a little anxious. He had left the school more than a year ago under a cloud after getting into several fights. It was Adrian himself who had asked Oliver to see if the school would take him back.

"Do you want me to help you settle in?"

The carriage drew up by a red brick building.

Adrian shook his head. "No. I'd rather do it alone."

Freddie clapped him on the shoulder. "Well, keep out of trouble this time, won't you?"

The young man flushed. "Everything is different now. I thought my sister dead, and I was angry that the man who claimed to be our uncle had sent her away." His eyes fell. "I was angry with myself too. I had not been kind to her the last time I had seen her, and I should have stopped him. I knew she could not be mad."

"You were but thirteen," Freddie said gently. "And your permission was not sought. There was nothing you could have done. Besides, he told you it was only for a short while until she was well again. As you say, everything is different now. I thought you happy this summer and was surprised that you wished to return to school."

"I was… am happy," Adrian said. "I don't know if you will understand, Freddie, but I feel as if I'm in the way. It is not because of anything Oliver or Win has done. It is just that…"

"That they look at each other as if they are the only people in the room," Freddie finished for him.

Adrian grinned. "You do understand."

"Don't I just," Freddie said. "It's dashed embarrassing sometimes. Happy for them though."

"So am I," Adrian said. "Oliver treats me like a little brother, and Win is the best of sisters. I wish to repay them in some way. I want them to be able to consider only themselves and not have to think about me. They will have a child soon, and then they will never be completely alone again."

Freddie felt a rush of fondness for the boy, and he marvelled that a young man who had turned fifteen but a few weeks ago should show such consideration.

"Well, that is excessively kind of you, not to mention perceptive. I would never have thought of it. Haven't I been haunting Oliver's and my sister's doorsteps for the past several months? I expect they are all wishing me at perdition."

Adrian grinned. "I cannot speak for your sister, but I am certain that Oliver and Win thought no such thing. You did them a favour by keeping me so well occupied. You have been very patient and kind and are not nearly as bacon-brained as you proclaim. Why, I daresay if you managed to get a decent night's sleep, you'd be awake on every suit."

Freddie laughed. "Perhaps I might, but as it is unlikely to ever happen, we will never know. Now, off you go. I would like to reach Town before nightfall." He took the hand Adrian proffered and shook it warmly. "Put that brain of yours to good use, but don't forget to have some fun! If you have a few minutes spare, perhaps you might write to me to let me know how you go on."

Adrian nodded, opened the door, and jumped down from the carriage. Freddie watched him walk away. The young man's spine was straight, his shoulders back, and his step unhesitating. He nodded to himself. Adrian would be all right. When he disappeared from view, Freddie thumped on the roof of the carriage, and it rolled on.

Since his friend and brother-in-law, Robert, Viscount Kirkby, had stepped into his father's boots, he had made his townhouse in Green Street available to Freddie whenever he found himself in Town. He had sent word of his impending arrival, but he barely glanced at the house as the carriage swept by and turned towards the mews at the back of the property. Knowing that Robert only left the housekeeper and a couple of maids at the house when he was not in residence, he always entered unannounced via the kitchen. Despite the housekeeper's protests, he generally took his dinner there too with his valet.

"Nonsense," was his invariable response. "There's no point in opening up the whole house when I'm only here for a few days."

This visit would be no different, although he might have to extend it to a week or two. Keeping up with Adrian had had its effect on Freddie. He was fitter, stronger, and slimmer than he had been in years. It was imperative that he visit his tailor. He had no great interest in fashion, but he liked his clothes to be comfortable.

Dusk had descended as he had reached the outskirts of the town, and Freddie made his way quickly through the dark garden behind the house, an intimate knowledge of its layout allowing him to avoid stumbling into the shrubbery or fountain that lay at its centre. He went down the few steps to the basement and let himself quietly into the house. The dark here was complete and he frowned as he realised Mrs Purdy had not left the candle on the small table by the door as she usually did.

Putting his hand on the cold wall he followed the short corridor, turned a corner, and felt the hairs on the back of his neck rise as he saw a light under the kitchen door ahead. He shook off the prickle of unease, knowing it to be nonsensical, and strode confidently forwards. The door opened just before he reached it, and he was bathed in warmth and light. A maid holding a candle gave a little shriek.

"I'm sorry, Peggy," he said. "I did not mean to give you a fright."

"I was just bringing your candle, Mr Ashton," she said. "I would have done it sooner but we're that busy."

He glanced over the girl's head and saw the veracity of her words. The kitchen was a hive of activity.

"Lord and Lady Kirkby and Lady Wirksworth arrived earlier today. You're just in time for dinner."

His eyebrows rose. "Have my valet and baggage arrived?"

"Yes, sir. You're in the blue bedchamber as usual."

"Thank you," he said, stepping past her into the kitchen, where several more maids tended to various pots on the cooking range or fire.

Mrs Purdy broke off her conversation with the cook and sent him a distracted smile.

"Forgive me, Mr Ashton, I am a little busy. I am sure Crimble will be happy to show you to your room if he is not busy in the dining room. Dinner will be served in half an hour."

"There's no need for any fuss," Freddie said. "I know the way."

He made his way swiftly to the ground floor and hurried up the next two flights of stairs, the prickle of unease stronger than it had been before. Lucinda was expected to be brought to bed in only three months, and he could only imagine that some extraordinary circumstance would have persuaded Robert to bring her to Town. He felt a twinge of guilt. He had known that his sister was not well when he had left Yorkshire, but she had assured him that the doctor was not overly concerned and that she would rather he went to Cornwall and enjoy himself than watch over her. His aunt had agreed, telling him in no uncertain terms that he was surplus to requirements.

"Freddie, you are not needed. You know nothing about women in your sister's condition, and you are not only fretting Lucinda, but you are adding to Robert's burden. I have always acted as a mother to Lucinda, and I will ensure she receives the best care. I will write to you if there is any need for concern."

As the only concern his aunt had expressed in her letter was his abandonment of her, he had assumed all was well. As he reached the second floor, he did not turn towards his room but went directly to Lucinda's. He knocked a rapid tattoo on the door. It opened, revealing a dark, powerfully built man with serious, grey eyes. They travelled over Freddie, a glint of amusement lightening them as they returned to his face.

"Good evening, Freddie. I see your trip to Cornwall did you a great deal of good. I have never seen your face so brown or your stomach so lacking."

Freddie relaxed. Robert would not have even a hint of a smile on his face if Lucinda stood in any danger.

"Freddie? Is that you? Let him come in, Robert."

Viscount Kirkby stepped back and Freddie entered the room. His sister rose from her dressing table and turned towards him, a warm smile of welcome on her face.

"I am happy to see you, brother."

He was relieved to see a little colour in his sister's cheeks, but he frowned as he saw the delicate bones of her shoulders jutting from her porcelain skin. Her face and arms were very thin and in stark contrast to her swollen stomach.

"You look so frail, Lucinda."

She laughed. "How unhandsome of you to say so. You, on the other hand, look to be in prime twig. I vow you are half the man you used to be!" When he did not give his customary good-humoured chuckle she came to him, lifting her hand to his cheek. "Do not fret, Freddie. I am much better. The nausea has finally passed, allowing me to make the journey to Town."

"But why did you come?" Freddie asked.

"She came because I and her aunt wished her to see a physician other than Doctor Trayton. He is a good enough man in his way, but I was not convinced by his advice that she should subsist on a diet of fruit and vegetables and abstain from drinking anything other than weak tea."

Freddie pulled a face. "I should hope not. She needs feeding up."

"And that is precisely what the London doctor advised," Lucinda said. "I may enjoy a little meat and even a glass of wine with my dinner. You cannot imagine how much I am looking forward to it, so do not keep me waiting, Freddie."

CHAPTER 3

It was dark when Lucy awoke, and she felt a moment's disorientation. It was odd, she reflected, that even though it was pitch black she knew she was in an unfamiliar room. Or perhaps it was not so strange. She had discovered that every house had a different atmosphere beyond that created by its furnishings, as if the very air within it held some residue of its dwellers past and present. The air at Talbot Hall had seemed taut and hard, that at Glasbury Heights still and a little stale. Ashwick Hall had felt different again, lighter, despite the secrets it held, and it had been easier to breathe there. She was not yet certain of this house in Brook Street. It was not oppressive, but it felt a little heavy, as might be expected of a house that had been unlived in for some time. Or was the impression of heaviness a reflection of her own spirits? It was entirely possible.

Her brother and sister were expected to arrive in Town any day now, and she still did not know how she felt about that, or what she would say to them. Sighing, she left her bed and padded over to the curtained window. Pulling back the drapes, she gazed out on the unfamiliar townscape. The dull, pewter sky was pierced by chimneys, rooftops, and spires. Her glance fell to the row of houses opposite. They were not uniform in character, some possessing more ornate frontages than others, but all were gracious, well-designed buildings with steps leading up to the front door or down to the kitchens and cellars. Lucy noticed that the knocker had been removed from many of the doors, as had her aunt's when she had sought her aid.

That explained why the street below was so quiet. She was glad of it. It must be very different during the season, and she wondered how people could bear to live in such close proximity. She could imagine the empty windows full of curious eyes watching every move their neighbours made, noting what they wore, or who paid a morning call. She shivered. Such an existence did not recommend itself to her. She and her sister had always been closely watched, and even at Ashwick Hall Lucy had been scrutinised. That had not rubbed as much because she had known the ladies were motivated by kindness.

She turned from the window and went to her dressing room, her hand trailing over the gowns that hung there. They were of simple cut and design, as befitted a young lady not yet out, but were of good quality, if a little worn and outmoded. That worried her not at all as she had no wish to draw attention to herself. She selected a long-sleeved, white muslin gown.

"Good morning, Miss Talbot."

She gasped, clutching the gown to her chest. She

had not heard the maid come into the room. The young woman was pretty, with large hazel eyes, a sprinkling of freckles over her nose and cheeks, and chestnut hair. She appeared to be close to her in age and had an open, honest countenance. She dipped into a curtsy, her cheeks colouring.

"Forgive me, miss. I didn't mean to startle you. I've brought up your water, and wondered if you'd like me to help you dress? Lady Frampton has directed me to act as your lady's maid whilst you are here. I was out on an errand when you arrived, but I came to you as soon as I returned. I was mortified when I saw you had already put yourself to bed and were fast asleep."

"I was exhausted from the journey and am quite used to taking care of myself."

The young woman gave a small shake of her head. "That doesn't mean you should have to, especially with you being the sister of a baron and all."

Lucy's bedchamber was her retreat, a place where she would not be disturbed, and she was not sure if she wished another to have unfettered access to it.

"I understand it's not what you're used to, ma'am," the maid continued, "but you are to have a new wardrobe and you will need someone to care for it. You needn't worry that I'm not up to the task; Lady Frampton's woman has been instructing me on how to go on, and if it's all the same to you, I'd like the opportunity to prove myself."

Her words were softly spoken but her eyes earnest. It was clearly important to her, and Lucy did not have the heart to dash her hopes.

"Very well."

The maid's eyes lit up. "Thank you, Miss Talbot.

My name is Dolly Bell, and you may be certain I will not disappoint you. If there is anything you require, you need only ask."

"Well, Dolly—"

"Lady Frampton refers to her maid by her last name, miss," the maid informed her in a conspiratorial tone.

That was true, and she recalled that her mother's maid had also been referred to by her last name. It seemed stilted and odd to her, especially having spent so long at Ashwick Hall where she had referred to the maids as well as her fellow residents by their first names.

"Not that I mind what you call me, but I thought you'd like to know."

The maid was obviously keen to embrace the new status she had been offered, however temporarily. On the other hand, Lucy had been encouraged to assert herself, and she might as well begin as she meant to go on.

"Shall we come to a compromise? When we are alone, I shall refer to you as Dolly, but when anyone else is present it shall be Bell."

The young woman smiled gratefully. "Thank you, miss. Lady Frampton won't come down to breakfast before ten, but after I've helped you dress, I can bring you a little something from the kitchen if you would like."

"A cup of coffee will suffice," she said.

After she had washed, dressed, and drunk the coffee, she again wandered over to the window. The sky remained leaden, and without the benefit of a wide swathe of countryside to counter its effect, she felt hemmed in. She turned her head as Dolly came out of her dressing room, a number of dresses draped over her arm.

"I thought I might wash and press these, Miss Talbot."

Lucy recognised the maid's desire to prove her worth, but she knew that the task was unnecessary. Flora had ensured that everything had been packed in such a way that her dresses had emerged unscathed from the journey.

"There is no need." When the maid looked a little crestfallen, she added, "Although there is something else you might do for me."

Dolly regarded her eagerly. "Of course, Miss Talbot. Anything."

"I would like to go for a walk, preferably somewhere with a stretch of greenery. Do you know of such a place?"

The maid's eyes were understanding. "Is this your first visit to Lunnon, miss?"

"It is," Lucy confirmed.

"Then I know just how you are feeling. I'm country born and bred, and when I first came to the city, I felt as if I could hardly breathe. Hyde Park is only a short walk away, and I am sure it will lift your spirits."

Lucy smiled ruefully. "Is it so obvious that I am in low spirits?"

Dolly shook her head, the hint of a smile on her lips. "I'm the youngest of five sisters, ma'am, and my ma was a feisty one. She ran an inn, and we were expected to clean, cook, or serve as soon as we were able. If I didn't know how to read a mood, I'd likely get a clout on the ear from Ma or a slip on the shoulder from one of the customers."

Lucy was not at all sure what that meant, but it did not sound pleasant. "I'm sorry to hear that."

The maid laughed. "There's no need for you to feel sorry for me. It was all I knew until I went into service, and it weren't too bad. We only know what we know until we learn different when all's said and done." She turned and went back into the dressing room, her voice drifting back. "There's some maids as complain of the hard work expected in a fine residence such as this, but I've no patience with them. What more can you want than to be safe with a roof over your head, food in your belly, and a few pence in your pocket?"

Lucy admired her maid's pragmatic outlook. A slow smile curled her lips. Her godmother had said that she had never had a friend, and although she was certain it was not quite what Lady Frampton had meant, she had an inkling that she might have just found one.

They walked slowly, Lucy's eyes widening as she took in the grand mansions of Grosvenor Square and the lovely garden at its centre. Many of the windows were shuttered and they passed only the odd wagon or servant going about their business. When they had first entered the city, it had been very different; everything had been noise and bustle.

Even at their dawdling pace it took them only fifteen minutes to reach the park. It was also quiet, only a lone rider visible in the distance. Lucy breathed in the air, her eyes roaming over the expanse of grass dotted with trees that seemed to stretch for miles.

"This is much better." She paused, looking over her shoulder. "Dolly? Am I walking too quickly?"

The maid shook her head. "No, Miss Talbot. But now I've showed you the way, it is only fitting that I walk behind you. It is how things are done."

Lucy's brow wrinkled. Rules. How sick she was of them. Her life had been governed by them. You must always sit with your back straight, you must walk at a decorous pace and never run, you must not be overfamiliar with the servants. You must be meek and obedient. She grimaced. That was one rule she had needed no instruction in. She was no longer Drucilla, however, but Lucy.

"Dolly," she said, "I wish you to walk by my side. Who is there to see you, after all? I would like to know more about you and your family."

The maid regarded her a little warily, as if she had said something outlandish.

"But why?"

Lucy was not entirely certain. It was not like her to be overly inquisitive, nor was it like her to take to someone so quickly.

"I simply wish it. You are my lady's maid, and we will be in each other's company often, after all."

"Very well, miss," Dolly said, stepping next to her. "What is it you wish to know?"

"You mentioned you had four sisters. Have they also gone into service?"

"Dora has, and Molly and Rebecca married farmers."

"Do you see them at all?"

The maid's face lit up. "I spent some time with Molly and Rebecca, as Lady Frampton gave us a holiday when she went to France." She smiled. "They've nipperkins now, and I enjoyed looking after them. Dora works for a family in Norwich."

"And your mother and other sister?"

She shook her head. "Ma's been dead these past three years, and Jane ran away from home."

Lucy's heart lurched. "That must have been difficult for you. Were you close?"

Dolly's lips drooped. "She was the next to me in age, and I missed her sorely, at first. I understood though. After Pa died, Ma became a little too fond of the gin. Jane is very pretty, and the customers were always bothering her, and Ma was not always in a fit state to set 'em straight. Jane came to me the night she left and said she was coming to Lunnon to find work. She said she would write to me when she was settled and that she would try to help me find a position."

"And did she?" Lucy asked.

The maid sighed. "None of us ever heard from her again. I always look for her when I'm running an errand, but what are the chances of finding her in a city so big?"

"Very small, I expect," Lucy said. She nibbled her lip. "Do you feel as if she let you down?"

"Perhaps I did, at first," the maid admitted. "But we've all got to shift for ourselves, after all, and I'm sure there was a good reason. Maids work long hours, and perhaps she didn't have the time, or perhaps she did write, and Ma didn't give me the letters. She was mad as fire when she discovered she'd gone. I only hope as nothing bad has happened to her."

Lucy's throat tightened. It appeared Dolly was more forgiving than she. Had Abby worried about her? Did she miss her? Did she regret what she had done? Was there a good reason for her actions? She was jerked out of her contemplation as the maid screeched.

"Lawks!"

"Dolly! Whatever…?"

Lucy broke off as she discovered the cause of the maid's alarm. She blinked, hardly able to believe her eyes. A few paces in front of them sat a small, brown monkey. A scar cut through the whiskers on its cheek, and it appeared to be missing the tip of one ear.

Lucy crouched. "Oh, you poor thing. Whatever happened to you?"

"Be careful, miss," Dolly said quickly. "I've heard as monkeys can be mischievous, capricious creatures. It's a wild animal, after all."

Lucy observed the animal's scarlet waistcoat. "It may once have been, but it appears to have been domesticated." She reached into her cloak pocket and retrieved the apple she had brought to sustain her until breakfast. "Are you hungry, little one?"

It cocked its head, its eyes flickering from her face to the apple.

"Come," she said softly, "do not be shy."

It suddenly darted forwards and snatched it from her hand before retreating and biting into the fruit.

Lucy laughed. "Your manners leave much to be desired."

The monkey raised its head, issuing a high-pitched sound as if mimicking her amusement. As it did so, she observed a silver disc dangling from its collar. Leaning closer, she saw it bore an inscription.

"Jacko," she murmured.

The monkey stopped chewing and again cocked its head.

"You recognise your name," Lucy said. "How clever you are."

The creature threw away the apple, let out another high-pitched screech, and executed a somersault as if to show her just how clever he was.

Lucy clapped her hands and laughed. She turned her head as she heard feet pounding on the path behind her. A footman carrying a leash came panting up to them.

"Keep your distance, ma'am. He's unpredictable with strangers."

The monkey bared its teeth and screeched.

"Come on, Jacko," the footman said, advancing slowly towards the creature. "Your mistress will be distressed if she wakes and discovers you gone."

He knelt and opened his hand. A few almonds nestled in his palm. He dropped them on the path in front of him. The monkey considered them for a moment and then darted forwards. The footman tried to grab its collar, but the animal was too fast for him. It swerved, leapt into the air, and plucked the wig from his head, before darting towards a nearby tree and climbing it.

Dolly's stifled laugh earned her a look of reproof from the servant.

"I'm sorry," she said. "It was very naughty of him."

A reluctant grin twitched the footman's lips. "He's that all right. I swear, he'll be the death of me."

"Does he often escape?" Lucy asked.

"No, ma'am. He has the run of the park at home.

He's not been in a city before. One of the maids left a window open, and he must have decided to explore."

Lucy regarded the monkey who sat on a branch, twirling the wig on one finger, an expression that looked very much like a grin on its face.

"He looks very pleased with himself," she said.

The footman sighed. "He's that all right. He delights in tormenting me."

They turned their heads at the sound of a cantering horse.

"It's Mr Ashton," the footman said. "What a stroke of luck."

"Is it?" she murmured, regarding the approaching horseman with some misgiving.

"Not a doubt of it," the footman said. "If anyone can get him down, it'll be Mr Ashton. And what's more, he won't rake me down for something that I couldn't help. He's as nice a gentleman as you'll ever meet."

Lucy retreated a few steps. She was torn. Part of her wished to leave, and part of her wished to witness Mr Ashton retrieve the monkey. In that moment of hesitation, the decision was taken from her, for the gentleman in question pulled up and dismounted.

"I thought it was you, Thomas." His eyes rested on the footman's head for a moment, and then he glanced up at the tree as Jacko started chattering. "He has your wig again, I see."

"He was showin' off to these ladies," the footman said, indicating Lucy and Dolly with a sweep of his hand.

The man turned his head, and Lucy found herself being regarded by a pair of forget-me-not blue eyes.

The gentleman removed his hat, revealing a riot of untamed blond curls that made him look a little comical. "Good morning, ladies. I hope Jacko did not frighten you? He is generally harmless, you know."

He either did not hear the footman choke, or he decided to ignore the irregularity. Judging by the amused twinkle in his eyes, Lucy thought it was the latter.

"He startled my maid, but I enjoyed making his acquaintance."

Mr Ashton's smile lit up his face, and the anxiety of meeting a strange gentleman receded. "Did you? How glad I am to hear it. Now, if you will excuse me, I must coax him down."

Lucy watched with interest as he approached the tree. Mr Ashton let out a few short, piercing whistles, and made several gestures with his hands. Jacko appeared to understand, for he dropped the wig. Mr Ashton caught it, briefly examined it, and passed it to the footman.

"No harm done, Thomas," he said cheerfully.

The footman placed it on his head grumbling, "Not this time, perhaps, but this is my third new wig this year."

"Well, never mind. At least you did not have to bear the cost."

He turned back to the tree, pursed his lips, and whistled once. To Lucy's surprise, the monkey immediately climbed down. When it reached the ground, Thomas came forward, but when he attempted to attach the leash to the collar, it began to climb again.

"You know he doesn't like the leash, Thomas," Mr Ashton said mildly, going to his horse.

"But how else am I to get him to go with me?" the footman asked, exasperated.

"I suppose I shall have to take him."

Mr Ashton mounted his horse and brought it up to the tree. He plucked the monkey from the trunk and sat it in front of him. The horse skittered sideways, but when Mr Ashton leant forward, patted its neck, and murmured something into its ear, it calmed.

"Blimey!" Dolly said in an awed voice. "This is better than the circus."

Lucy laughed. "Are you not afraid of what people might say, sir?"

"No," he said simply, raising his hat. "Good day."

"I'd best be off too," the footman said.

"Wait a moment," Lucy said. "How is it that Mr Ashton can communicate with Jacko?"

"Oh, they're the best of friends. Mr Ashton saved the pesky creature. He came upon some gentlemen who had set the monkey to fight a dog twice its size. It was mortal injured—"

Lucy gasped. "Oh, that is horrible."

"It weren't a fair fight," the footman acknowledged. "And being as Mr Ashton's aunt makes a habit of collecting injured animals, he took it home. Must have been eight years since."

"How kind of him," Lucy said.

"I told you he was a nice gentleman." He glanced at the lowering sky. "I'd best be getting back, and I suggest as you do the same, miss. If I'm not much mistaken, there's going to be a downpour before long."

The rain began to sheet down as they reached the upper half of Brook Street. Dolly had insisted on walking behind her mistress when they left the park, but Lucy now reached behind her, gripped the maid's hand, and they ran the final hundred yards together. By the time they mounted the steps and Dolly rapped the door knocker, they were both gasping and laughing. They tumbled over the threshold in an undignified sodden heap when Shield, Lady Frampton's butler, opened the door.

"Lucy! Wherever have you been?"

She looked up, still chuckling.

Lady Frampton's brow cleared as she saw her goddaughter's smiling face.

"For a walk in Hyde Park," she said, handing her sodden cloak to her maid, and reaching for the ribbons of her bonnet. "We have had quite the adventure. There was a monkey who stole a footman's wig, and a very pleasant gentleman who talked it down from the tree and then rode off with it on his horse."

"Oh?" Lady Frampton said, the frown returning. "And who was this gentleman?"

"Mr Ashton."

Lady Frampton's brow once more cleared, and she gave a dry laugh. "I should have guessed. If anyone would do anything so cork-brained it would be Mr Frederick Ashton."

Although she was used to Lady Frampton's acerbic tones, Lucy did not feel that the gentleman she had met in the park deserved to be so maligned. "Cork-brained? I thought it was very clever of him, and the monkey seemed to know precisely what Mr Ashton wished him to do."

Lady Frampton gave a bark of laughter. "Then the creature has the advantage over most of Mr Ashton's human companions. He is a good sort, but…" She tapped the side of her head with her finger. "He hasn't much up here. Indeed, I expect a monkey is the perfect companion for him."

That was unkind. Although Lucy did not voice the words, her expression gave her away. Lady Frampton's eyebrows rose.

"Perhaps that was a little harsh, but I have known Mr Ashton for far longer than you. He is a distant connection of mine, as is his aunt, Lady Wirksworth. She is an eccentric and prefers animals to people, Frederick and his sister, Lucinda, excepted, which is hardly surprising as she has had charge of them since Lucinda was a babe and Freddie was still in short coats. However, you must make up your own mind on the matter. If Mr Ashton was retrieving an escaped monkey, Seraphina must be in town. We shall, of course, pay her a morning call. As she rarely comes to Town, she does not keep a house here. I shall send a footman to discover where she is staying." She held up a finger. "I am not best pleased that you spoke with him, Lucy. You should not speak to any gentleman you have not been introduced to."

When Lucy coloured, she laughed and pinched her cheek. "Never mind. Frederick Ashton is harmless, so we will say no more about it."

CHAPTER 4

Freddie walked through the dark, his eyes fixed on the sliver of light beneath the door on the opposite side of the room. He felt a little afraid but knew that it was important that he reach it. Each time he drew close, however, it seemed to recede into the distance. He tried to run towards it, but his legs refused to obey. The darkness felt suffocating, and his heart began to pound in his chest.

His eyes snapped open, the disturbing feeling that followed the dream remaining with him for some minutes as it always did. He sighed, turned onto his side, and closed his eyes, although he knew sleep would not come. He had suffered the same dream since childhood, although he had not used to be able to recall any specific details, only the fear of being alone in the dark. He found it curious that he never dreamt when he fell asleep during the day. Perhaps that is why he awoke so refreshed from his daily naps.

Accepting the futility of waiting for slumber to claim him once more, he slipped from the bed, lit the candle on his bedside table, and donned dressing gown and slippers. He stepped onto the landing, intending to go down to the library. He did not have the concentration for novels but had discovered, in recent years, a liking for poetry. Their shorter format and suggestive imagery enabled him to grasp the meaning more easily and to his surprise, he found that he could often remember the lines. He had bought several volumes when last he was in Town and added them to Robert's library, neither the viscount nor his predecessor apparently sharing his affinity for verse.

A faint light peeked underneath a door ahead of him. It appeared his aunt was also awake. He berated himself for a fool when his chest tightened. This was one door he could open. He paused outside it and knocked softly.

"You may come in, Freddie."

He opened the door, smiling a little sheepishly. "How did you know it was me?"

His aunt sighed. "Who else would be prowling about at this time of night?"

"True," he acknowledged. "I thought I should check if you had fallen asleep without blowing out your candles."

Lady Wirksworth peeked over the rim of her spectacles and put down the book she had been reading.

"I am not in my dotage yet, Freddie."

"No, of course not. Your mind is as sharp as ever, Aunt Seraphina."

He thought she looked a little fagged, however. Her faded blue eyes seemed edged with strain, and the creases on her face deeper. Caring for Lucinda these past months had clearly taken its toll. He walked towards the bed.

"Now that Lucinda is so much improved, would you like me to escort you back to Wirksworth Hall?"

"I would like nothing better," she said. "But I cannot face the long journey just yet."

"No, of course not. I didn't think. Try and get some sleep; you look tired."

Lady Wirksworth's eyebrows lifted, disappearing under the flounced edge of her cap. "Being tired and sleepy are two different things, as you well know."

He nodded and turned to go.

"Wait, Freddie," she said, her tone softening. "I do not believe you came only to snuff out my candles. Is something troubling you?"

He glanced over his shoulder. "Just the usual."

She patted the bed, and he turned once more and perched on the edge.

"Why do I have the feeling there is something more?"

He smiled at her fondly. "Because you have a nose for such things. It is just that the dream has changed recently."

Her eyes grew sharper. "Go on."

He told her of the light under the door he could not reach. "I know it sounds nonsensical, but I have the oddest notion that if I can somehow open the door the dream will cease to plague me."

Lady Wirksworth's brow creased. "An interesting thought."

He sighed. "But a pointless one. It is impossible to control a dream."

"Perhaps." Her frown deepened. "Have you

thought about what you wish to do with Ashton Manor now that old Mr Ramsey has died?"

That gentleman had leased his family home when Freddie had gone to live with his aunt and uncle as a small boy. He had several times asked to purchase it over the years, but his aunt would not hear of it.

"It brings in a respectable income, Freddie, and it may be that you will one day wish to live there. It has been in our family for generations, after all."

That day had never come, however, and he did not think it ever would. He hardly remembered his parents, and his aunt and uncle had long held that position in his heart and mind. Wirksworth Hall had been left to him, and he loved it. He could not imagine living anywhere but Yorkshire. He had no attachment to the house he was born in, but his aunt had grown up there, indeed, she had lived there until after his father had wed, and it stood to reason that she might be fond of the house.

"I saw Putnam today," he said cautiously. "Mr Ramsey's son wishes to return to Derbyshire. He has expressed a desire to purchase Ashton Manor, but he does not wish to lease it."

"It is understandable," his aunt said. "He grew up there and wishes to be able to guarantee that his children and grandchildren will also be able to do so."

"It is more his home than mine," Freddie said. "He has said he will not offer again, and that if I don't sell it to him, he will buy another property in the area. He has made a very good offer, far more than I could have hoped for, and given me two months to make up my mind."

He looked down in surprise as his aunt grasped his

hand. She was not naturally demonstrative, finding it easier to show affection to animals than people.

"I did not wish you to do anything you might regret, Freddie. Landowners do not generally sell their property unless they must."

She closed her eyes and winced. Freddie leant forwards.

"Aunt? Are you ill?"

She withdrew her hand and rubbed her chest. He noticed how paper-thin her skin appeared, clearly showing the bulging green veins underneath.

"Do not fuss. I should not have eaten the buttered lobster at dinner. It does not agree with me, but I am so very partial to it."

He relaxed, knowing this to be true. "Nor should you have had a second glass of claret."

"Nonsense," she said querulously, "I thought it would help me sleep."

He grinned. "It appears you were wrong."

"Do not state the obvious!" she snapped, before sighing. "Forgive me. I have had a lot on my mind. I too have been thinking of Ashton Manor. Selling your heritage is not something to be taken lightly, Freddie. I am of the opinion that before you decide anything, we should spend a little time there. Lucinda should also visit, or she will be able to tell her children nothing of where she was born."

Freddie jumped as he felt something touch his shoulder, but it was only Jacko. He often slept at the foot of his aunt's bed. The monkey crawled onto his lap and put his finger to his lips.

Lady Wirksworth chuckled. "He is right. Sleep on it, Freddie. We will talk again in the morning."

She stifled a yawn. "You may blow out my candles now."

He gently put the monkey back on his rumpled blanket at the end of the bed, did as she asked, and left the room. He went to the library, selected a volume from the shelves, and opened it at random. He stared unseeing at the page in front of him for several minutes and then closed it again. His aunt's suggestion had some merit, and yet he felt strangely reluctant to visit the house where his parents had died.

A portrait of them hung in the gallery at Wirksworth Hall, but he rarely glanced at it anymore. Not because he wished to deny them but because whenever he stood in front of it, he felt nothing but a sliver of unease and guilt that he could not even summon a measure of sadness. It troubled him that although his mind acknowledged their early demise to have been a tragedy, he felt so little. He told himself that it was hardly surprising as he had only been five years of age when they had been murdered by burglars, yet he somehow felt it was disrespectful of him.

Standing, he slipped the book back onto the shelf. He would go. Perhaps being there would stir lost recollections and enable him to feel more of a connection to his parents. The decision made, he felt something ease within him, and to his surprise, he slept the rest of the night through.

At breakfast, Lucinda listened with interest as Lady Wirksworth mentioned her idea. She showed none of Freddie's hesitation. She had always been a bold, adventurous sort of girl who knew her own mind.

"Why not?" she said. "I certainly do not think Freddie should even consider selling the estate without first paying it a visit." She glanced at him, a twinkle in her blue eyes. "There is still time for you to marry and have a nursery full of children, brother mine. You might wish to leave it to one of them."

Freddie laughed a little self-consciously. "I might, of course, but I think it an unlikely chance. I have never yet met a woman I wished to marry; besides, it would not be fair to inflict myself on anyone. I cannot imagine a woman looking at me like you do Robert, or Winifred does Oliver. Why should they when I've no brains and fall asleep in the middle of a conversation?"

Lucinda's eyes softened as she glanced at her husband before returning her attention to her brother. "Oh, Freddie. Brains aren't everything, and I am sure there are many women who would prefer their husband was loyal and kind, and you have both of those qualities."

He noticed his aunt slip her hand under the table, no doubt to feed her pug a slice of ham from her plate.

"You can say the same of most dogs, but unlike my canine friends, I have no desire to be patted on the head and told to run along by someone who would no doubt run rings around me. Besides, I am quite comfortable on my own, you know. Although if you like Ashton Manor, perhaps I shall keep it. I can always leave it and Wirksworth to one or other of your brood." He glanced at his aunt. "You wouldn't mind, would you?"

"No, Lucinda is as a daughter to me, as you are

my son in all but name. But I agree with your sister. You underestimate yourself, and you should never close your mind to the possibility that you might one day meet someone who will suit you. As you know, I did not meet Lionel until I was forty and he almost fifty. That being said, I never tried to push your sister into marriage even though she had several offers, and neither will I try to force your hand."

"I have more than ample means to provide for my own children, Freddie," Lord Kirkby said. "And I agree with Aunt Seraphina; there is time enough for you to find a wife."

Lucinda smiled prettily at him. "If you would allow me, Freddie, I am sure I could find a nice girl who would not try to take advantage of your good nature."

"No, Lucinda," Lord Kirkby said, his voice stern. "Freddie is quite capable of doing that himself if he so desires. A man must be allowed to make his own choices."

Freddie glanced at his brother-in-law in some surprise. He had half-expected him to agree that he should not inflict himself on a female, for historically he had teased him mercilessly.

Lucinda gave a tinkling laugh, seemingly unperturbed by her husband's warning tone and sent him a saucy smile. "So says the man who was oblivious of his attraction to me until I kissed him."

"You, my love," he said, his eyes grave but his lips twitching, "were a veritable minx. And I am shocked that you should admit such behaviour in front of your aunt."

Lady Wirksworth gave a bark of mirth. "Who do

you think put the idea in her head? I could not bear to see her waiting for you to notice her in that way any longer. Even the brightest of men sometimes do not see what is under their nose. And it is not as if she tried to entrap you; she merely hoped the infatuation that had followed her into womanhood would be resolved one way or another."

"And it was," she said, smiling warmly at her husband.

"Well, that is all very well for you," Freddie said. "But it's not as if a man can test if a woman is suited to him by kissing her. Not only is it disrespectful, but he'd find himself in the basket! He would have to marry her regardless of whether he liked it or not."

"That it is true," Lady Wirksworth said. "And I would never have allowed your sister to kiss anyone but Robert." She sent him a wicked look. "I knew he would not be constrained by such honourable principles."

The viscount laughed softly. "Thank you, Aunt, but I would remind you that it was Lucinda who kissed *me*. I assume what you really mean, is that you knew I, as an old family friend, could be trusted neither to take advantage of Lucinda nor to ever speak of her indiscretion." He rose to his feet. "As to your proposal that we visit Ashton Manor, as it is not far out of our way when we return to Yorkshire, I have no objection. It will be as good a place to break our journey as any other. We will not leave, however, for at least another week or so. I wish to be certain that Lucinda's health continues to improve." He cocked an eyebrow at Freddie. "Ready for that ride?"

To Freddie's knowledge they had made no such

arrangement, but he leapt to his feet. "Certainly, old fellow."

As they cantered through the park, Freddie turned to his friend. "Thank you for taking my part, Robert. Once Lucinda takes an idea into her head, it can be hard to shift it."

The viscount grinned. "I doubt I've succeeded in doing that, but I hope I may have prevented her from putting it into practice."

"Yes, well, that's what I'm grateful for. Apart from anything else, I wouldn't wish her to get up some poor gal's hopes."

"Yes, it was the poor young ladies I was thinking of."

Freddie chuckled, happy they were on familiar territory. "Thought you might have been."

They were approaching the Cumberland Gate when Freddie thought he saw a familiar figure bending over to observe some late-blooming flowers. She turned her head as they approached, and he knew he had not been mistaken.

"Do you know that young lady?" Lord Kirkby asked.

"I met her yesterday when Jacko escaped. She seemed quite entertained by his escapades."

"Then she is in a minority," the viscount said dryly.

"Oh, you cannot blame him for being out of sorts when he is out of his natural environment."

His friend raised an eyebrow. "I am all for sending him back to his natural environment. I am sure he would much prefer to be in the forests of South America."

"Well, you're out there," Freddie said. "It would be a cruel thing to do. He would not know how to go on at all. I don't hold with animals being captured and taken from their natural habitat, neither does my aunt. The climate does not always suit them, and they are often cruelly treated, but they cannot always be sent back. Jacko would not be accepted by a strange pack of monkeys. We are his family now, and he is perfectly happy when we are at Wirksworth."

"Then it is a pity Lady Wirksworth did not leave him there, along with her ill-featured pug."

"I say," Freddie protested, "so would you be ill-featured if you had your eye poked out." He shook his head. "I will never understand why some people are so cruel."

Lord Kirkby's lips softened, curling up at the edges. "No, I don't suppose you can. There is not a cruel bone in your body. I find it interesting, however, that whilst you will never ride with the hunt or frequent a cock fight, you have no qualms about watching two men beat each other to a pulp."

"You're out there, too," Freddie said. "I do not frequent those sort of bouts, only the mills where there are two well-matched opponents and a referee who ain't afraid to stop the fight if it becomes too bloody. That is sport and a fair fight, but the poor animals who are mistreated have no say in the matter."

The viscount laughed softly. "Well said, my friend. I do not think I have ever heard you express yourself so eloquently as you have today, both at the breakfast table and just now."

"I had more sleep than usual, and my brain seems a little less foggy, apart from that, both topics under discussion were something I knew about. Makes a difference you know."

"Clearly," his friend said.

Freddie pulled up his horse as the lady who had so approved of Jacko straightened and turned towards them.

"Mr Ashton," she said shyly. "I do hope Jacko was not quite in disgrace for his antics yesterday."

"No, I assure you," he said, raising his hat. "I see you were admiring the *Astrer-novi-belgii* and *Impatiens balsamina*. I'm glad to see the gardener who tends this part of the park had the wit to plant something which will flower into the autumn."

"Oh, is that what they are?" Lucy said, her brow wrinkling. "I am afraid I am quite ignorant of such things. I quite thought they were Asters and Busy Lizzies."

Freddie beamed at her. "Then you are not ignorant at all. That is precisely what they are, but my uncle always referred to flowers by their Latin names. It is the strangest thing, you know, because I was terrible at Latin at school, and yet I remember them."

"I do not think it strange at all," she said. "Perhaps you remember them because they mean something to you, or at least because they were taught to you by someone who did and who was perhaps patient and understanding." She sighed. "It is much more difficult to learn when your teacher is impatient or tries to rule you by fear."

A flush of delicate colour enlivened her cheeks, and the thought that she knew of what she spoke entered Freddie's head. As he was not quite sure how to respond to her assertion, he was pleased when

Robert spoke, at least, he was until he realised he could not answer his question.

"Would you do me the honour of introducing me to your friend, Freddie?"

"The thing is, I can't." He glanced apologetically at Lucy. "Forgive me, but I have forgotten your name. I do it all the time, forget names that is. I've a terrible memory."

As his new acquaintance glanced at the viscount, she took a step back. She reminded Freddie of a nervous animal who was unsure if it was observing a friend or a foe.

"Do not worry about Lord Kirkby. He is my brother-in-law, and a very decent fellow, I assure you."

Her eyes flicked back to Freddie.

"You did not forget my name, sir. We were not introduced. It was your footman who told me your name. I am Miss Drucilla Talbot. I am staying with my godmother, Lady Frampton, who I believe is a distant relative of yours and of Lady Wirksworth. She had intended to call on her, but her footman could not discover her at any of the hotels."

"I am pleased to make your acquaintance, Miss Talbot," the viscount said, bowing from his waist and raising his hat. "It is a fortuitous meeting, for I am happy to inform you that Lady Wirksworth is residing at my house in Green Street. You may inform your aunt that both Lady Wirksworth and my wife will be pleased to receive her, and you, of course, if you intend to accompany her."

"Lady Frampton, eh," Freddie said. "She is a formidable lady."

"You need not fear," the viscount said dryly, "I am

sure Aunt Seraphina will not allow her to ride roughshod over you."

"Oh, I'm not afraid," Freddie said. "But what is the point of being in someone's company if you cannot please them?"

"I could not agree more," Lucy said.

Freddie turned back to her. "You couldn't?"

Her shy smile once more tilted her lips. "No, and I would not blame you at all if you find yourself busy this afternoon, but I hope Jacko will be there."

Freddie looked dismayed. "I hate to be disobliging, but I do not expect he will be allowed in the drawing room."

"You may be sure he won't be," Lord Kirkby said sternly. "He has already ruined one set of curtains by climbing up them." His eyes swivelled back to the young lady. "Are you any relation to Baron Talbot?"

"Y-yes," she said hesitantly. "I am his sister. Are you acquainted with my brother?"

"Barely," he replied. "He is a few years younger than I, but I believe I met him and your father once a few years ago. I was not aware he had a sister. Is the baron also in Town?"

"We are expecting him and my sister any day," she said softly.

"I say, Miss Talbot," Freddie said, "are you feeling quite the thing? You have gone as white as a sheet."

"I am perfectly well, but if you will excuse me, I must return to my aunt's house. She will worry if I am out too long."

"Curious," the viscount murmured as they left the park.

"What is?" Freddie asked.

"One, that you never mentioned that you had met such an attractive young lady—"

"Well, dash it," Freddie interrupted. "Why should I have mentioned her? Come to think of it, I couldn't have if I wanted to because I didn't know her name. I suppose she is pretty enough, but to be honest, I never gave it any thought."

"No, I suppose I should not have expected you to. Having spent your life with a menagerie of the least attractive animals it has ever been my misfortune to meet, and yet you seem to be inordinately fond of, I should have known that beauty is not the first thing you look for."

"It is not," Freddie said. "And you should be glad of it. Did you not tell me only last year that pretty things come in deceptive packages?"

"Touché," the viscount said. "Again, you surprise me, Freddie. Your memory is clearly not as bad as I thought."

"Generally, it is," he said. "But you can hardly expect me to forget an episode so shocking. I believe the woman who tried to ruin Oliver, can't remember her name, is now the mistress of Bevis."

The viscount grinned. "Her name is Mrs Thruxton, and you are quite right. I begin to think that I may be guilty of underestimating you. The second thing I find interesting about Miss Talbot is that she is clearly old enough to have had a season or two and yet I have never met her or her sister."

"Perhaps the family don't like Town," Freddie said.

"And yet Miss Talbot is in Town, and her brother and sister soon will be," the viscount mused. "Perhaps Lady Frampton had the task of bringing them out, in which case, the Talbot girls had to wait for her to return from abroad."

"Well, that is too bad, but I expect they will get their turn this year."

"And the final thing that I find curious, is how the colour drained from Miss Talbot's face when I mentioned her father and brother."

Freddie shook his head. "If ever there was such a fellow. If her brother is the baron, it stands to reason her father is dead. Dashed insensitive of you to mention it."

"You may be right. She was not in mourning, however, so his death cannot have been of recent date."

"That does not mean she don't still mourn him," Freddie said. "She looks like a sensitive sort of girl. Why, she looked at you as if you were an ogre."

The viscount grinned. "I will allow that she is perhaps a little shy, but I cannot accuse her of being sensitive."

"Why ever not?"

"Because, my dear friend, she made it perfectly clear that she would prefer Jacko's company to yours."

CHAPTER 5

Lucy would have been mortified if she had overheard this comment. Her intention had been merely to convey to Mr Ashton that she would not expect him to be present when she and her godmother called. She had wished to spare him from an encounter that might prove embarrassing for them both. Lady Frampton had made it clear that she did not hold him in esteem, worse, that she thought him a buffoon, and as Mr Ashton appeared to be fully aware of her opinion, it seemed she did not try to hide it.

Lucy's desire to shield Mr Ashton from Lady Frampton's barbed tongue had soon been superseded by the anxiety she had felt when Lord Kirkby had mentioned her father and brother. She had not been prepared to answer questions about her family. Her aunt had assured her on their journey to the metropolis that Town would be very thin of company as parliament would not resume until January. Those with country estates would remain there to enjoy the shooting and hunting seasons, and those who were not so fortunate would not yet have returned from Bath, Brighton, or whatever other resort they had chosen to visit, especially with the weather remaining so mild.

"You will have the opportunity to reunite with your brother and sister away from the public gaze, acquaint yourself with London, and replenish your wardrobe. Then, perhaps we might visit Bath, which although no longer a very fashionable resort, will at least offer us some entertainment and allow you to flutter your society wings in a quiet way."

Having neither the courage nor desire to argue with her godmother, she had accepted her plan. It was her hope that Lady Frampton would be slowly brought to realise that she meant it when she said she did not wish for a London season. She had not fully realised, however, how awkward going into society might be. It was quite natural that people would feel curious about her, and how was she to deflect their interest without telling a host of lies?

When Lucy voiced her concerns to Lady Frampton, she merely waved them away. "You need only give vague replies, my dear, and you can use my illness to explain that you did not go much into society. There really is no need for you to worry."

But Lucy did worry. The thought that her new life was to begin with deceit troubled her, but what was the alternative? She could hardly speak the truth. No, she must maintain the fiction, not only for her sake but also for her family's. If the truth of her flight ever became common knowledge, she would be ruined, if she wasn't already.

She would even have to lie to her sister and brother, for Lady Frampton had insisted that she must maintain the fiction that she had spent the last two years under her wing.

"It was very good of Lady Westcliffe to keep you until I returned, and I can see that it has done you a great deal of good, but it would not do for her philanthropy towards genteel ladies in a difficult situation to become generally known. It would put her in a very awkward position. Only a few of my most trusted servants know that you did not travel with me, and that must remain the case."

Lady Frampton ordered the carriage to be brought round shortly before two o'clock.

"It is not far, but it looks like rain, and the wind whips about one so unpleasantly. I will not meet Seraphina looking a fright, not that she ever gives a fig about how she appears. I sometimes think, however, that she enjoys putting people out of countenance. Do not allow yourself to be intimidated by her; she will think more of you if you stand up to her."

Not so very long ago, this advice would have made her quake, but a long acquaintance with Flora and time spent in her godmother's company had, she believed, cured her of such craven impulses.

She reminded herself of this when she was shown into the drawing room at Green Street and announced. Lady Wirksworth did not rise from her chair, but a beautiful lady who bore a strong resemblance to Mr Ashton did.

"Please, do not stand on our account," Lucy said quickly, noticing how frail she looked despite clearly being with child.

The woman smiled. "I am perfectly well, I assure you, Miss Talbot. I am Lady Kirkby, and I am very pleased to make your acquaintance. I have been starved of company these past months."

"And food, by the looks of you," Lady Frampton said dryly. "I hope you have not been so concerned with keeping your figure that you have been eating like a bird."

Lady Kirkby's eyes flashed, and her hand went to her stomach. "No such thing. I was until very recently suffering from sickness."

"If you think I would allow Lucinda to do anything so foolish, you've more hair than wit, Honora," Lady Wirksworth said irritably. "And that, I may tell you, is something I never thought to accuse you of. I suggest it is you who should sit down; you look as if a puff of wind would blow you over." Her eyes turned to Lucy. "Come closer child and let me look at you."

Lucy took a few steps into the room and offered the old woman a curtsy, a self-conscious blush infusing her cheeks.

"Closer," Lady Wirksworth said. "My eyes aren't what they used to be."

As she neared her chair, Lady Wirksworth's unfashionably wide skirts rippled, and a short black muzzle emerged followed by a crumpled face. One large brown eye regarded Lucy appraisingly, the other was missing, only scar tissue remaining where it had once been. Lucy forgot her self-consciousness and dropped to her knees, holding out her hand.

"Oh dear. Whatever happened to you?"

"Lucy!" Lady Frampton exclaimed, clearly horrified by such a lapse of decorum.

She jumped, her face turning crimson. "I apologise—"

"Let her be," Lady Wirksworth snapped. "Why should she not greet him?" Her gaze returned to Lucy, and she said in a kindlier tone, "Some horrid youths attacked him with sticks, and when he lost his eye, his owner had no more use for him."

The dog's stocky neck emerged, and after cautiously sniffing Lucy's hand, he licked it. Lucy smiled and ventured to stroke the pug's head.

"His name is Jasper," Lady Wirksworth said. "And it appears he likes you. You are honoured."

Lucy raised her face. "I am very pleased to meet him, as I enjoyed meeting Jacko yesterday in the park."

Lady Wirksworth scrutinised her closely and then smiled. "Good girl."

"Come and sit with me, Miss Talbot," Lady Kirkby said. "And tell me all about it. Jacko is very naughty. My husband despairs of him."

"And you may bring your chair a little closer, Honora," Lady Wirksworth said. "Now you are here, you may as well tell me all your news. It appears France did not agree with you, for it is you who looks as if you have been eating like a bird."

Lucy smiled shyly and joined Lady Kirkby on a sofa. "Did Mr Ashton not tell you of the encounter?"

Lady Kirkby laughed, affection softening her clear, blue eyes. "No, but that is hardly surprising. He is a dear, but he has a shocking memory." A wrinkle creased her brow. "No, perhaps that is unjust of me. I do not think he would have forgotten you precisely, but he is not a gabster and is quite matter of fact. He has a simple way of looking at things that I sometimes envy. If you were not introduced and he did not think he would meet you again, he most likely put it from his mind."

Lucy's cheeks warmed. "I did not mean our meeting, but Jacko's antics."

Lady Kirkby touched her arm gently. "Forgive me, I did not mean to put you to the blush. He merely said that he had found him in the park and brought him home. He is not one for details. But tell me the whole."

Lucy did so, and they were both soon overcome with laughter.

"Poor Thomas has much to bear," Lady Kirkby said when she had recovered. "He is my aunt's footman, but he is tasked with caring for both Jacko's and Jasper's needs as much as her own. The former is forever stealing his wig, and the latter has been known to nip his ankles if he is displeased with him."

"He was perhaps a little annoyed," Lucy admitted. "But he soon recovered his temper." Her voice shook as she concluded her tale. "A-And then Mr Ashton rode off with Jacko on his horse, and my maid thought it better than a trip to the circus. Yet your brother did not appear to care in the least what anyone might think."

Lady Kirkby smiled at this observation. "He would not. Why should he? Neither my uncle, who preferred plants to people, nor my aunt, who much prefers animals, ever did. That is not to say that Aunt Seraphina is blind to the proprieties, and she made sure that we were both well versed in them." A mischievous twinkle lit her eyes, and she leant a little closer to her new acquaintance. "Especially Freddie and it is just as well, for several females have tried to put him in a compromising position, you know, although I am sure he is sublimely ignorant of it. But my aunt has so impressed upon him that he must not, under any circumstances, risk a lady's reputation by being alone with them, that it is quite useless of them to try."

Lucy's eyes widened. "I am glad to hear it. It is odious to try to entrap someone in so underhand a manner."

"I see that I have shocked you," Lady Kirkby said, smiling ruefully. "Am I correct in assuming you have led a very sheltered life?"

Lucy nodded.

"Well, then, of course you would feel that way. But you must realise that a lady's lot is a precarious one indeed if she does not possess an independent fortune, and few do, you know. But such a match would not do for Freddie."

As if summoned by the use of his name, the door just then opened, and Mr Ashton appeared carrying Jacko as if he were a child.

"Oh no, Freddie," his sister cried. "You must know that Robert has forbidden him to be brought to the drawing room."

"He won't do any damage, I assure you," he said. "Miss Talbot mentioned that she would like to see him again, and I thought I'd oblige her. Just for a moment, and then I will take him up to the attics. He seems to like it up there." He gave as much of a bow as he could with the monkey settled on his hip. "Good afternoon, Miss Talbot, Lady Frampton."

"Frederick," the latter said with some asperity,

"take that odious creature away, at once. If it is not just like you to do something so… so—"

Before she could find an appropriate expression, Lady Wirksworth intervened in a tone quite as scathing. "I would remind you, Honora, that you are in no position to give orders under this roof, and I do not appreciate you referring to Jacko as odious. He is, perhaps, a little spirited, a fact we must rejoice in after all he went through."

Jasper, who had retreated once more beneath his mistress's skirts, now emerged, springing up and adding his might to hers. Jacko, startled by the pug's sudden barking, leapt from Freddie's arms, raced across the room, and climbed one of a pair of very expensive curtains made from blue silk and fringed with gold tassels. When he reached the golden rod from which they hung, Jasper raced across the room and barked even louder. Jacko took a sudden leap towards the elegant chandelier that hung from the ceiling. He missed his mark, only succeeding in clasping one of the cut glass pendants that dangled beneath it. The chandelier began to sway, and then the pendant came away in his hand. He fell into Lady Frampton's lap, and when she screamed, he leapt off just as the pug raced by. He landed on Jasper's back. Understandably, the pug took exception to this and began to race around the room in an attempt to dislodge the monkey. And into this scene of chaos walked Lord Kirkby.

He quirked an eyebrow, saying softly, "Freddie, if you do not remove that monkey at once, I will not be responsible for my actions either towards him or you."

"There's no need to be in such a pucker," his

friend said, plucking Jacko from the dog's back as he rushed by. He took the pendant from the monkey and dropped it into his friend's hand. "I'm sure that can be re-attached quite easily. There's no real harm done."

Lady Wirksworth, also seemingly unruffled by this incident, called Jasper. He went to her, collapsing in a panting heap at her feet.

Thomas appeared at Freddie's elbow. "I'll take him, Mr Ashton."

"Yes, do that," he said, passing him over. "I would never have brought him down if I had realised Jasper was in here. I thought you'd taken him for a walk. In fact, I know you did, for I saw you leave."

The footman looked sheepish. "He didn't want to go very far. Indeed, he sat down and wouldn't budge, and I hadn't taken him above two hundred yards."

"You need to be firmer with him, Thomas, but never mind that now. Take Jacko up to the attics; he likes climbing amongst the beams up there, and I've made him a sort of swing from rope that he particularly enjoys."

"I hope it strangles him," Lord Kirkby muttered.

Lady Kirkby crossed the room and laid a hand on her husband's arm, a dimple peeping in her cheek and amusement lighting her eyes. "Do not be cross, my love. It was not Freddie's fault."

"I told your brother only this morning that I did not wish that creature in my drawing room," he said, exasperated. "And if you mean to inform me that we cannot blame him for his memory lapse, do not. I won't believe you."

Lucy rose to her feet, her attempt to look contrite quite ruined by the amusement still brimming in her eyes. "I am sure he did not forget, but if anyone is to blame, my lord, it is I. If I had not expressed a wish to see Jacko again this morning, Mr Ashton would not have brought him in."

Lady Kirkby grinned at her. "If only your maid had been here, Miss Talbot."

To the bemusement of all, both ladies once more became convulsed with laughter.

Lady Frampton, recovering her composure, said, "I feel as if I am in a madhouse."

"You have my sympathy, Lady Frampton. I know just how you feel," Lord Kirkby said dryly, although his expression gentled as he observed his wife wiping her streaming eyes. "It is good to hear your laughter again, Lucinda. I have not heard it near as often as I would like of late."

"Yes, I must admit Miss Talbot's visit has done me a great deal of good." She smiled at her new friend. "I do hope you will come again."

Before Lucy could answer, Lady Frampton rose to her feet. "Perhaps it would be better if you all came to us, and just to be clear, neither the pug nor the monkey is included in the invitation. Shall we say Wednesday evening for dinner?"

"Oh, don't go yet," Lady Kirkby protested. "Why, Crimble has not yet brought in the tea tray."

"Perhaps that is just as well," Lady Frampton said crisply. "Or I imagine there would be spilled tea and broken crockery on the carpet."

As they took their leave, Lucy found herself next to Mr Ashton. "Thank you," she murmured. "It was very kind of you to grant my wish, and I hope you will not long be in disgrace with Lord Kirkby."

"It was my pleasure, and don't give it a thought," he said cheerfully. "He never stays on his high ropes for long; there's no point as I never pay him any heed."

How she wished she shared his disregard for disapproval. She tilted her head. "Why don't you mind when you are in his black books? He is your friend and brother-in-law, after all."

"There is no point," he said. "We have known each other practically all our lives, and neither of us is likely to change now. He cannot help becoming irritated with me any more than I can help annoying him because he is a serious, knowing sort, and I'm not, but he don't mean anything by it."

"I see," she said, a little uncertainly. "Until Wednesday, then, Mr Ashton."

Lady Frampton ordered Shield to bring a tea tray as soon as they returned to Brook Street.

"We may enjoy a cup in peace, my dear. My nerves are quite shattered."

Lucy giggled. "Aunt Honora, how can you say so?"

A reluctant smile twitched her godmother's lips. "Well, if they are not, they ought to be. And I can assure you I was never so near going into hysterics as when that monkey landed on my lap." She covered her eyes with her hand, and her shoulders began to shake. "What a roaring farce! I did warn you that Lady Wirksworth was eccentric, but even I did not expect such a scene."

"I liked her," Lucy said, leaning in and kissing her godmother's cheek. "And I wish you were truly my aunt, for I like you very much too."

Lady Frampton laughed dryly. "But then you like one-eyed pugs and scar-faced monkeys."

"True," she said airily. "There really is no accounting for taste."

Lady Frampton chuckled. "Do I detect Flora's influence?"

"Perhaps." Lucy's brow wrinkled. "What is your relationship to Flora?"

A wry smile touched her godmother's lips. "I am constrained by Lady Westcliffe's and Flora's wishes, but I see no harm in admitting that I know her for you must already have guessed as much. We did not always get along. She is older than I, after all, and she can be censorious, but when we lost our husbands, everything changed." She sighed. "When you are fortunate enough to marry someone you hold in affection, you think your future happiness is assured. But things do not always turn out as you would wish."

Lucy glanced around the elegantly furnished drawing room. "But you were well provided for, were you not?"

A gentle smile curved Lady Frampton's lips. "Oh, yes. My lord left me this house for my lifetime and a generous jointure." Her voice hardened. "His successor was not pleased, for he is a grasping upstart. It pains me that he now has possession of Frampton Court. However, I have no one but myself to blame as I did not provide my husband with an heir." She shook her head. "I still miss Anthony; he was taken from me too soon, and no word of blame ever passed his lips, you know."

"I am pleased to hear it, for you could not help it,

after all. Could it be that you are lonely, Aunt Honora?"

She patted Lucy's hand. "When I spend any amount of time alone, perhaps, but that is a thing of the past for you are here."

"But I will not be forever. Why do you not hire a companion?"

Lady Frampton laughed dryly. "I have had three, and all of them were insipid and dull. Thank heavens I am past the age when it is thought necessary, for I do not have the patience for mild-mannered creatures without a thought in their heads but to please me, and who are forever cluttering up the place with yards of knitting."

Lucy felt a moment's pity for the three companions. "But, Aunt, surely that is the ideal companion?"

"Not for me. Anthony was the ideal companion because he would spar with me." She chuckled. "I rarely got the better of him as he was sharp of tongue and wit, but I enjoyed trying."

Lucy shuddered at the thought of such a relationship. "I hope you do not find me insipid and dull."

Lady Frampton snorted. "I believe there is little chance of that. You have too much of your mother in you, and I shall enjoy watching you come out of your shell."

Lucy's brow wrinkled as various memories of her mama came back to her; her laughing gently, holding her and Abigail close and whispering words of love and affection in their ears, of her expression changing to wariness when their papa came into the room before she sent them away.

"Mama was quiet, kind, and gentle," she said.

Lady Frampton sighed. "Your mother was all of those things and very beautiful. But beneath her quiet dignity lurked a sense of humour, a joy in the ridiculous. Before your father buried her in the country, I often caught her eyes and saw them brimming with laughter at some absurd thing someone had said or done. I saw the same expression in your eyes today." She laughed softly. "Your mama would never have thrown herself at the feet of a new acquaintance, however, to pet their dog, but I believe it would have amused her had she witnessed it." As Lucy blushed, Lady Frampton squeezed her hand. "Do not worry, my dear, as much as I might deplore such hoydenish behaviour, there was nothing more you could have done to earn Seraphina's regard."

CHAPTER 6

Freddie slept well again the following night and woke refreshed, his mind clear and his body possessed of a restless energy. He sprang out of bed as his valet drew back the curtains, eying the clear, blue sky.

"What time is it, Lipton?"

"Half past nine, sir."

Freddie's eyes widened. "Good grief! I must have slept for ten hours straight!"

The valet raised his eyebrows. "It must have been the first occasion in the eleven years I have been in your employ that I have ever known you to sleep the night through, sir. I am delighted for you."

Freddie chuckled. "What you mean, Lipton, is that you are delighted to discover everything just as you left it for a change."

A hint of a smile touched the valet's lips. "I will admit that it is refreshing to discover no random clothes scattered about after you have enjoyed one of your nocturnal rambles, nor even a dressing gown in a rumpled heap on the floor."

"Yes, well, do not be surprised or disappointed if it doesn't last, will you?" Freddie said.

"I doubt anything any longer has the power to surprise me, sir, and I am sure that once the novelty of discovering your room as I left it had worn off, it would become tedious and not at all refreshing."

"You are a good fellow, Lipton," Freddie said.

The valet bowed. "Thank you, sir."

Freddie was the last down to breakfast. The viscount offered him a sympathetic smile as he entered the room.

"Bad night, Freddie? You missed our morning ride."

"Sorry about that, Robert, and I've no excuse. Never slept better." He filled his plate from the various dishes laid out on the sideboard and took his place at the table. He did not pay much attention to the gentle chatter going on around him, his mind trying to grasp a nebulous thought.

"Freddie?" his sister said insistently when he did not reply to her.

He glanced up. "What was that, Lucinda? I wasn't attending."

She laughed softly. "I am quite used to that, dear brother. What I am not accustomed to is seeing that contemplative look in your eyes. Could it be that something…" She smiled. "Or should I perhaps say, someone, is occupying your mind? Could it be that a good night's repose has brought with it some clarity about your feelings towards…"

His eyes lit as he suddenly grasped the elusive thought. "That's it. Fancy you realising it before me."

Lady Kirkby's expressive eyes shone with sudden tears, and she raised her napkin, dabbing at them. "Forgive me," she said, her voice trembling with emotion. "I had no notion that carrying a child would turn me into such a watering pot. It is just that I am so happy that you have finally…" She broke off, wiping again at her eyes.

"Agreed to go to Ashton Manor," he helpfully finished for her. "But there's no need to cry about it. I had no idea it meant so much to you, Lucinda. If I had, I would have suggested it sooner. We could have spent the summer there. At least we could have if you hadn't been so below par."

She stared at him blankly for a moment, her tears evaporating. "That is what you were thinking about?"

Freddie swallowed a mouth of ham. "I thought we had just established that."

"Had we?" she said faintly.

He waved his fork at her. "I'll tell you what it is. Carrying that child has addled your brains into the bargain."

Lucinda regained her spirit, her eyes flashing as she said, "It has not. And how you… you of all people could accuse me of such a thing."

"I never thought to," he said, unperturbed by the dangerous gleam in her eyes. "I've always thought you a dashed clever chit, but here you are forgetting what we have only just spoken of."

"Freddie," she exclaimed. "I did not forget—"

"I hesitate to contradict a lady, but you did."

"I thought you were speaking of something else entirely!"

Freddie looked nonplussed. "Eh? What else would I be speaking of?"

Lady Kirkby just then intercepted a warning glance from her husband. She sighed. "Never mind. But if you were not thinking what I thought you were thinking, whatever made you look so? It was as if you had had a blinding revelation."

"I wouldn't go that far," he protested. "It was just a thought, and I might very well be wrong. I often am, you know. Only time will tell."

Oblivious to the two pairs of eyes regarding him with interest, he carried on with his breakfast. Inevitably, it was his sister who first cracked, saying impatiently, "Freddie. Are you going to leave us all in suspense?"

He winced. "I say, Lucinda. You should not screech like that at the breakfast table. Not at all the thing. It is enough to rob a man of his appetite." He sent his brother-in-law a reproving glance. "You ought to be stricter with her, you know."

Lord Kirkby raised a sardonic brow. "Two blinding revelations in one morning, Freddie? I am all amazement." He eyed the dwindling mound of Freddie's breakfast. "I am relieved to see, however, that the second appears to have fuelled rather than impaired your appetite."

Freddie grinned. "You've got me there. I awoke ravenous this morning."

"If sleeping so soundly makes you so hungry, we had best hope it is a temporary glitch in your habitual pattern or the new clothes your tailor is even now preparing will no longer fit by the time he has finished them."

Freddie wiped his mouth with his napkin and jumped to his feet.

"That reminds me, I have an appointment with him this morning. He had two coats he had prepared for someone else that only needed slightly altering, but as the fellow doesn't need them for a month or two yet, he said I might have them."

"Freddie," his sister said exasperated. "If you leave this room without telling me what revelation you had about Ashton Manor, it will be too bad of you."

"Oh, that," he said. "It is probably all nonsense, but it occurred to me that the moment I decided to go there, my stupid dream stopped plaguing me, and I've been sleeping like a baby. It is almost as if it was trying to tell me to go there, and the door I couldn't reach represented the house."

As he left the room, Lucinda glanced at her aunt, who had, to all outward appearance been paying scant attention to the conversation.

"Well, that was an odd thought, even for Freddie. It doesn't make the remotest sense."

"Perhaps that is irrelevant," Lady Wirksworth said. "Perhaps all that matters is that Freddie believes it to be true. The mind is a mysterious thing."

"And Freddie's more mysterious than most," Lord Kirkby said dryly.

He held up his hands as Lady Wirksworth skewered him with a glare.

"I apologise. You know I did not mean anything by it. I am really very fond of him."

"That and the fact that you appear to have made

Lucinda happy, are the only reasons I shall not raise several unsatisfactory episodes that would make you appear ridiculous."

Lady Kirkby looked intrigued. "Do tell, Aunt."

"Freddie was right," the viscount murmured. "I have indulged you too much, my dear." He appeared impervious to her dimpling smile, adding sternly, "He was also correct when he brought up your failing memory."

A hint of colour warmed her cheeks, and her gaze dropped from his.

"I see you have finally recalled that I told you in no uncertain terms that you were not to promote a match between your brother and Miss Talbot."

"I did not," she protested. "But when he brought Jacko down to see her against your wishes, I thought perhaps he liked Miss Talbot. And when I saw him with that faraway look in his eyes…"

"You put two and two together and made five. You goose, Freddie has always done precisely what he wishes regardless of what I think. He was just being kind, and he probably thought it would be as much a treat for Jacko as Miss Talbot."

Lady Wirksworth rose from the table. "You may be right, Robert, and I wish Freddie to make his own choice as much as you, but I will say this; I was very impressed with that girl. She had no airs or graces and had no idea of being anything but herself. He could do a lot worse."

"If you will forgive me for saying so, that is a rather large assumption to make on so little evidence. We hardly know her."

Lady Wirksworth snorted. "That can easily be remedied."

"Perhaps," the viscount allowed. "But as far as I can tell, she is more enamoured of a monkey and a pug than Freddie."

Lady Wirksworth smiled. "That is why I like her. And it is a very good start."

As she left the room, Jasper trailing in her wake, the viscount shook his head. "On occasion, your aunt cloaks her words in as much obscurity as your brother."

∽

Lady Frampton and Lucy sat in the drawing room discussing their plans for the day.

"We shall make a start on our shopping this morning, my dear. I refuse to take you to Bath looking like a dowd."

Although Lucy was not particularly enamoured of the Bath scheme, a little thrill of excitement ran through her at the prospect of this expedition. Mrs Wardle had never taken them shopping, choosing herself such things as she thought suitable from the few shops available to her in Glasbury, and arranging for a local seamstress to make up their dresses. This unsatisfactory circumstance had been ameliorated, however, by the few hours unsupervised freedom her absence had afforded Lucy and Abby. Not that they had been able to do much with it as Glasbury Heights had been some miles from the town, but they had enjoyed running through the house and grounds making as much noise as they wished.

She felt quite giddy as her godmother reeled off a list of the mantuamakers, linen drapers, haberdashers, and milliners they must visit.

Lady Frampton chuckled at her awed expression. "It will be quite the experience for you, I am sure."

"It will," Lucy agreed, "and I am very much looking forward to it, but will not such an expedition exhaust you? And think of the expense."

Lady Frampton dismissed her concerns with a wave of her hand. "Nonsense. It will give me great pleasure to spoil you, and I am much stronger than I look, my dear."

Their eyes turned towards the door as the butler entered.

"Lord Talbot and Miss Abigail Talbot."

Lucy was frozen into immobility for a moment, but as her sister stepped into the room, she rose so quickly that she became dizzy. She felt a steadying hand on her arm, and her godmother whispered in her ear, "No die-away airs, if you please. Flora would be most disappointed."

And then Lady Frampton was stepping forwards to greet her visitors. As she embraced Abigail, the tall, slender figure of her brother appeared, and their eyes met. His expression was grave but gentle as it had been the last time she had seen him. She felt colour infuse her cheeks and tears start to her eyes. She blinked rapidly and when her vision cleared, she found her sister standing before her. They stared at each other for a moment, their likeness so complete it was almost like looking in the mirror. Almost, but not quite, for her sister's eyes were brighter, keener, and harder. They softened as she stepped forward and embraced her sister.

"Cilla, oh, Cilla. How I have missed you."

As Lucy remained stiff and unyielding in her arms, Abigail took a step back. Her smile seemed a little forced, brittle even, and her eyes roamed over her sister's attire.

"I recognise that old dress. I am surprised you did not take the opportunity to update your wardrobe whilst in France."

Lucy only stared at her, stung by the criticism and amazed that she could talk of anything so trivial when so much that was unspoken lay between them. Fortunately, Lady Frampton stepped into the breach, explaining that her daughter's and then her own illness and painfully slow recovery had made shopping out of the question and that they had kept very much to themselves.

"I am sorry to hear you were so ill, Aunt Honora." Abby's eyes turned to Lucy. "Apart from worrying about our godmother, which I expect you did as you always were one to fret about the smallest of things – not that it was a small thing, of course – I imagine you were quite content, sister. You only ever needed a pianoforte or a book to be quite content. But it will not do for you to bury your nose in a book now you are in Town. You must go shopping. My own wardrobe needs a few embellishments, so perhaps we can go together. It will be such fun."

"You will, of course, join us, Abigail," Lady Frampton said. "Lucy and I had intended to begin this very morning."

Abigail blinked at this. "Lucy? Surely you mean, Cilla?"

Lucy felt heat infuse her cheeks, sure that her sister would perceive a slight in her preferred form of address. It was true enough that she had not wished to be addressed by the name only her sister had habitually used. Her brother broke the awkward silence, regarding her with solemn eyes.

"It has been two years since we last saw our sister, and it is only natural that her preferences may have changed." He smiled ruefully. "Not that I would know, of course, never having been privileged enough to know either of you but superficially when we were children. My knowledge of you is based only on the week you spent at Talbot Hall and the various things Abby has shared with me. I hope very much that such an unsatisfactory situation will soon be remedied, however, and I am sure I will enjoy getting to know you as much as I have Abby."

Abby raised her brows at that. "I seem to recall you telling me I was stubborn, interfering, and secretive."

Her brother's rather serious face made him look older than his four and twenty years, but as he laughed softly at this dry comment, Lucy glimpsed the boy he must have been.

"And was my admittedly unflattering description entirely erroneous?"

Abby's arch look was belied by the twitching of her lips. "Not entirely, I will admit."

Lucy felt a swift, unexpected pang of jealousy. In her absence, her sister and brother had apparently forged a closeness that had previously been hers and

Abby's alone. She wondered if her sister had told him the truth of what happened two years ago.

"I have never had the opportunity, Lord Talbot, to thank you in person for having the good sense to send Lucy to me," Lady Frampton said.

Lucy felt the colour drain from her face. It appeared the moment she had been waiting for had finally arrived, and yet she felt unprepared for it.

It seemed her brother was perceptive, for after a moment's pause and a worried glance at Lucy, he said, "I had been on the receiving end of my father's temper many times, ma'am, and I thought it best for all concerned that we give it time to cool. None of us could have imagined what was to follow. It may have been that my actions were unnecessary, as he was a changed man after his stroke. He never regained either his speech or his memory and was content to allow me to order things as I wished." His eyes returned to Lucy. "If I had not had so much to do and Abby had not assured me that you would not wish to return to Talbot Hall so soon, I might have been tempted to come to France and bring you home."

Stephen was dark like his mother and sisters, but his eyes were grey like their father's, and something in his stern expression as he turned them again on Lady Frampton reminded Lucy of that gentleman. She repressed a shiver.

"If you had written to inform me that my sister might be exposed to typhoid fever, I would certainly have done so, however."

"It was an unfortunate circumstance," Lady Frampton admitted, not missing a beat. "But whilst I was still too ill to write, the source of the infection was identified as emanating from a nearby well and the danger had passed. I saw no advantage in worrying you after the event."

For the first time, Lucy saw something akin to anguish in Abigail's eyes.

"We never received but one letter from you, sister, shortly after your arrival in Town, informing us that you were safe and well and were about to depart for France with our godmother. Surely, you must have known we would wish to know how you went on."

Lucy drew in a shaky breath, firmly repressing the anger that bubbled up from a place deep within her. In truth, she had written to her brother, not her sister, the words dictated by Lady Westcliffe when she had realised Lucy was still too upset to complete the task with any coherence. And afterwards, she had baulked at the idea of writing a host of make-believe lies about her time in France.

"I believe our godmother wrote when she could. I am not a great letter writer as I have never been in the habit of it, but I believe I might have replied if you had first written to me."

And offered an apology and an explanation, she added silently. She had the satisfaction of seeing a dull flush stain Abigail's cheeks.

"I did suggest she do so," her brother said. "But it seems you are as stubborn as each other. Abby would have it that you should be the first to write, and it seems you felt precisely the same way. I assumed there had been a falling out of some kind between you before… well, the events of that day. I have tried to discover the cause of the rift so that I might suggest a way to heal the breach, but Abby refused to enlighten me. Do you care to?"

Lucy felt her sister's eyes upon her and glancing at her saw a strange mixture of fear, pleading, and defiance in them.

"There is no time, now," Lady Frampton said quickly. "We have shopping to do. Will you come with us, Lord Talbot?"

"No, I thank you," he said. "I insist, however, that you send all the bills to me."

Lucy was stunned by Lady Frampton's interjection. She knew what had happened, and yet she did not appear to wish Abigail to be confronted with her actions. Judging by his frown, her brother was not overly pleased with Lady Frampton's dictate either.

"Lucy," he said gently, "I would like to take you for a drive in the park tomorrow afternoon, if that is acceptable to you?"

"Thank you," she murmured. "It is."

"Well, go on, Lucy," Lady Frampton said. "Run up and fetch your hat and cloak."

CHAPTER 7

Lucy went upstairs with lagging steps, the excitement at the shopping trip gone.

"Whatever is wrong, miss?" Dolly asked as she entered her chamber. "I heard as how your sister and brother had come. Are you not pleased to see them?"

"Yes and no," she said. "It is complicated."

The maid looked wistful. "I'd give anything to see my sister."

"Part of me is glad," she said. And it was true. She loved Abigail but hurt and resentment bubbled within her. "We are to go shopping."

"You'll enjoy that, miss, and whatever it is your sister has done, try to forgive her. Blood is blood, after all. I'll fetch your bonnet and cloak."

Lucy sighed. Blood was at the heart of the problem. She found Lady Frampton waiting for her on the landing.

"Ah, there you are, my dear. I can see you are not best pleased that Abigail is to come with us, and I am sure you would like to have everything out with her straight away, but I do not think that wise."

"Why not?" she asked. "Not only did she lie by omission, but she has clearly not informed our brother of the truth."

Lady Frampton sighed. "Give her a chance, Lucy. Things cannot have been easy for her either. I do not doubt that she loves you and has missed you greatly. I am sure that she regrets her actions, but was she not planning to save both of you from your father's plans before things were taken out of her hands?"

"Yes," Lucy admitted.

"And from what you have told me, she had but a moment to tell the truth, and she must have been as shocked as you. As no one but your father believed any ill of you, and he only for a few moments, what real harm was done?"

Lucy gasped. "Imagine if my father had not suffered a stroke, what then, Aunt?"

"Imagining what might have been is pointless. Now, come, let us go, and if you cannot be friendly towards your sister, at least be civil. All I ask is that you spend a little time with Abigail before you demand the truth from her. To do so in anger would be a mistake. You have had almost two years to paint her as black as you wish, give her at least a few hours to remind you of how things used to be between you, and then perhaps you will listen to her with a more reasoned ear."

Lucy reluctantly nodded. She would not repay Lady Frampton's kindness by making a scene.

"Good girl."

Although Abigail had claimed that she wished to

go shopping, when she learned of the Bath scheme, she paid scant attention to her own needs, but appeared to take great delight in helping choose suitable materials and fripperies for Lucy.

"Oh, is this not a pretty colour, sister? You will look ravishing in it."

"No, do not choose that reticule, for I have one just like it, and do you remember how we hated always to have everything the same? This one is far superior."

In short, her sister was at her most charming, and Lucy found herself softening by degrees as the day wore on, even though she was fully aware that was precisely what her sister intended. When Lady Frampton commented that Abigail had purchased only a fan and a few ribbons, her sister merely shrugged.

"Oh, I have dresses enough. It is not I who will be attending balls, and concerts, and going to the theatre, after all."

This was said without rancour, and yet the Abby Lucy remembered had always longed for parties and gaiety.

"Would you not like to?" she found herself saying.

Her sister shook her head and gave the brittle smile she had seen earlier that day. "Not anymore. Besides, Stephen needs me at Talbot Hall."

It seemed Lucy was not the only one to have changed. It occurred to her that Abby might be so happy for her to go to Bath because she did not wish her to intrude on the life she and Stephen shared at Talbot Hall. She put the uncharitable thought to the test.

"I am not particularly enamoured of the idea

myself. Perhaps I will come with you when you return."

Genuine warmth entered her sister's eyes. "That would be wonderful, but as it seems you have not been to any parties whilst abroad, I think you should enjoy yourself a little first."

"As do I," Lady Frampton said firmly.

As Lucy had no real desire to return to Talbot Hall nor to abandon Lady Frampton, who she was convinced would be lonely when she was once more alone, she did not demur.

They had just stepped out of a shop on Bond Street when Lucy heard herself being hailed.

"Good day, Miss Talbot."

Both she and Abigail turned towards the voice. Mr Ashton came to a halt halfway across the street, his eyes growing round. A blur of movement made Lucy turn her head, and she saw a curricle bowling towards him. She pointed her finger and shouted a warning. "Be careful, sir."

Seeing the danger, Mr Ashton hurried across the road. It was a close-run thing as the driver of the vehicle showed no inclination to slow down. He did, however, rudely call out as he passed.

"Keep what few wits you have about you, Cherub. I nearly had you there!"

"Better luck next time," he called back cheerfully before sweeping off his hat and executing a creditably elegant bow. "Good day, ladies. I apologise for standing there like a regular gapeseed, but I thought I was seeing double. You did not mention that your sister was your twin, Miss Talbot."

"Oh, did you speak of me, Cilla?" Abigail said, surprise and pleasure lacing her words.

"Only to say you were coming to Town," Lucy murmured.

"Allow me to introduce my other goddaughter, Miss Abigail Talbot, to you, Mr Ashton."

He bowed again. "Delighted to make your acquaintance, Miss Talbot, or should I say, Miss Abigail?"

"I am the eldest by ten minutes," she informed him coolly.

"Miss Talbot, then," he said, eyeing the two footmen who were weighed down by a number of packages. "I see you have been shopping."

Lady Frampton raised her eyebrows and said with some asperity, "Clearly. You should have given Lord Bevis a set down, Frederick. How do you expect anyone to respect you if you accept their rudeness with such complaisance?"

"I do not expect or desire him to respect me," he said. "If he or anyone else wishes to behave in such a fashion, let them, I say. Bevis and others of his ilk are no friends of mine, after all."

"I think it very wise of you," Lucy said quietly. "I detest brangling. And I expect it irritates the people who wish to demean you very much that you do not allow their rudeness to upset you."

He chuckled. "You have it, Miss Drucilla. It drives them wild. I won't keep you. I just thought I would let you know that both I and Jacko have been forgiven."

She smiled. "I am glad to hear it. He has been behaving himself, then?"

"More or less. He has done nothing to signify at all events." He bowed. "Have a pleasant day."

"What a peculiar gentleman," Abigail said as he strode away. "Is it his good temper that has earned him the name Cherub or that ridiculous mop of blond curls that cover half his face?"

"Both," Lady Frampton said thoughtfully. "And he used to be quite stout and his face rather round." She glanced at Lucy. "Do you know, until today, I had no idea that he was baiting his detractors as much as they him."

"Perhaps you underestimated him, Aunt Honora."

"We shall see," she said noncommittally. "Oh, good. Here is our carriage. I will admit to being a trifle fagged."

When they and their packages were safely inside, Abby asked, "Who is Jacko?"

She enjoyed the tale of his antics as much as Lady Kirkby had, and by the time they pulled up in front of Lady Frampton's house, the constraint between the sisters had eased a little more.

"I need to lie down on my bed for an hour or two," Lady Frampton said. "I will instruct my coachman to take you home, Abigail. Why your father insisted on keeping a house in such an out-of-the-way place as Charlotte Street, I do not know."

"Of course." She glanced at Lucy and then leant forward and grasped her hands. "May I come tomorrow morning after breakfast? We have much to discuss."

Lucy nodded. "Come before. Weather permitting, I usually take a walk before breakfast. Shall we say nine o'clock?"

By the time she had escorted her godmother to her room and satisfied herself that she was comfortably settled, Dolly had already unwrapped the majority of her packages.

"Well," she said, "you look a little more cheerful, miss, and I'm not surprised. You did find some pretty things."

The maid opened another box and gasped. "But this must be one of the loveliest." She lifted out a fan and opened it, displaying its finely carved ivory sticks and the silk leaf decorated with colourful sequins and exotic birds.

"There has been a mistake," Lucy said. "That is one of my sister's purchases."

The maid lifted a small piece of paper from the box and handed it to her. Lucy opened it.

I hope you like my gift, dearest Cilla, and will receive it in the spirit it is given. It is not meant to persuade you to forgive me, although I hope you will, but is a reminder of my love and affection. Abby

"Oh, Abby, you wretch," she murmured, sitting on the edge of the bed. "You are making it very difficult for me to remain angry with you."

This peace offering and Lady Frampton's words had their effect on her, and when she retired to bed that evening, she tried to look at things anew.

She had shrunk from being amongst strangers when she had first arrived at Ashwick Hall and had remained closeted in her room for weeks. She had been in a state of shock, and as it slowly wore off confused feelings of betrayal, grief, and shame had spun her into a deep melancholy. Her thoughts had turned dark, and she had laid the blame for everything that had happened to her at Abby's door, becoming by turns angry and then ashamed because of where those thoughts took her. Such horrid, surely impossible thoughts had begun to creep in that she had become frightened and finally left her room.

She had slowly inserted herself into the life of the house and blocked them out, and she had not permitted herself to visit the events of that fateful day again. Spending time with her sister that day had made her remember how amusing and kind she could be, and the creeping suspicion that she had been unjust was beginning to take root. Taking a deep breath, she allowed herself to remember.

They had been drinking tea in the small parlour allocated to them at Talbot Hall, discussing Mrs Wardle's recent departure.

"Why do you not look happy, Abby?" Lucy said.

Her sister drained her cooling tea and pulled a face. "Urgh! This is quite horrid."

"But not as horrid as Mrs Wardle," Lucy said with a small smile, hoping to coax Abby from the black mood that had been with her for days. "We are free of her, at last."

"Free from Mrs Wardle, certainly," she agreed. "But I am not sure our father will prove any better. He has not had a kind word for either of us. Not that I expected him to be kind, but perhaps civil, at least, now that we are grown women. He has only barked questions, and there is something in his eyes when he regards us that makes me uneasy."

"Perhaps we need not see much of him," Lucy said. "Our brother, at least, has been welcoming."

"That is true," she conceded. "In his serious, quiet way."

"And Mrs Hawkins and Collins can't do enough for us."

"Yes, we are fortunate, indeed, that our housekeeper and butler seem to think more of us than our own father," she said bitterly.

Lucy's heart began to pound as she recalled what had followed.

Their father strode into the room, and without preamble, informed them that they had been betrothed since infancy.

"Viscount Gaines will be paying his respects to you in the next week or two, Drucilla, and I hope that Anthony Fairbrass will soon follow. He is with the army still in France, but his father has requested he sell out and return home."

He frowned as they exchanged shocked looks.

"I want no missishness from either of you," he said sharply. "You may think yourselves fortunate that I have been able to arrange such advantageous matches for you. Gaines is heir to an earldom, and Fairbrass a baronetcy."

Abby gasped. "Think ourselves fortunate—"

"Yes, fortunate," he barked. "The regular reports Mrs Wardle has sent to me have been borne out this past week. One of you is both sullen and impertinent, and the other almost mute. You have only your beauty and virtue to recommend you." A rather ugly look came into his eyes. "Fortunately, that is all that is required. But I will take no chances. I will risk no slur being cast upon our good name. My doctor will examine you to make sure you are chaste."

Lucy had been speechless, but Abby had not been so shackled.

"Are you mad? How could we be anything else when we have been shut up like lepers at Glasbury Heights?"

"As Mrs Wardle has not succeeded in instilling a civil tongue in your head, I can put no faith in her. Since the time of Eve, women have been disobedient, sly creatures who tempt men to transgress."

Abby jumped to her feet. "We will not be so violated, nor have we escaped one prison only to be forced into another before we have had a chance to step foot into the world."

His eyes narrowed and his colour heightened. "You, my girl, will do as you are bid. You are the image of your mother, and her virtue proved to be an illusion."

Abby's cheeks turned as red as her father's, and her hands clenched by her sides. "Our mother was good and kind, and you shall not sully her memory with such slanderous lies."

"You know nothing!" he snapped, banging his fist against the back of a chair. "And you will submit to this examination. Mrs Hawkins will remain with you for the entirety of it. Now, go to your rooms!"

Lucy, terrified by his explosive temper, pulled Abby away. Halfway up the stairs, Abby halted.

"This is insupportable. We will neither submit to the examination nor being wed to complete strangers. I will search our brother out and see if his promise to stand our friend will hold. If he cannot change father's mind, he must help us run away and seek refuge with our godmother. Did she not say we were always welcome? Wait for me in my room."

Lucy had hardly stepped into Abby's chamber when she began to feel strange. She stumbled to the bed and lay upon it. Her rapid breathing began to slow, and her sense of panic recede. She felt strangely detached from herself, and her eyelids grew so heavy she could no longer keep them open. She came to herself too soon, the drowsiness that still engulfed her dissipating as she realised what was happening.

Lucy squeezed her eyes closed, forcing her mind to skip over the ordeal of the doctor's examination. His words of apology had made it no less awful nor had the kind words of the housekeeper.

They were summoned to their father's study some time later. Abby appeared as shocked as Lucy and was uncharacteristically quiet, clinging to her arm as they descended the stairs. They had found the doctor and their brother waiting there. Lucy had not been able to look at either of them.

"I am so sorry," Stephen murmured as he showed them to the two chairs set before the desk. "You do not deserve such treatment."

However suspicious their father's nature, he had been confident enough to closet himself with his bailiff whilst his daughters underwent their ordeal. Or perhaps he had conscience enough to wish to distract himself, although Lucy doubted it. When he deigned to join them, she kept her eyes downcast, her hands clasped on her lap so that he would not see the anger, humiliation, resentment, and shame swirling within her.

"Ah, Stephen, you are here, are you? Perhaps it is

just as well to have a witness. Gaines must then be satisfied."

"You do not mean to say he asked for this archaic measure?" he said, aghast.

"His father did at any rate, which amounts to the same thing. I do not know why you are so surprised. Our families pride ourselves on our ancient lineage, after all, and we would not have it tainted."

Lucy heard the trace of bitterness in his voice and risked a look at her brother. His jaw was set, and his lips drawn into a thin line.

"So, Doctor, let us know the results of your examinations. It is a formality, I am sure."

Lucy grasped her sister's hand. It felt cool and clammy and lay limp in her grasp.

"I went first to Miss Talbot's room, and all was certainly as it should be." He paused and cleared his throat. "However, when I examined Miss Drucilla, the results were inconclusive."

She raised her head then and quailed before her father's steely gaze.

"What do you mean, man?" Lord Talbot barked. "Either she is a virgin, or she is not."

"As I told you before, my lord, it is not so clear cut. I have not been called upon before to conduct such an examination, and the hymen is not always easy to detect. Also, its absence is not always an indication of… er… having fallen from grace. I cannot tell you with certainty that Miss Drucilla is a virgin, but neither can I tell you with any certainty that she is not."

Lucy looked at her sister, her eyes wide as she realised the import of what he was saying.

"Tell him," she whispered, nudging her.

But Abigail only shook her head. And then her father was before her, yanking her from her chair and shaking her until her teeth rattled.

"You have brought disgrace on this family, and you will pay for it, my girl."

Stephen had acted quickly then, pulling him off her, and suffering a blow to his jaw for his trouble. And then Lord Talbot had fallen to the ground, and with a swift order to the doctor to see to him, Stephen had bundled her out of the room and told her to pack her things.

"Is there anywhere you can go that is safe?" he asked.

She could hardly speak for the shocked tears rolling down her face, but he had somehow understood her.

"M-my godmother, L-Lady Frampton. I did not… am not guilty of…" was all she had managed to say.

"I know it. This is madness. Write to me to inform me that you arrived safely."

She had not had much to pack, and a bare fifteen minutes later had been bundled into the carriage with Mrs Hawkins who was instructed to buy her a ticket for the mail coach and put her on it.

Her hands went to her chest, which rose and fell rapidly. She breathed deeply trying to slow her racing heart and order her mind, but old confused feelings were roiling through her, and it was difficult. It was true that Abby had only a few moments to respond, but that did not excuse her silence afterwards. However much her brother said he thought no ill of her, surely a tiny seed of doubt must remain, as it must in the doctor's mind. What if a servant had been hovering at the door and overheard? They must have wondered at her sudden departure.

Whatever their godmother said, the fact remained that Abby had chosen to protect herself and, in the process, risked ruining Lucy. Of course, it was also unfair that her sister might have been ruined by so inexpert and unreliable an examination.

Lucy rolled over and her fingers went to her lips as a thought came to her. If it had to happen to one of them, might it not be better that it had been her? She had no wish to take her place in society. Abigail might say that she was happy to remain at Talbot Hall, but Lucy could hardly believe it. Did her sister feel so guilty that she was punishing herself by once more burying herself in the country and keeping house for their brother? She yawned, suddenly exhausted and her thoughts scattered. These reflections were pointless, and only the morrow would bring any clarity.

CHAPTER 8

Freddie returned to Green Street to find his family enjoying a light luncheon. He helped himself to an apple and a slice of cheese.

"I thought you might be wearing one of your new coats," his sister said, brushing some lemon cake crumbs from her fingers. "Were they not ready?"

"They were," he said. "But they are evening coats and will be sent round later."

"Are they very smart?" she asked.

"What an odd question," he said. "Any tailor who made evening coats that were not smart would soon go out of business."

"Oh, Freddie," she said, smiling. "Did you even look in the mirror?"

"Now you mention it, I did not. A coat is just a coat, after all."

"Beau Brummel would not agree with you," Lord Kirkby said dryly.

"He can't as he's holed up somewhere in France,

and as he's penniless, I doubt his dress is as smart as it once was."

"Or his tongue so quick," Lady Wirksworth said. "Clothes do not make the man, and he is a prime example. I never rated him above half. To run through the fortune his father left him so quickly was foolish indeed, and to call the Prince Regent fat to his face was the act of an imbecile, even if it was quite true."

"His success certainly went to his head," Lord Kirkby agreed. "But I cannot deny that he could be very amusing."

"You would not say so if you were one of the poor girls whom he raised an eyebrow at, thereby signalling his disapproval," his wife said. "I think it heartless and cruel that he should use his influence in such a way."

"He could not have done so if society had not allowed him to have so much sway over them," Lady Wirksworth said dryly. "I am afraid the *ton* is made up of a great many fools."

Freddie decided it was time to change the subject before his aunt launched into one of her scathing attacks on the state of humanity in general. He glanced at the viscount.

"Did you know Bevis is in Town, Robert?"

He raised an eyebrow. "I did not. I wonder what brings him here?"

"Tattersalls, I suspect. He was driving a fine pair of chestnuts I've not seen before down Bond Street. They were a bit fresh. He nearly ran me down."

"Bevis? In Town?" Lady Wirksworth said. "I believe it has been years since he has visited the metropolis. Well, if it was him, I expect he did not see you. He has hardly been able to see beyond the end of his nose for as long as I remember. He should not be driving at all, and so I shall tell him if I have the misfortune to see him."

"Although I would very much like to witness that altercation, I believe you are suffering a misapprehension, Aunt," the viscount said. "Which is perfectly understandable as you rarely come to Town and do not follow society news as a rule. Old Lord Bevis died last year. His son, who was formerly Viscount Gaines, is now the earl."

"I may not have realised the earl had died," Lady Wirksworth said querulously, "but I hope I know who his son was. There is nothing wrong with my memory."

"Forgive me, Aunt," the viscount said. "It is my memory that is at fault. You have so long lived in Yorkshire that I forgot that you must have once known the family well." His eyes narrowed. "The current Lord Bevis has his faults, but his eyesight is not one of them."

Lady Kirkby's eyes sparkled indignantly. "Do you mean he purposefully tried to run my brother down?"

"Don't get in a pucker, Lucinda," Freddie said. "He would not go that far. He just wanted to give me a fright, I expect."

"That is horrid," she said.

"His father was no better," Lady Wirksworth said. "Worms breed worms, I've always said so. Well, I'll put a flea in his ear, if I see him."

"As shall I," Lucinda said. "I have never liked him. He has always looked at me in a cold, mocking sort of way."

"I beg you will not," Freddie said. "I do not need

anyone to fight my battles for me. It will only make him worse. Robert and Oliver put several fleas in his ears when we were at school, and even a toad down his trousers, and it made not a ha'porth of difference."

"You never said anything of it to me, Freddie," Lady Wirksworth said, frowning.

"Nor to me," Lucinda said.

He chuckled. "A fine fellow I would have been to run home with tales to my aunt and sister. Besides, it was nothing. I rarely run into him these days and have my own way of dealing with him when I do."

"What you mean," Lucinda said, sighing, "is that you laugh the whole thing off as if it is a very good joke."

"It is as effective a way as any other," he said. "And better than having to call him out."

"I agree," Lord Kirkby said. "As you're not a good enough shot to pick your spot, you'd either kill him or miss him altogether, and you could not trust him to toe the line. You could, of course, plant him a facer, but that would end up with him calling you out. It is time he gave up these childish games, however."

"Oh, I daresay he will marry presently and settle down," Freddie said.

"Perhaps," Lord Kirkby said, "but until then, try to keep out of his way. You were not the only one he tormented at school, and some, who did not have Oliver or me to take their part, came off far worse than you. Do you remember poor Hopkins?"

Freddie's brow wrinkled. "Hopkins… now let me see. I think I've got it. Didn't the poor fellow fall from the dormitory window and break his leg?"

"That was the story that was put out, but he

claimed someone had pushed him. As he and Gaines had had an argument earlier that day, the viscount was suspected. He denied it, of course, and as neither Hopkins nor anyone else saw him do it, it could not be proved."

"Good God!" Freddie said. "He might have killed him. I did get off lightly considering he has always despised me so thoroughly. I've never understood why, but I begin to think he's unhinged."

Lady Wirksworth sighed. "This puts today's events in a different light. Perhaps it is time for some plain speaking. I am loathe to rake up old history that is better forgotten, but it seems that I must." She dabbed at her lips and set down her napkin. "I had hoped that time and distance would allow the resentment between our families to die down, at least between the younger generation, but it seems that was a forlorn hope. He dislikes you because he has been taught to do so, and having a mean-spirited disposition, he carries it to excess. I am afraid I am to blame. I was supposed to marry his father."

Lucinda gasped. "Aunt! You never mentioned that you had a suitor other than our uncle. What happened? Did he fall in love with someone else and jilt you? Is that why you swore you would not marry until Uncle Lionel changed your mind?"

She gave a crack of scornful laughter. "Love never came into it. The match was arranged when we were still in our cradles, although I did not know it until I was almost one and twenty." She gave a bitter little smile. "It came as quite a shock to discover my father considered me betrothed to Roger Gaines."

"It seems foolish not to have prepared you for the

union," Lord Kirkby said. "You may have formed an attachment to another."

"There was no chance of that. The Gaines were the only family of note that we were acquainted with for miles, and Roger Gaines was the only boy outside the family I knew." She blew out her cheeks. "What was foolish beyond permission, was to allow me to know him at all. He delighted in teasing me; in a cruel rather than a humorous way, I might add, and never made the slightest push to engage my affections. His worst crime, however, was to hang my cat from a tree when I made it clear I preferred her company to his."

"But that... that is..." Lady Kirkby trailed off, apparently unable to find words to express her feelings.

"The act of a madman," her brother put in for her. "Must run in the family."

"It is certainly an odd way to treat your future wife," the viscount said dryly.

"I can only assume he was as ignorant of our circumstances as I," Lady Wirksworth said. "I managed to save my cat, but my dislike of him became implacable afterwards. I felt sure he felt the same and would not come up to the mark, but when he came down, or rather, was sent down from university, he came to pay his addresses. I refused to marry him, of course."

"I should hope so," Freddie said. "Surely your father could not have expected you to marry a man who would hang a cat?"

"That, my dear Freddie, was merely a schoolboy prank, inadvisable perhaps, but the result of high spirits not any inherent wickedness."

"Poppycock!"

"Quite. We were sixteen when it happened, and I made my feelings abundantly clear. I suspect that is why my father did not inform me where my future lay until the last minute. He probably thought time would lessen the impact of Gaines' actions. A foolish notion."

"You have never spoken much of our grandparents," Lucinda said. "But from the few things you have let drop, I gained the impression that our grandfather was a rather forbidding man. It cannot have been easy for you to defy him. Did your mother offer you her support?"

A sad smile tilted Lady Wirksworth's lips. "My mother was a timid creature who jumped at shadows and could only weep and wail and do my father's bidding."

Lady Kirkby stroked her round belly, unable to comprehend how a mother could not do everything in her power to protect her child. "Was the pressure he brought to bear on you very terrible?"

"He tried to cajole and bully me by turns. He was obsessed with genealogy—"

"Many families are interested in their antecedents. We have a family Bible," Lord Kirkby said.

"I did not say interested, Kirkby, I said obsessed. He, and several of his friends believed themselves to be what they called the true *Companions of the Conqueror*, claiming that their ancestors fought with him when he came to England. It is a very difficult thing to prove, of course, especially as their names are not mentioned in the few remaining documents from the period. Family records only go back so far, and not every generation is meticulous in keeping them, and others are lost by carelessness, fire, or some other disaster. However, my father gathered what evidence he could and was admitted into their ranks soon after he finished university, I believe.

"They hatched a scheme between them to allow their sons only to marry the daughters of members of this club." Her lips tightened. "When I thought my father had finally accepted that I would not be moved, he resorted to deceit of the most heinous kind."

She said nothing more, seemingly lost in her recollections. The tension in the room was palpable, but Lord Kirkby broke it. "I believe that means you are descended from a worm, Freddie, ergo, you must be a worm."

"Robert!" Lucinda protested. "That jest is ill-timed and unwarranted." She turned to her aunt. "Forgive him, Aunt Seraphina, and finish the story, do."

A wry smile twisted that lady's lips. "I do forgive him, for it is a timely reminder that I have already said too much on that head. Fate made a timely, if rather final intervention. Whilst trying to impress Roger's father, mine took a fence he should never have attempted and broke his neck. Soon afterwards, I turned one and twenty. Your father, who was some ten years younger than I, grew up with my and my mother's guidance. We had no more to do with the Gaines family until after your father wed."

"What happened then?" Lucinda asked, her eyes wide.

"I think I can guess," her husband said, his lip curling. "As I have never heard of it, I imagine there could not have been that many members of this club, and as time wore on their choices must have dwindled. I imagine Roger Gaines wished to persuade your father to make a match between his first-born daughter and his son."

Admiration brightened Lady Wirksworth's eyes. "I will say this for you, Robert, you are not at all slow. Roger Gaines had to wait another nine years before a suitable girl became old enough to wed him, and she bore him a son. He was by then the earl; his father having died some two years earlier. Lucinda was no more than two weeks old when he had the audacity to pay us a visit. Needless to say, he did not get his wish. So, as you see, Freddie was not born of a worm. His father was both honourable and principled."

"Well, that is a relief, I can tell you," Freddie put in. "I could not bear for Lucinda to be married to Bevis."

"No, indeed," his sister murmured. "I begin to think that he really did mean to run you down."

"Nonsense," Freddie said. "I was largely to blame. I was crossing the road when I saw Miss Talbot, or rather, Miss Drucilla. I stopped, thinking I was seeing double, for next to her was another young lady who resembled her completely. At least, she did from a distance. When I drew closer, I could tell them apart. It was Miss Drucilla who called out a warning and brought me to my senses."

"Then we have much to thank her for," Lady Wirksworth said.

"Yes, indeed," Lady Kirkby agreed. "You said the sisters look very similar?"

"Almost identical. They are twins."

Lady Kirkby tipped her head to one side, a

thoughtful smile on her lips. "How delightful. I do hope we will have the privilege of meeting Miss Talbot."

"I expect she will be present when we go to dinner," Lord Kirkby said.

"Oh, but why wait so long? I could call on Lady Frampton and beg an introduction."

"You will do no such thing," her husband said. "As it appears that Miss Drucilla has spent the last two years in France, she will no doubt like to have her sister to herself for a little while. Apart from that, you are expecting a visit from the doctor tomorrow afternoon."

Lady Kirkby sighed. "Very well."

Freddie once more slept soundly that evening and joined Lord Kirkby bright-eyed for their morning ride. They had barely entered the park when they saw two young ladies walking together, two maids trailing behind them. They turned their heads as they approached.

"Good grief," the viscount murmured. "You said they were almost identical, but if there is any difference between them, I cannot discern it."

"Can you not?" Freddie said. "It is not so much in their looks as in their expressions, although Miss Drucilla does have a tiny mole on the side of her neck that Miss Talbot lacks."

The viscount looked closely at his friend. "How is it that in all the years I have known you, I never realised quite how observant you are."

"I am not *always* observant, as you well know, but I do sometimes notice little things. Growing up with a host of injured animals, who could be quite unpredictable, taught me to pay attention to little details when I must."

They raised their hats as they came up to the sisters.

"Good morning, Miss Talbot, Miss Drucilla," Freddie said. "Miss Talbot, may I introduce my brother-in-law, Viscount Kirkby?"

Abigail stepped a little away from the horses but returned his nod. "Good morning, sir."

"How pleased you must be to once more be in your sister's company, Miss Talbot," the viscount said.

This only drew a small, tight smile from her.

"Do you make a long stay in Town?" he persevered.

Her eyes darted to her sister. "I am not sure of our plans, but I hope a week or two, at least."

"Is Lady Kirkby well, sir?" Lucy said.

"She is much improved and is looking forward to seeing you again and meeting your sister."

After a few minutes of polite, if stilted conversation, Freddie raised his hat. "I can see you are wishing us at Jericho, and I do not blame you in the least. I am sure you have much to say to each other."

"You hit the nail on the head," the viscount said as they rode away. "They were not best pleased to see us, were they?"

"What of it?" Freddie said. "I've a notion they have something important to speak about."

"I agree," the viscount said. "There was a palpable tension between them. And you, my friend, have many more notions than I had any idea of."

CHAPTER 9

Lucy drew in a long breath as she watched the gentlemen ride away. She had been both relieved and frustrated by the interruption. It had put off the moment when she must confront her sister. She was aware that Abby's words would once more change things between them for better or worse. When she had first been separated from her twin, she had felt as if a part of her was missing, almost as if she had lost a limb. The ache in her heart had lessened over time, but it now throbbed almost as fiercely as it had when they had first been parted. Her sister walking beside her felt so familiar and yet so different. They had used to be able to read the other's mood and thoughts, but that was no longer the case.

Abigail had filled their walk thus far with inconsequential, bright tattle about the forthcoming trip to Bath and Lucy had not been able to see beyond it. Was she really as unconcerned as she appeared? As they entered the park, it had begun to grate on her nerves. She had been about to beg her to stop and come to the point when Lord Kirkby and Mr Ashton had arrived on the scene. She had been distracted throughout the encounter, something she felt a little guilty about, for she liked Mr Ashton. She hoped she had not offended him, but no, his cheerful disposition had not faltered, and his parting words proved that he had understood.

She felt a spurt of surprise as she realised he had not hesitated in his greeting of her and her sister, looking at each of them in turn. He had somehow been able to tell them apart. The thought pleased her.

But the interaction had somehow taken the wind from her sails, and as she met her sister's gaze, she was unsure of how to proceed. It seemed that Abby had more insight into Lucy's feelings than she of hers, for she took her arm and began to lead her away from the path.

"Let us ensure we are not interrupted again. This might take some time."

Lucy pulled her arm free and began to walk quickly, suddenly angry that Abby apparently had an advantage over her and was taking control of the situation as she always had. She would not allow her to conduct this conversation on her terms. Abby had always been able to make the unreasonable somehow appear reasonable, and she had been too easily persuaded. She would not be this time.

"Cilla! Wait!" she cried.

Lucy did not slacken her pace, if anything, she quickened it until she was almost running, not stopping until she reached a stand of trees. Ahead of her, she saw a glimmer of water in the distance that suddenly blurred into a formless shimmer. She blinked rapidly, drawing in long slow breaths.

"Cilla!" her sister panted, leaning against the trunk of the nearest tree.

The roiling emotions of the evening before once more rose to the surface and suddenly overwhelmed Lucy.

"Cilla is gone." The words rasped over her dry throat, her eyes stinging with unshed tears. "Whether that happened the moment I awoke to find the doctor violating me, or later, when you did not speak up for me, I do not know."

A stunned expression crossed Abby's face, and it took on an ashen hue. "Cilla… Cilla… I am so sorry," she whispered. Her lips twisted in a grimace. "I did not mean for it to happen. I did not realise Father would move so quickly. I was going to look for Stephen to beg his aid when I began to feel odd, weak. I sat on the bottom step of the stairs to catch my breath, and Mrs Hawkins found me there. She helped me up to my room… your room, although I was not really aware of where I was." She put her hands to her brow as if her head ached. "I discovered later that it was she who laced the tea with laudanum to make us sleep. She was trying to protect us. I think I drank more of it than you, and I did not wake until after the doctor had seen me." She bit her lip. "Even now, the thought of it makes my skin crawl. When we were summoned to father's study, I still felt groggy and detached from everything."

Her eyes went flat and blank as if she were reliving the events, and Lucy felt sympathy stir in her breast, but then she remembered the little shake of Abby's head had not been one of confusion but a denial of Lucy's request that she tell the truth.

"Why did you not tell our father that we were in the wrong rooms?"

Abby blinked slowly, as if coming out of a trance. "It all happened so quickly. When I saw the look in Father's eyes, the fog lifted. The thought that once he calmed down, he must realise that meek, quiet Drucilla could not have been deflowered flashed through my mind, but I felt sure he would easily believe it of me." She gulped. "I did not imagine for a moment that he would lay hands on you, and I was about to blurt out the truth so that he would let you go and direct his anger at me when Stephen pulled him away." Her lips trembled and her eyes dropped to the grass. "I wish I had followed you from the room to explain my theory and talk it through with you, but I could not move or take my eyes from Father. It was horrible. His mouth drooped to one side as did one of his eyes, and his mouth opened and closed like a fish but no sound emerged."

Lucy shuddered at so lurid an image but would not allow herself to be distracted. "And if you had followed me from the room, what then? You would have bullied me into agreeing to maintain the deception so that your reputation remained unsullied."

Abby's head jerked up, exasperation sparking in her eyes. "I would not have bullied you, and was it really so much to ask? All our lives I have protected you from a host of little unpleasantnesses that I thought might overset you. Would you then baulk at returning the favour?"

Lucy gasped. "I hardly think what you would have asked of me a little unpleasantness."

Abby batted this away with a wave of her hand. "It would have become so when Father came to his senses. And if he had not, I would have owned the truth and faced the consequences. As it turned out, it did not become necessary for me to do so."

Lucy noticed Dolly and her sister's maid inching towards them and began to walk again.

"Do not be angry, Lucy," Abby said gently.

It was the first time she had heard that name on her sister's lips, and it sounded all wrong. Tears again blinded her, and she could not speak.

"When Father was carried to his room, Stephen informed me that he had sent you to our godmother. I felt bereft and pleaded with him to send me after you. But he said that could wait because there was no immediate danger to me, and that he would write to put off the visit of Lord Gaines." She shook her head sadly. "And by the time we received your letter, you were on your way to France, and it was too late."

Lucy heard the wistfulness in her words and did not doubt their sincerity. She was not prepared to forgive her quite yet, however.

"As our father apparently forgot the whole, I accept the futility of telling him anything, but what of our brother?"

Abby stopped walking and kicked at a blade of grass, the blush infusing her cheeks an indication of her guilt.

"He has made it clear that he does not believe any ill of you. What sane person would? You have always been the well-behaved one who would not say boo to a goose. Do you know how many times Mrs Wardle threw your goodness in my face? How many times she bemoaned that I was not as like you in character as I was in looks?"

Lucy blinked in surprise. "Did she? It is a pity she did not say so to my face. I thought she disliked me excessively."

Abby shrugged. "I think she enjoyed her situation as little as we did ours. She had little more freedom. Perhaps it was only natural that she resented us. I imagine she only accepted the position because she was offered an unusually high wage."

Lucy could hardly believe her ears. "That is uncommonly forgiving of you, sister."

A small smile twisted Abby's lips. "I have frequently reflected on the importance of forgiveness since that time. But I digress. Our father was dangerously ill for some time after his stroke, and the burden of running the estate fell firmly on Stephen's shoulders. He was ill-prepared to take on the responsibility, and I did what I could to aid him, but I would not sit with Father. I was afraid that seeing my face would spark his memory. The doctor said that it would be some time before we would know if he would recover his faculties.

"At first, there seemed no opportunity to tell Stephen anything, and as time went on it became more difficult." She briefly touched her sister's arm. "No one could completely fill the gap left by you, but as each week passed Stephen's good opinion became more precious to me. Our brother is one of the few people who has ever accepted me as I am. He does not expect me to be a paragon of maidenly modesty but laughs at the dry and even cutting things I say. What good would it have done to have told him? It would not alter his good opinion of you, but I feared it might alter his perception of me, not least because I did not immediately own up to the mistake. He has always admired what he calls my brutal honesty."

They began to walk slowly towards the ribbon of water ahead, the remnants of Lucy's anger ebbing with every step. The vulnerability her sister had revealed both touched and surprised her. Abby had always been the strong one, and it had never seemed to Lucy that she needed anyone's approval, but it appeared she had been mistaken. She could understand such feelings, of course, for had she not always sought approval even if it had not often been given? And if she was honest, did she not still wish for it? Had not her anger and melancholy been fuelled by the desire that no one should think any ill of her?

They came to a wide path that ran parallel to the water. Abby turned to her and took her hands, her eyes shining with emotion.

"I have told you only the truth, sister. Can you forgive me?"

A small sliver of mistrust still lodged in Lucy's heart.

"Would you tell our brother if I asked it of you?"

Abby smiled. "I have already done so. I explained the whole this morning."

Lucy felt a weight lift from her heart. "How did he react?"

"In his usual solemn, thoughtful way. He said it was not well done of me, but that the ultimate blame lay with our father, and as no true harm came of it, perhaps it was best forgotten."

"But it is not only he who knows of it," Lucy said.

Abby sighed. "You always were morbidly sensitive, and I expect you have spent the last two years turning a molehill into a mountain. Apart from our brother, only the housekeeper and the doctor are aware of what occurred, and neither have nor will say a word about it. Mrs Hawkins was very attached to our mother and has some fondness for us, and the doctor did not wish to do father's bidding in the first place. Besides, he retired soon afterwards and moved away." She smiled wryly. "I think our brother had a hand in that, although he would not tell me how he accomplished it."

"And how did he explain my sudden disappearance?"

"Stephen put it about that you left so precipitously because our godmother was on the point of leaving for France and she had invited you to go with her. Your tears were easily explained as not only had you witnessed Father's collapse, but you had to leave me behind. You are not ruined, sister, and, if anything, had the better outcome. Whilst you were with our godmother, I was living under our father's roof, and until he died, I was always afraid that he would wake up one morning and remember the whole."

Lucy was about to disagree that she had had the better outcome when she remembered that she could not without explaining that she had not gone to France. Besides, although it was true that she had hated to be surrounded by strangers when first she went to Ashwick Hall, she had slowly become accustomed and found some happiness there. The truth was, she probably had been better off. If Abby had been afraid of their father regaining his senses, Lucy would have been terrified.

"Why did you not write and tell me all this?"

Abby sighed. "I did sit down with quill and ink on several occasions, but it was hopeless. The words sounded stilted, forced, and insincere. This is a conversation we needed to have face to face, and I had no idea that you would be away so long. Besides, I did not think it wise to put anything in writing. Letters do go astray, after all."

Lucy again blinked away tears. Her sister's arguments made sense.

"I forgive you, Abby." She bit her lip, colouring as she forced herself to voice the black thoughts that had sometimes plagued her. "But I also need your forgiveness. When in a deep melancholy, I did wonder if you had intentionally sent me to your room… that you knew all would not be as it should be. But I knew that could not be so, for it would mean that you… that you…"

She was clasped in a fierce embrace, and hot tears streaked her face. "Hush, sister. I forgive you freely. I too have suffered black thoughts at times. Melancholy has a way of taking one down dark paths that are better left unexplored."

"I don't mean to interrupt, and I'm happy you are reconciled, but I thought you'd like to know that there is a curricle approaching."

"Thank you, Dolly," Lucy said, stepping back and wiping her tears away.

They moved to the edge of the path, expecting the

curricle to pass, but it slowed as it approached. Lucy gasped as she saw it was the gentleman who had nearly run Mr Ashton down and then insulted him. She had caught but a brief glimpse of him, registering only a flash of auburn hair and a hooked nose, but she felt certain it was him. As he came abreast of them, he drew his beautiful horses to a stop, and his hard green eyes fixed on them in a most impolite way.

The sisters glanced at each other and then, linking arms, turned and walked away from the path.

"That is the man who might have killed Mr Ashton," Lucy murmured.

"Yes, I know," Abby said.

"Why did he stare at us in that way? It gave me the shivers."

Abby squeezed her arm. "Do not be so melodramatic. The sight of two ladies who are not only identical but young and pretty is bound to attract attention. Did not Mr Ashton also stare at us?"

"Yes, but in surprise, not in that horrid, rude way."

"But as we saw yesterday, Lord Bevis is rude and horrid."

The sound of galloping hooves made them turn their heads. Lord Bevis was still looking in their direction, and Mr Ashton and Lord Kirkby were bearing down on him. Mr Ashton turned from the path some hundred yards from the curricle and came towards them.

"It seems Mr Ashton wishes to avoid Lord Bevis," Abby said. "It is understandable, of course, if a little cowardly."

"It is not cowardly in the least," Lucy protested. "But very sensible."

Freddie saw the sisters embrace in the middle of the path and then Bevis's curricle approaching. Even though they were too far to hear, he opened his mouth to shout a warning, but the curricle slowed perceptibly and they stepped back. The sound emerged in a strangled croak.

"Calm down, Freddie," Lord Kirkby said laconically, "I hardly think Bevis would treat two young ladies as he did you."

The curricle slowed even further and a rare frown crossed Freddie's brow. "He will not speak to her."

He spurred his horse to a gallop as he spoke. It took the viscount a moment to come up with him.

"Freddie," he said laughing. "Bevis must have seen us; there is no need for these heroics."

"He has no right to speak to her… to them," he said. "They have not been introduced."

"Neither had you when you first spoke with Miss Drucilla," his friend said grinning.

"The circumstances were entirely different. I was concerned that Jacko may have frightened her." His face relaxed. "They have turned their back on him and are walking away."

"Good," his friend said, "I suggest you follow them whilst I speak with Bevis."

"I will," Freddie said. "And I will ensure he does not get another opportunity to come near them."

He dismounted as he reached the sisters, bowed, and raised his hat. "Forgive me for once more interrupting you, Miss Drucilla, Miss Talbot, but I saw you turn away from Lord Bevis, and it occurred to me you might like my escort. The thing is, two such pretty girls are bound to attract attention, and not every gentleman can be trusted to behave as he should."

Abby raised an eyebrow as she glanced over her shoulder. "And that gentleman in particular?"

Being a fair man, Freddie said, "I've never heard that he has behaved badly towards a female, but what he was about pulling up like that, I do not know. I hope he said nothing to distress you."

"He did not say anything at all," Lucy said. "He just stared at us in an odious way, and so we walked away."

"A very good notion," he said. "I see you have brought your maids with you, but might I suggest a footman would be better?"

"Surely you are refining too much on a trivial incident, sir," Abby said. "Is the park such a dangerous place?"

"A lady is always safer with a male servant or better still a male relative in attendance," he said.

A secretive smile touched Abby's lips. "We are not as defenceless as we appear, sir."

Lucy frowned at her sister before smiling shyly at Freddie. "Your concern is appreciated, and I thank you for offering us your escort."

Freddie bowed, returning her smile. "It is my pleasure."

Lord Kirkby pulled up next to the curricle and nodded. "Good day, Bevis. That's a fine pair of horses you have there. Are they a recent acquisition?"

The earl inclined his head. "Kirkby. Yes, I have had them but a few days."

Lord Kirkby's smile did not reach his eyes. "Ah, perhaps that explains why they got away from you yesterday on Bond Street."

The earl sneered. "Ashton ran to you with that tale, did he? He was standing stock still in the middle of the street like the fool he is. If I had wished to knock him down, I might easily have done so." He glanced in his direction. "It is time he fought his own battles and stopped hiding behind your coat tails."

"Ashton does not hide behind me or anyone else, Bevis, and it is time you learned that your antics worry him not at all and only make you look like a fool."

The earl did not appear to have heard him, his eyes were still following the progress of Freddie and the sisters.

"Who are those ladies?" he said abruptly. "Beautiful twins are a rarity, and yet I do not think I have had the pleasure of making their acquaintance."

"It appears that they do not wish you to, Bevis."

He gritted his teeth. "Who are they and how does Ashton know them?"

The viscount raised his brows. "I can answer neither question. I am his friend and brother, not his keeper."

CHAPTER 10

Although Freddie was not known as a great conversationalist, he could generally summon something or other to talk about, and yet now his initial burst of verbosity had subsided, he was at a loss. Until that morning, Miss Drucilla had conversed with him quite naturally, and he had expected that once she had cleared the air with her sister, she would once more. Yet she seemed fascinated by the grass underfoot and her sister had edged a little away and appeared disinclined to talk. His wilting neckcloth suddenly felt too tight. He loosened it with a finger, willing himself to say something.

"It is a fine day, is it not?"

"Yes, it is quite warm," Lucy agreed.

"Are you enjoying your time in Town?"

"It is very quiet," Lucy said. "Not that I object to that, but it seems very strange to walk through streets that seem deserted."

"This part of Town is quiet, of course, although not quite deserted. It is not a pleasant place to be in

August, you know. The summer heat becomes oppressive, and everyone of note leaves. It is only early September, and the majority will not return for some time yet. It is very different during the season, of course."

Miss Talbot found her voice. "Have you enjoyed many seasons, Mr Ashton?"

"Well, yes."

"You surprise me," she said dryly.

"How so?" he asked, mistrusting her smile.

"I would have thought that you would have learned to discuss something other than the weather. As you have been so chivalrous as to escort us, I might expect you to comment on my sister's pelisse, for example. It is very fetching, is it not?"

"Abby," Lucy hissed, her cheeks growing pink. "I do not desire fulsome compliments about my attire, nor would I expect Mr Ashton to notice it."

He noticed it now. The pelisse's buff sarsenet was enlivened by rich brown and gold silk threads which formed a feather pattern down the centre and around the hem and cuffs. This colour scheme was matched by the ribbons that decorated her leghorn bonnet. When she raised her blushing face to him, he thought she looked charming. Her obvious embarrassment alleviated his, and he smiled ruefully.

"You are quite right, Miss Drucilla. I only noticed how well you looked when we met earlier, but then you always do, and so I did not pause to consider why. I rarely notice the details of a person's attire."

A mischievous glint came into Miss Talbot's eyes. "That perhaps explains why you look as if you have dressed all by guess, or like a little boy who has stolen his big brother's clothes. Do you not have a valet, Mr Ashton?"

"Abby!" Lucy once more protested. "What Mr Ashton chooses to wear when he is riding is his business. I expect loose-fitting clothes are more comfortable."

Freddie was no stranger to teasing and merely laughed. "I do, indeed, have a valet, Miss Talbot. I never give much thought to fashion, I admit, but the case is, I am still awaiting a host of items from my tailor, including new riding clothes. It is why I came to Town."

"Ah, yes," Abby said, "Lady Frampton mentioned that you had lost weight. I hope you have not been ill?"

"Far from it," he said. "I have spent the summer running about the Cornish countryside with a young man who has boundless energy. It did me a great deal of good."

They had just come to the Cumberland Gate when the viscount rode up to them.

"Ah, here is Lord Kirkby," Abby said. "Thank you for your company, Mr Ashton, but we are quite capable of walking the short way to Brook Street with our maids in attendance."

"I am not sure—"

"Do not worry, Freddie," the viscount interrupted, "Bevis has gone in the other direction. The ladies will be quite safe."

When he still did not look convinced, Lucy stepped forward and offered him her hand, saying as he bowed over it, "You have been very kind, Mr

Ashton, but my sister is right, we will do very well now. I look forward to seeing you the day after tomorrow."

As they walked away, Miss Drucilla bent her head towards her sister and whispered something indistinguishable in her ear. It came as no surprise to Freddie that Miss Talbot did not share her sister's preference for discretion, and her voice drifted clearly back to them.

"I spoke only the truth, sister, and if Mr Ashton did not mind, why should you? Yes, I know you will say that he cannot help it, but that is nonsense. What self-respecting man would countenance being seen abroad looking like a groom who has stolen his master's clothes? I am only glad there was no one apart from his brother and the detestable Lord Bevis to see us in his company."

"Well," Lord Kirkby said, "Miss Talbot is not one to mince her words, is she?"

Freddie mounted his horse. "What care I if she is embarrassed by my appearance? Besides, she exaggerates."

The viscount's gaze swept over him. "A little, perhaps. I know that you have never set any great store in appearances, Freddie, but perhaps it is time that you did. You might not care what Miss Talbot thinks of you, but I have a notion you set more store by Miss Drucilla's opinion."

"I do not think she gives a fig for my appearance," Freddie said.

"As she found no objection to either Jacko's or Jasper's, perhaps not, nevertheless, it is time you stopped hiding behind your eccentricities."

Freddie's head whipped around at this. "I do not hide behind them."

The viscount smiled wryly. "I did not think so, but I begin to think I was wrong and you are not quite the gudgeon you appear."

"When you start talking deep, Robert, you lose me completely. Now, tell me what Bevis was about."

"He seemed very interested in the Misses Talbot. He wished to know their name, how you knew them, and why he had not seen them before."

Freddie frowned. "I hope you did not enlighten him."

The viscount sighed. "I was wrong. You are most certainly a gudgeon."

❧

When Lucy sent her a disapproving look, Abby took her arm. "Very well, I apologise. I admit I was having a little fun at Mr Ashton's expense." She sent her sister a sideways look. "You like him, don't you?"

"Why should I not?" Lucy said. "He has been nothing but kind."

"Kindness is certainly a virtue in a man," Abby conceded.

Lucy met her sister's gaze steadily. "Not only in a man, Abby."

She gave the brittle little laugh that Lucy now realised she used when on the back foot. "I suppose I am not always kind, but then life has not often treated me kindly, so perhaps it is hardly surprising."

Lucy's eyes softened. "I am beginning to realise just how difficult you found our time at Glasbury

Heights and what happened afterwards, but do not let it make you bitter, sister. Your life is better now."

"Yes, that is true," she said.

"And you are happy at Talbot Hall, are you not?"

Abby sighed. "I am happy enough. I like being mistress there, but one day Stephen will wish to marry, and what will become of me then?"

"Perhaps we could set up house together."

Abby laughed. "It will be years before we are old enough for that to be thought a respectable thing to do."

Lucy smiled. "I did not think you would care for that."

"I do not, but I do not think you would enjoy the disapproving scrutiny such a step would bring on our heads and neither would Stephen. Besides, you will one day meet a man who will capture your tender heart and you will fall head over ears in love."

"So might you, sister."

Abby looked away, saying lightly, "I think that extremely doubtful."

"Perhaps, if you stay at Talbot Hall. Why don't you come to Bath with us? I am sure our brother can do without you for a month or two."

Abby turned to her, her eyes softening. "That you wish for my company warms my heart, but—"

"Do not say no just yet," Lucy said as they reached their godmother's house. "I am not particularly enamoured of the scheme, but if you were by my side, I think I could face it with more equanimity."

Abby raised a quizzical eyebrow, mischief brightening her eyes. "Would you not be on tenterhooks lest I say something outrageous and embarrass you?"

"Perhaps, but you could moderate your tongue or say those things only to me." She laughed softly. "When Mrs Wardle uttered something cutting, you used to whisper outrageous comments about her in my ear to make me smile. She was a fusby-faced old crone, a harridan, a butter toothed spinster—"

"And so she was," Abby said, smiling wryly. "It was perhaps cruel of me to make fun of her spinsterhood, however. Although she could have been kinder to us if she chose, that, at least, was not her fault." The smile slipped from her face. "A woman's fate is too often decided by the whims of fate or the decisions made by men. It is they who have all the power."

"You are thinking of our father," Lucy said softly. "But not all men are like him."

Lucy's thoughts went to Lady Westcliffe. She had never met Lord Westcliffe, but it seemed to her that he granted his wife a great deal of freedom and power which she used to benefit those less fortunate than herself. Lord Kirkby did not try to rule his wife with tyranny, and Lady Kirkby was certainly not powerless. One coaxing comment and smile from her had dispelled his annoyance when he had walked into the drawing room to discover the animals causing chaos, and Lady Frampton spoke fondly of her husband, who had been both her companion and sparring partner.

"It is true women have little power outside marriage, but—"

"And within it," Abby said dryly. "What power did our mother have?"

"But not all marriages are like our parents'," Lucy

said. "Where there is equal affection between man and wife, surely—"

"There would still be a disparity of opportunity and power," Abby interpolated. "You might not mind that. Indeed, your gentle character is bound to attract a man of strong will who wishes to shield you from every ill wind, and such a man would, I am sure, make you happy. That would not do for me, however. If I were to wed, I should choose a man whom I could bend to my will."

Lucy frowned. "That sounds so cold, so calculating. How could you love such a man?"

"I do not seek or expect love, only perhaps kindness." She shook her head as if to clear it. "But this is all pointless conjecture, what man, no matter how kind, would remain so when he discovered all my faults?"

Lucy embraced her sister. "One who truly loved you."

Abby's arms tightened about her. "That would truly be an unequal match, for I could not return such a love." She chuckled. "You see how hopeless my case is. I wish for a man who does not love me and yet is kind and will not dictate to me or object to my flaws. Such a man does not exist."

Lucy was beginning to realise just how fragile her sister was behind her confident exterior.

"You exaggerate your flaws as much as I did when we were apart. You use them as both a shield and a weapon. Your tongue cuts and slashes indiscriminately. You must stop trying to shock and allow people to know you, Abby, truly know you. You can be brave, bold, and amusing without being unkind, and they are all qualities that might be admired by a gentleman worthy of you. Does not our brother love you?"

"Stephen is a singular case. He also suffered at our parent's hands. Apparently, Father was never sure if Stephen was really his, and he never let him forget it."

"But why did he think it?"

Abby shrugged. "I do not know, nor does Stephen. Perhaps he did not need a reason. He was not the most rational of men." She kissed Lucy on the cheek. "I must go or I will be late for breakfast."

Lucy watched her walk away with a frown in her eyes. She could not be satisfied. All the unhappiness wrought on their family stemmed from their father's belief that his wife was unchaste, and she could not help but wonder how different their lives might have been if such a thought had not poisoned his mind.

Lady Frampton did not come down to breakfast, indeed, she did not emerge from her chamber until shortly before Lucy was due to go for a drive with her brother. She found her in the drawing room wrapped in a shawl.

"You look very fetching, my dear. That carriage dress becomes you. Match it with the pelisse with the fur trim that I gave you; it has turned chilly."

Lucy looked closely at her godmother, concerned. It was still unseasonably warm.

"Are you, ill, Aunt Honora? You look pale."

"Do not fuss, child. I am a little tired, but it will pass. It always does. If I am quiet today, I will be perfectly well." She patted the sofa. "Come, sit, and tell me how your talk with your sister went."

Lucy smiled. "We are reconciled."

Lady Frampton took her hand. "I am glad. I knew that if you listened with a reasoned ear, you must see that it is your father who was the real villain of the piece."

"But why, Aunt? What made him think ill of my mother, of all of us?"

"He was a fool," she snapped, her spirits momentarily reviving.

Lucy frowned. "That is not answer enough."

Lady Frampton sighed. "Very well. I expect you know little of what happens between a man and a woman, although I am sure you have an inkling. When a woman lays with a man for the first time, she sometimes bleeds a little. Not every woman, however, and so I told your father, but he doubted me, and when Stephen was born a month early, he felt his suspicions had been confirmed."

Sadness and shame mingled in Lucy's eyes. She had spent so long feeling sorry for herself, but she was not the only member of her family to suffer at their father's hands, and perhaps she had suffered least of all.

"Poor Mama and poor Stephen."

Lady Frampton sat up. "Now, Lucy, do not become maudlin. Your mother's lot was a difficult one, but she loved all of her children. Your father spent weeks at a time in Town, and I believe at those times she was happy. As for Stephen, he benefited from being sent away to school, and if your father sometimes threw his suspicions in his face – which I am sure he might have done when in a temper – his pride, at least, ensured that he did not share them with anyone else."

The butler entered the room. "Lord Talbot awaits outside, Miss Drucilla."

Lucy rose swiftly to her feet. "I will come directly, Shield. Thank you." She glanced down at her godmother. "I am not maudlin, Aunt Honora, although I will admit that I have been guilty of self-pity in the past. I am realising, however, that my pity is best reserved for those who truly deserve it. And also my respect. I would have shrivelled under my father's critical eyes whereas my mother and brother endured, as I would have been terrified to live under his roof whilst he still breathed as my sister did."

Lady Frampton smiled. "Perhaps that was true once, but I do not think it is any longer. Your time away from your sister has changed you. It is not that you lacked character, Lucy, so much as that character was smothered by your sister's larger one. Now, go, and enjoy getting to know your brother."

Stephen handed her up into the curricle, a slight smile on his face. "I am glad you and Abby are once more friends. She returned to Charlotte Street lighter somehow."

"As am I," she said. "Thank you for taking such good care of her."

He climbed up beside her and set the horses to a trot, his smile turning wry. "It is rather she who has taken care of me. Our sister has a managing disposition."

"And a good heart although she does not always show it. I think she likes to feel needed."

He sent her a sideways glance. "Perhaps you are right. I think she took our father's rejection of you both to heart. I am sorry for it, and that I was neither allowed to visit Glasbury Heights nor write to you, although I frequently asked for permission."

"I understand that Father was not always kind to you," Lucy said. "And when you were a boy, I can quite see that he might have cowed you. But—"

He finished her sentence. "Why did I not come once I reached my majority?"

She nodded.

His brow drew into a frown. "Father did not wish me to be close to any of you. He tried to keep me from mother, to punish her, I think, although Mrs Hawkins found ways to sneak me in to see her. Mama knew she was dying, and before I was sent back to school, she asked me to try and protect you and Abby." His mouth twisted into a bitter line. "I was allowed to return for her funeral, at least. You were sent to Glasbury soon afterwards, and I watched you and Abby, already the image of our mother, get into the carriage. I am not ashamed to admit that tears were pouring down my face. I felt I had failed her, but then I realised you were better off away from Father. I did receive regular news of you, however."

Lucy's heart ached for the boy who had felt so powerless. "How?"

"Father's pride ensured you were schooled in all the accomplishments that were required in a lady. What did you think of Mr Evans?"

"My music teacher?" Lucy said. "He was wonderful. So kind, so gentle, and endlessly patient."

Stephen laughed gently. "With you, perhaps. I made him pull his hair out when I first attempted to learn the violin."

Lucy gasped. "I do not know what is more surprising, that you play an instrument or know Mr Evans."

"I had private lessons when I was at Eton for a time." He grimaced. "Father never knew, of course. It was Mama who funded them. Father would have scoffed at my interest in music. Mr Evans left the school in my third year and went to Glasbury to live with his sister. My loss was your gain. I corresponded with him. I still do." He smiled. "He informed me that you were far more talented than I. I look forward to hearing you play."

"I will gladly play for you, brother." She looked thoughtful. "Could you not have communicated with us through Mr Evans?"

"I thought of it, but I decided it was too risky. I collected my letters from Mr Evans from the inn in Madley and so Father was none the wiser, but if I had written to you and Mrs Wardle had discovered our subterfuge, she would have informed him. Mr Evans would have lost a valuable client, and there was every possibility you would have been moved somewhere far less comfortable than Glasbury Heights." He sighed. "It is what he always threatened when I pleaded with him to allow me to visit or correspond with you. He did not wish me to develop a fondness for my sisters lest I try to interfere in his plans, I think." He sighed. "I did not know the whole. I would certainly have tried to persuade the doctor to refuse my father's demands. I would no doubt have failed, however. Father paid him a healthy sum for his services that he could ill afford to lose."

"I can see that it was very difficult for you to do

anything, and I thank you for putting off our prospective suitors," she said quietly.

"Father's illness and death gave me the excuse, but now that your period of mourning is up, Gaines, at least, may well make an approach," he said gravely. "Fairbrass has never contacted me. Rest assured that I feel no obligation to uphold the agreement made by our father."

CHAPTER 11

Generally, Freddie wore whatever his valet laid out for him, that personage being fully conversant with what would be acceptable to his master. On the evening he was to dine with Lady Frampton, however, his trusted servant found him unusually hard to please.

"No, not the black coat, the blue one."

Lipton's eyebrows rose by the veriest fraction. "Very well, sir."

He tied his master's cravat in the simple style he always sported, but after his easy-going employer had contemplated this article of clothing in the mirror for several minutes, his efforts were rejected.

"Do you know, Lipton, I think a change might be in order. Shall we try something else?"

This time, Lipton's eyebrows rose discernibly, although Freddie was too busy untying his cravat to notice.

"By all means, sir. Is it perhaps a special occasion?"

"Not at all, just a quiet dinner with Lady Frampton and her guests. You do know some other styles, I take it?"

Although this was said without any hint of disparagement, the question left the valet momentarily speechless. Although he was very fond of his generous, undemanding employer, it had always irked Lipton and stung his professional pride that his master had never done him justice, but he had long since given up any hopes in that quarter. Even if Mr Ashton had developed a sudden interest in sartorial elegance before now, there was only so much he could have done. The form-fitting clothes of the day were not kind to those without the figure to carry them off. Things had changed, however, and a long-dormant desire to prove his mettle suddenly burst into life.

"Several, sir, and it will be my pleasure to send you out in a way that does me credit."

The implication that he did not generally do so did not appear to strike home. Freddie merely nodded.

"Set to it, then, before I change my mind."

It took the valet's nimble fingers only a few minutes to arrange a fresh cravat in the complicated folds necessary to achieve the style known as the waterfall. He waited as Freddie regarded it intently for a few moments, wondering if he had been too ambitious. He let out the breath he had unconsciously been holding when he smiled.

"Well, that's bang up to the mark, isn't it?"

Lipton thought his master had never looked better, and yet he was still not satisfied. His finger's itched to tame Mr Ashton's riotous curls.

When the valet did not return his smile, Freddie's

eyes turned again to the mirror, uneasiness creeping into them. "Be honest, Lipton. You don't think it suits me, do you? I think you are right; it makes me look like a regular coxcomb!"

"Not at all, sir," the valet said quickly. "You look very well, it is only…" He paused, searching for a persuasive argument. In the early years of his employment, he had frequently suggested that a much shorter haircut might suit his master, but he had invariably received the same reply.

"Nonsense, besides, my aunt is very fond of my curls, and I would not look like me without them."

No amount of gentle persuasion or the assurance that merely cutting his blond locks would not eradicate his curls had moved his gentle master. He could be extremely stubborn when he chose. A flash of inspiration came to the valet. Mr Ashton had been very pleased when the chamber they presently occupied had been allocated for his use and transformed from the rose room to the blue room.

"Well, sir, if, when this room was freshly decorated, matching curtains had not been hung, they would have ruined the effect, would they not?"

Freddie looked baffled. "Of course they would have. They were old, faded, and pink! What has that got to do with anything, Lipton?"

The valet's gaze became fixed on the curls framing Freddie's cheeks and jaw. "Well, sir, if you don't mind me saying so, when your face was plumper, your current way of wearing your hair suited you and went someway to hide the lack of discernible cheekbones. Now, it only covers them and looks unruly. The effect is only made more apparent by the change in your figure and apparel. In short, sir, it ruins the look of elegance we have been at pains to achieve."

Only one word of this speech appeared to make an impression.

"Eh? Unruly? Why did you not say so before?"

Lipton smiled wryly. "I am loathe to admit it, sir, but your lack of interest in your appearance, has, over the years, perhaps encouraged me to become rather lax." He sighed. "The disappointment at having my ideas rejected has discouraged me from any longer making the attempt."

Freddie regarded him with surprise. "You are gammoning me. You have never seemed particularly disappointed."

"It is not fitting that I should appear anything but pleased to obey your wishes, sir."

Freddie was dismayed at the thought his valet had not been entirely happy in his employ. He was very fond of Lipton and had thought they understood each other perfectly.

"What a trial I must have been to you. You would have been happier in the employ of a fashionable gentleman, I dare say."

"Not at all, sir," he said quietly. "It has been my honour to serve you, and I have no desire to work for anyone else, I assure you."

Freddie regarded him uneasily. "So you say, but I can see that I had better let you have your way."

The valet smiled. "Thank you, sir."

Not wishing to startle his master, Lipton sat him far from any mirror and went to work with a will. Some half an hour later he stood back, nodded, and removed the towel he had draped around his master's shoulders.

Freddie eyed the quantity of curls littering the floor with some misgiving. "Good God, man. You have fleeced me, indeed."

Not possessing any vanity, he rarely even glanced in the long cheval mirror, but a nagging suspicion that he might be about to make a cake of himself in front of Lady Frampton and the Misses Talbot took him to where it stood in the corner of the room. A stunned, arrested look came into his eyes. He felt almost as if he were looking at a stranger. His hair was swept away from his face, his curls clustering in an orderly fashion above his ears and atop his head, although one or two had been allowed to fall artistically over his forehead. Two neat sideburns arrowed downwards, highlighting strong cheekbones. He raised his hand touching them tentatively as if he did not quite believe they were real, and then his fingers followed the chiselled line of his jawbone. His eyes dropped to the form-fitting coat that emphasised his shoulders and newly trim waist. He laughed a little self-consciously.

"Well, well. Who is this fine fellow?"

Lipton smiled. "You do indeed look fine, sir, but if you will permit, there is one final finishing touch necessary."

He moved in front of Freddie and set a sapphire tie pin in his cravat.

"Steady on, Lipton," he said. "I am not going to a ball."

"No, sir, but you will both honour and please Lady Frampton by looking so smart."

He quirked an eyebrow. "I doubt it. I may

resemble a fashionable fribble, but I am still me, after all."

"You look quietly elegant, sir, no more, no less."

When he entered the drawing room, he doubted the truth of these words. The conversation stopped abruptly, and his sister, brother, and aunt regarded him in silence for longer than was comfortable.

"I knew it was too much," he said, shaking his head. "But Lipton would have his way."

Lady Kirkby gave a tinkling laugh. "Freddie! He is to be commended. You look so handsome and elegant."

Knowing well his sister's partiality, he sent a glance not wholly free of anxiety at his brother-in-law. The viscount gave a lopsided smile, a hint of approval in his charcoal eyes.

"It is quite a transformation, Freddie. Are you trying to put me out of countenance? My valet will be most displeased. He will no longer be able to make sly digs at yours."

"Does he do so?"

"Certainly, he does, but there is no real malice in it. There is a friendly rivalry between most valets."

This revelation made his capitulation to Lipton's wishes more palatable. He was the last to enter Lady Frampton's drawing room, as both his rank and preference dictated. He hoped that in the melee of greetings and introductions, he might make an unobtrusive entrance. Miss Talbot had suggested in the park that he had looked as if he had donned his big brother's clothes, the irony was, now that he wore ones that fit him perfectly, that is precisely how he felt. He was not yet comfortable with this new version of himself.

Unconsciously, his eyes scanned the room looking for Miss Drucilla.

～

Lucy moved forwards to take the hands Lady Kirkby held out towards her. She was pleased to see that the angular planes of her face had filled out a little and a healthy glow sheened her skin.

"Lady Kirkby," she said, smiling. "I am happy to see you again and in such good looks."

That lady laughed. "You are very kind, Miss Drucilla. My glass tells me I am not looking quite so hagged, and the doctor is satisfied with my improvement. I have found eating little and often the key, and I am hoping that country air and Mrs Godley's cooking – she is my aunt's cook – will restore me further. She, and several other of my aunt's servants are preparing my brother's property in Derbyshire for our arrival. We leave in two days."

Lucy felt a little stab of disappointment. "So soon?"

She was not sure that her new friend had heard her, for her eyes moved to her shoulder, her eyebrows rose, and a surprised gasp escaped her.

Lucy stepped to the side and introduced her sister.

"I am very pleased to make your acquaintance, Miss Talbot. Freddie did, of course, mention that you and Miss Drucilla were twins and very alike, but to see you standing side by side quite takes my breath away. I vow I might easily have mistaken you for Miss Drucilla. What a pretty pair you make."

As Abby made her reply, Lucy felt a prickle of

awareness and turned her head. Mr Ashton stood just inside the doorway. Her eyes widened, her cheeks grew warm, and her heart fluttered in the strangest of ways. This unusual and confusing reaction was compounded by a faint feeling of disappointment. She had liked how he looked before and was not sure what to make of his new, polished appearance. When she finally met his gaze, his blue eyes seemed to hold a rueful apology. She relaxed a little and was about to go and greet him when Abby swept past her, her hand held out.

"Mr Ashton," she said, in her cool, clear voice. "I did not expect you to take my words so much to heart or for them to have such a transformative effect. I hope you know that I was only funning."

Lucy blinked. Had he cut off all those beautiful curls merely to please her sister? She felt an odd sinking sensation in the pit of her stomach at the thought.

It seemed that Abby's voice had penetrated the murmur of greetings, and all eyes turned towards them. Mr Ashton bowed over Abby's hand murmuring a muted greeting.

"Frederick," Lady Frampton said, "This is certainly an improvement."

"Freddie needed no improvement," Lady Wirksworth snapped.

Her eyes turned towards Abby when she stifled a laugh. "You, I assume, are Miss Talbot?"

Abby executed a neat curtsy. "I am. Although how you can tell my sister and me apart, I do not know."

"No, I don't suppose you do."

This was said in a tone calculated to throw her into confusion, but Abby merely laughed again.

"You mean, I suppose, that I lack her good manners. I admit it freely and that I deserved to be snubbed. A person should not be judged on so early an acquaintance, and as Mr Ashton has behaved as the perfect gentleman whilst in my and my sister's company, it was not well done of me to tease him about his appearance. I cannot regret my comments, however, for whilst I agree that a smart, well-fitting coat and a haircut cannot alter a person's character, it must please any discerning lady's eye."

Lady Wirksworth gave a crack of laughter. "You are an impertinent chit. So, you rate your discernment above mine, eh?"

"Not at all," she said, her chin rising a fraction. "My discernment has proved woefully inadequate on more than one occasion. It is to your credit that your affection for your nephew cannot be altered by such frippery things as being a la mode, but you cannot expect those who know him only superficially to feel the same way. How can a stranger or new acquaintance be expected to know that a carelessness in appearance does not also denote a carelessness in character?"

"Are you suggesting, Miss Talbot, that a finely dressed gentleman must then be viewed as having a good character? That his wish to turn heads somehow speaks of a meticulously honourable disposition?"

"Not at all," she said. "It might indicate, however, respect for both himself and those he honours with his presence."

A begrudging amusement crept into Lady

Wirksworth's eyes. "I have only ever known a handful of people who were deserving of respect, Miss Talbot."

Abby's brow wrinkled in apparent contemplation. "I wonder if that is because you have been unfortunate in your acquaintance or if it is merely that you are very difficult to please."

Lucy's eyes darted to Lady Frampton, but instead of the reproach she expected to see etched into her face, she was surprised to see she was biting her lip as if to hold back a laugh. Sensing that her godmother's enjoyment at seeing her distant cousin matched in a battle of wits would prevent her from intervening, she sent a beseeching look in her brother's direction. Stephen was standing with Lord Kirkby, and she was surprised to see a hint of amusement in the grey eyes he turned on her. It faded as he saw her anguished expression. He nodded and addressed Lady Wirksworth.

"Forgive my sister, L—"

Lady Wirksworth raised her hand, silencing him, her eyes regarding Abby in a fascinated manner.

"You speak of respect, Miss Talbot, and yet you show very little yourself. Whilst matrons of my and your godmother's age are generally granted the indulgence to utter what they please, the same freedom is not offered to green girls who are neither married nor yet out."

Abby flushed, although whether from embarrassment or anger was unclear. "Then perhaps it is fortunate that I do not expect to marry or come out, if, by that, you mean enjoy a season." She glanced briefly at Lucy, and seeing her chagrin, softened her words.

"However, I apologise for my unruly tongue. I kept it for so many years more or less under control that I find it hard to still it now."

Lady Wirksworth tilted her head, a faint, unreadable smile touching her thin lips. "You begin to interest me greatly, Miss Talbot. Perhaps you will sit with me a while."

Lucy let out a slow breath. Not only did she dread scenes, but she had wanted Abby to make a favourable impression on her new acquaintances. It seemed that her outspokenness had not alienated her, however.

"Your sister is a breath of fresh air."

Lucy turned her head and looked into Lady Kirkby's laughing blue eyes.

"Do not look so worried, my aunt is not easily offended. She believes in plain speaking, the word with no bark on it as she calls it. If your sister had not stood up to her but become covered in confusion she would have soon lost interest in her." Her eyes turned to where they sat together on a couch. "As it is, she will see her as a puzzle she wishes to understand."

"And what happens once she has unravelled the puzzle?" Lucy asked.

Lady Kirkby smiled wryly. "That depends on what she discovers. She will either decide she is worth the trouble of knowing or not."

"And if she decides not?" Lucy asked, perturbed.

Lady Kirkby shrugged. "Nothing terrible. She is not a malicious gossipmonger. She will merely forget her existence, as she does with anyone who no longer interests her. Very few people do, you know."

Her eyes went to Mr Ashton who was in conversation with Stephen.

"That could prove awkward if your brother one day weds someone his aunt has no interest in."

Lady Kirkby smiled. "Oh, however much my aunt claims that she will not interfere in his affairs, I think you will find she will make it her business to be interested in any female who wishes to marry Freddie." She smiled fondly. "She has only ever wished for us to be happy, and if Freddie chose someone she felt would not suit him, I am sure she would find a way to intervene." She took Lucy's arm. "Come, introduce me to your brother."

She allowed herself to be led towards Stephen and Mr Ashton, feeling unaccountably shy when they came up to them. She made the introduction, and then turned to Freddie, although her eyes did not rise above his beautiful tiepin.

"How do you do, Mr Ashton?"

His soft chuckle encouraged her to meet his eyes. They were a few shades lighter than the sapphire that nestled in his neckcloth but held a warmth that the gemstone lacked.

"I am much happier now that everyone has stopped looking at me as if I were an animal that had escaped a menagerie. Generally, you know, I do not draw so much attention, and I prefer it that way."

She smiled her understanding. "You look so very different that it was only to be expected, but at least the glances you drew were admiring."

He smiled wryly. "Well, that makes a change, at least."

Lucy did not usually speak without thinking, but the question that had been repeating itself in her head for the last several minutes popped out before she could stop it. "What made you do it? I hope it was not because my sister embarrassed you."

"Not at all," he said. "It turns out my valet has been itching to smarten me up for some time, poor fellow." His hand moved to his face as if to brush his hair from it, and then fell. He sighed. "He said my hair was unruly, but between me and you, Miss Drucilla, I miss it."

Yes, so do I. She could hardly say it aloud, of course. "It is very smart."

Was that disappointment she saw in his eyes?

"You don't like it, do you?"

She blushed, sorry that she had hurt his feelings. "It is just that I am not yet used to it, and I agree with your aunt that there was nothing wrong with how you looked before."

He smiled. "You are in a minority, but I have known that almost from the moment we met. There are not many ladies who would not be put off by Jacko's or Jasper's appearance. I think the more of you for it."

She felt inordinately pleased at the compliment. "Does Lady Wirksworth have other animals?"

"There have been many over the years, but most of them have died. Now, there are only Jacko, Jasper, and Juniper."

She laughed. "Who is Juniper, and why do all the animals' names begin with J?"

He grinned. "Do you know, I haven't any idea why. It has always been that way. I think it is just my aunt's habit. Juniper is a one-legged popinjay. We went to Whitby for a few days when I was a boy and found him lying on top of a drunken sailor. He was in a sorry state and so my aunt picked him up and carried him off. He is bad tempered, rude, and uses language unfit for a lady's ears on occasion. He is quite old now and does not like to travel and so he was left at Wirksworth Hall."

Lucy's eyes went to Lord Kirkby and she giggled. "Perhaps that is just as well."

CHAPTER 12

As most of the party were related in some way, it was perhaps not surprising that no great formality attended the meal. The conversation was not restricted to those either side but ranged across and up and down the table. Inevitably, the Bath scheme came up.

"Having not experienced a London season, I suppose you might enjoy it," Lady Kirkby said.

"You do not rate the city?" Abby said. "I only ask because my sister is trying to persuade me to go with her."

"That might make it more palatable, I suppose," Lady Kirkby said. "A friend of mine spent a month there recently on her doctor's advice and she thought it a dull place. She alleviated her boredom by writing me lengthy, satirical letters describing the amusements on offer and the people who frequented them. You will find no one of any note there."

"That is all to the good," Lady Frampton said. "It

will give Lucy a chance to flutter her social wings a little, and Abigail, of course, if she so desires. No young woman should be thrust into the *ton* without some experience. It is better that they learn how to go on in a quieter and perhaps more forgiving place than Town."

Lady Wirksworth snorted. "Miss Talbot will certainly give the old tabbies fodder for gossip within a week, and her actions must impact her sister. If you think any whisperings will remain in Bath, you are much mistaken. However unnoteworthy the current residents are, you may be sure several of them will be related to others who are not."

Lady Frampton bristled. "I do not envisage either of the girls causing me any embarrassment."

Lady Wirksworth looked across at Abby, one eyebrow raised. "What say you, Miss Talbot?"

Abby smiled. "I think it better that perhaps I do not go. I think I am likely to make both my godmother and sister uncomfortable to some degree however good my intentions. Besides, my brother will be returning to our home in Herefordshire in a few days, and I think I will be more useful there." She glanced at Lucy. "I am sorry if you are disappointed, and it will be a wrench to part from you so soon, but I think it will be for the best."

Lucy felt saddened at the thought but recognised the truth of her sister's words. Her own feelings aside, she did not think their godmother well enough to cope with both of them. Despite her assurances that her tiredness would pass, Lady Frampton still did not look perfectly well.

"I understand, Abby." She glanced at her

godmother. "Perhaps the waters will help you feel better, Aunt Honora."

"I am perfectly w—" She raised her napkin to her lips, her words interrupted by a bout of coughing.

"One has only to look at you to know you are not yourself, Honora," Lady Wirksworth said brusquely. "The last thing you need is to be escorting Miss Drucilla to a host of balls and concerts or being bored to death by the regular attendants of the pump room. What you need is some fresh country air, plenty of rest, and your family about you. As I know you won't go to Frampton Court, I suggest you and the girls come with us to Ashton Manor. We will spend several weeks there, and Buxton has a pump room if you wish to take the waters." She glanced at Lord Talbot. "And you may also come if you wish."

A twinkle of amusement lurked in the baron's eyes at his belated and somewhat reluctant inclusion in the invitation. "Thank you, Lady Wirksworth, but I have some outstanding business at home that I cannot delay much longer." He glanced at Abby. "Although I have appreciated your help and support, I believe I can do without you for a few weeks." He then glanced at Lucy. "I hope you will feel ready to return to Talbot Hall before too long, however. It is where you belong, and much has changed since your last visit."

She murmured a non-committal response. She knew that must be so, but the thought of returning there still did not appeal to her. The prospect of spending a few more weeks in the company of her sister amongst a group of people who would not be either embarrassed or affronted by Abby's outspokenness was appealing, however. She would also enjoy furthering her acquaintance with Lady Kirkby.

"I think it a splendid idea," Freddie said. "The more the merrier."

Her eyes flicked towards him, and she acknowledged that she would also like to know him better.

"Oh, do say you will come," Lady Kirkby said, her gaze moving between the sisters. "You may bear me company whilst Robert and Freddie are busy surveying the estate." Her gaze moved on to Lady Frampton, and she smiled sweetly. "You do look a little delicate, ma'am, and I am sure it will do you a great deal of good. However distantly connected, we are family, after all."

A small frown wrinkled Lady Frampton's brow as if she were weighing up the pros and cons of the invitation. Her eyes turned to Abby.

"Would you come with us?"

She nodded before smiling at Lucy. "A small house party in the country amongst people we are already acquainted with is a very different proposition."

A satisfied smile curled Lady Wirksworth's lips. "Well, that's settled," Her voice became unusually gentle. "Can you be ready in two days, Honora?"

"Of course, I can," she said, her sharp tone suggesting that she was not best pleased to have been manoeuvred so adroitly into accepting the invitation. "Although why you think three or four days in a carriage will be good for my health, I cannot imagine."

"We will travel in easy stages," Lord Kirkby said. "And stay in only the best inns, of course."

Lady Frampton snorted. "You can't trust the linen

in any of them. I shall take my own." She rose to her feet. "Come, ladies, we will leave the gentlemen to their port."

Lord Kirkby sat back in his chair, a wry smile twisting his lips. "Did you know our aunt was going to proffer the invitation, Freddie?"

His eyebrows rose. "No, she said nothing about it. What of it?"

"It has just occurred to me that it was rather high-handed of her to do so without conferring with any of us, especially you. It is your house, after all."

Freddie shrugged. "Aunt Seraphina lived there for far longer than I. Ashton Manor is her home as much as mine."

Lord Talbot put down the decanter that had just been passed to him, a small frown creasing his brow. "Do you have any objection to the invitation?"

"Not at all, Talbot. My wife spoke the truth when she said she would enjoy the company of your sisters, and whatever makes my wife happy must also make me happy." The viscount grinned. "Within reason, of course."

The baron relaxed and returned the smile. "I'm glad to hear it."

"And we are honoured that you would entrust them to our care when you know us hardly at all."

"I do not, but Lady Frampton is their godmother and related to you, so I must trust her judgement." A grave look came into his eyes. "My sisters have had very little control over their lives, and I would not interfere with their pleasure. They must be free to make their own decisions." The hint of a smile softened his expression. "Within reason, of course. Abby is rather impulsive, but I trust Lady Frampton will be able to manage her with the able assistance of your aunt."

"Oh, I doubt there will be any need for that," Freddie said. "We will be very quiet, you know."

"Tell me about Ashton Manor," Lord Talbot said. "From Lady Wirksworth's comments, I gather it is in Derbyshire."

"It lies in a dale some thirteen miles north of Buxton," Freddie said. "It has been tenanted since I was a small boy but is now empty. We are to spend a few weeks there whilst I decide what to do with it."

Lord Talbot looked surprised. "Then I hope you will find it in good repair."

"There's not a doubt of it. I may not have visited but our steward at Wirksworth has every year. I expect to find the house and grounds in good order."

"And do you intend to remove there permanently? I assume as it bears your name, it is your main seat."

"I have no such plans. I have lived at Wirksworth since I was five years old, and I am very fond of it. I will either find another tenant or sell it." Freddie tossed off the remnants of his drink. "Shall we join the ladies?"

"You go ahead, Freddie," the viscount said. "We will join you in a minute. Lord Talbot has had no time to enjoy his port."

"Very well," Freddie said. "Port makes me sleepy, so I shall not have another. I will not risk nodding off in front of Lady Frampton. If she is to be with us for the next few weeks, I had better attempt to annoy her as little as possible." He gave a rueful smile. "I would not lay odds on my success, however."

"It seems an odd thing to consider selling the estate," Lord Talbot murmured as he left the room. "Have Mr Ashton's fortunes…" He paused. "Forgive me. It is not my affair."

The viscount smiled. "I understand your confusion. Mr Ashton does not need to sell the estate, but his parents died there when he was a small child, and he feels no attachment to it."

The baron's eyes widened. "I am sorry to hear it. If he and his sister are to return there for the first time since this tragedy, surely they will not wish near strangers in their midst?"

"It happened almost twenty-five years ago, Talbot, and Sir Lionel and Lady Wirksworth became as parents to them. I do not foresee any great upset, but I begin to think my aunt was wise to invite Lady Frampton and your sisters. A family party might be tempted to dwell upon things best forgotten, but they are unlikely to succumb to the temptation when they have visitors to attend. I believe it is a fine old house, and the appreciation it is likely to receive will perhaps bring Freddie to a realisation of just how lucky he is to own it."

"Ah," the baron said, "You do not approve of him selling it."

"I do not." Lord Kirkby sipped his port. "A gentleman generally wishes to add to his assets not diminish them, although I have to admit that Freddie is a singular sort of gentleman." He paused, and then said, "Do I detect a reluctance to return home in Miss Drucilla?"

Lord Talbot's eyes dropped to his wine glass. "You are perceptive, sir."

"I have that reputation," the viscount acknowledged. "However, I will echo your words; it is not my affair."

"No, it is not." The baron sipped his drink. "But you are correct. There are some unfortunate memories at Talbot Hall, and my sister does not wish to face them." He put down his glass. "She must do so at some point, however, and she does not have the luxury of waiting twenty-five years to do so."

"I did not know your father well," the viscount said. "But I gained the impression that he was not an easy man. I met you once, years ago, in his company, and you looked so contained it made an impression on me. You were not afraid, but you were most definitely wary."

Lord Talbot rose to his feet. "You are correct in your assumption, but however difficult a man, he was still my father, and I will not air our dirty linen in public."

The viscount stood. "It is right and proper that you should not. I should not have pried, forgive me." He smiled wryly. "Your sisters are a different matter, however. We will take very good care of them, I assure you, but it might help if I knew a little more about their history. I admit, they intrigue me. Despite their similar appearance, they are not at all alike, and yet both share one trait that is plainly obvious."

Lord Talbot raised an eyebrow. "And what is that?"

"Neither of them has any idea of how to go on in company. Miss Drucilla looked at me as if I might be an ogre when first she met me and cast herself at my aunt's feet to pet her ill-favoured pug when they were first introduced. Miss Talbot was not afraid to enjoin battle with my aunt, which speaks of an intrepidity or ignorance most uncommon, and yet they are not schoolroom misses." He held up his hand at Lord Talbot's gathering frown. "I do not mean to denigrate them. I find them both… interesting, and if I am not much mistaken, both please my eccentric aunt in their own ways, and yet I cannot help but wonder how they are quite so unmoulded by societal expectations."

The baron grimaced. "Neither of my sisters has spent much time in company. When they had just turned twelve our mother died. They were sent to our property in Wales and did not return until they were eighteen. Due to my father's and Lady Frampton's illnesses, followed by my father's death, they have had little opportunity to practise the social graces since. The only expectations they learned to fulfil were those taught by their strict governess, but they never had the opportunity to put them into practice. Their behaviour is both a reflection of and a rebellion against the constraints put upon them, I believe. But they will find their way."

"Ah," the viscount said. "That is illuminating. Thank you. Now, shall we join Freddie before he sets Lady Frampton all on end?"

Lord Talbot followed him from the room. "Why should he? He seems a pleasant enough fellow."

"He is, but she has no patience with people she regards as stupid."

"I only spoke with him for a few minutes," the baron said, "and although we spoke of nothing of any great import, he seemed quite sensible."

Lord Kirkby laughed softly. "He is becoming ever

more so. He has for years suffered with sleeplessness, which has inevitably affected his ability to concentrate and caused him to fall asleep at the most inopportune moments, but he is enjoying a rare respite from the malady."

∽

Lady Frampton approved of Freddie's early appearance.

"I am glad to see that you are not one to linger over the port," she said.

This promising start was somewhat spoilt by her next comment.

"Having seen you fall asleep at a ball, a concert, and the theatre, I doubt you able to hold your drink."

"I'll have you know, Honora—"

"It is quite all right, Aunt," Freddie said. "It is an easy assumption to make, after all."

Lady Wirksworth nodded briefly before turning back to her relative and speaking to her in such low tones that Lady Frampton was forced to lean forward to catch her words.

"The tea tray has just been brought in, would you like a cup, Mr Ashton?" Lucy said brightly.

"Yes, thank you."

He followed her to a sideboard.

"Sugar? Milk?"

"A little milk, if you please."

As she bent her head, he could not help noticing the graceful curve of her neck. A strand of ebony hair had come loose from her knot and lay curled against it. He had the oddest urge to reach out and touch it.

As she turned and handed him his cup, her large, soft eyes regarded him earnestly. She spoke quickly and quietly. "Mr Ashton, I am sorry that my godmother—"

"Do not give it a thought," he said softly. "I am guilty of what she accuses me. Drink is not the source of my frequent somnolence, however."

"It would not matter if it was," she said. "Perhaps I should not do so, for my godmother has been nothing but kind to me and my sister, but I feel I must speak. She should not take every opportunity offered to snap at you."

Freddie found himself quite enchanted by the indignation sparking in her eyes.

"Please, do not concern yourself, Miss Drucilla. I am quite used to it."

She drew in a deep breath as if gathering her resolution. "Be that as it may, I do not like it. As you said once before, one would not choose to be in the company of a person one cannot please. I think, perhaps, it would be better if I told my aunt that I would rather go to Bath, after all, because I do not wish you to be subjected to her barbed comments in your own home."

He had only a moment to notice the curious sinking sensation in his stomach before words formed on his tongue and spilled from his mouth. "No, don't do that, Miss Drucilla. It would disappoint your and my sister, my aunt… and… well, me."

As her eyes widened and she blushed, he felt the colour rising in his cheeks. He realised he had made a blunder and hurried on in some confusion.

"My sister has been sadly flat, you know. I am

really very fond of her, and I would not like to see her cast once more into the dumps. You must not worry about Lady Frampton, she will be company for my aunt, who, between you and I, is also rather pulled. She was very worried about Lucinda, and she needs a rest as much as Lady Frampton, so you and your sister will be doing me a great favour if you come."

A sweet smile trembled on her lips, and there was a curiously warm light in her eyes as she said, "Then we shall, of course, oblige you."

At that moment, Lords Kirkby and Talbot entered the room. He felt a wave of relief. In future, perhaps he should forgo port altogether. He had never given any lady a reason to think he had fixed his interest with her, but he had just come mighty close. It would never do.

Lord Talbot observed them closely for a moment and then smiled. "Lucy, as it seems we are soon to be parted, please, sit with me."

CHAPTER 13

As there was much to do if they were to be ready to leave, it had been agreed that Lucy would take breakfast at Charlotte Street the following morning. It would give her a chance to spend a little more time with her brother. She had never visited the house and looked about her with some interest as a footman admitted her. The hall was a little dark and very much like any other. It had a musty air similar to Lady Frampton's abode when she had first arrived. She expected the house to be a very masculine domain and was surprised to find the breakfast parlour decorated in primrose yellow with bright blue curtains framing the windows.

It seemed she was early for the room was empty. A creak behind her made her look over her shoulder, and she saw her brother running lightly down the stairs. She turned smiling, and he came to her.

"May I kiss you, sister?"

She offered her cheek. "Of course, you may. You need not ask my permission."

He glanced at the footman. "You may serve breakfast, Peter. My sister will be down momentarily."

He led the way into the room and pulled a chair out for her. "I like your new friends."

She smiled ruefully. "As they are my only friends, I am glad."

Stephen's grey eyes darkened. "I hope you count me as your friend as well as your brother."

She put out a hand, and he grasped it firmly.

"Of course, I do. It is a shame we are to part so soon. What is this business that is so urgent it calls you home?"

He paused and then said, "Father left a great many ends for me to tie up. He was not as careful a steward as I had assumed."

Her eyes widened. "Do you mean he left you with debts?"

His lips twisted. "A few, but nothing for you to worry about. Some careful management has allowed me to come about, but I do not like to be absent for too long. I have had a letter informing me that the roof of the east wing has sprung a leak. It will need repairing, of course, but I wish to see for myself the extent of it before I give permission for repairs."

"I understand," she said. A horrid thought crossed her mind. "Stephen, was father depending on us marrying well to fill his coffers?"

"Do not think about that, Lucy. I hope you and Abby will find someone you wish to marry, but you may be sure that I have the means to care for you until then."

She remembered that Abby had wondered what would become of her when he married. "And what of you?" she asked gently. "Do you wish to marry? Did… did Father arrange a match for you?"

His eyes darkened and a small frown pinched his brow. "Bevis had a sister, but she drowned shortly before her sixteenth birthday."

Lucy sighed. "The poor thing. Would you have gone through with it if she had not?"

A dull flush crept into his cheeks and his eyes dropped to the table. "I did not agree to it but said that I would meet her to appease Father. It was not wise to say no to him outright. I must admit I hoped that something would occur to prevent… I was but one and twenty… but I never wished for any harm to come to her."

"Of course you did not," Lucy said quickly. "It is very sad, but at least you may now make your own choice with a free conscience."

He smiled wryly. "I think it will be a few years yet before I can or need consider the wedded state. I am but four and twenty, after all."

"Yes, of course. I hope you will not be lonely without Abby."

He laughed. "I will have little time to be lonely; I have much to occupy me. I will admit, however, that she has been helpful for the most part. I turned off several people once I had come to grips with the mess Father had left me, but I asked Abby to be present at many of the meetings I had before I came to that decision. It was not a step I took without a great deal of thought, and I felt a second opinion would be valuable." He smiled ruefully. "I had for so long been told I was quite useless that I was not, at first, confident in my decisions, and I wished to keep Abby busy and make her feel useful.

"She was not slow to share her opinions in her inimitable way. Mr Ferris, our bailiff, was a lying weasel, Father's valet, Kent, a light-fingered toady, and Jacob, one of the grooms…" He shook his head. "I will not repeat what she said of him."

"And was it true?" Lucy asked. "You know our sister can be rather judgemental."

He nodded. "Mr Ferris had been lining his own pockets, a little at a time, for years. Kent had a surprising number of expensive 'gifts' from our father, and Jacob…" He sighed. "Well, Jacob had got one of our maids with child, and she claimed he had forced himself on her."

Lucy gasped. "Oh, no! Whatever became of her?"

"Abby would not have the maid turned off. She persuaded one of our tenant's wives to take her in and look after the babe when it was born so the girl could return to work."

"That was very good of her. I hope Jacob was punished."

"I do not think that would have been fair. Jacob insisted she had willingly lain with him."

"You believed him?"

The baron looked grave. "Yes, I did. Another of the stable hands informed me they had been carrying on for some time and the girl was jealous because she thought he had turned his affections elsewhere. If only Abby had been present at my interview with Jacob, she might have seen reason, but she claimed she could not bear the smell of the stables.

"He looked me straight in the eye and reeled off a list of when and where they had met. He even offered to marry the girl, but when I informed Abby, she insisted that it would be the ultimate cruelty to force her into wedlock with such a man." He sighed. "And the girl could hardly agree to marry him without looking guilty of making a false accusation, especially after our sister had championed her so fiercely. I believe Abby's judgement was faulty on that one occasion and it prevented a happy conclusion. I found Jacob another position." He smiled wryly. "But not too far away. I still hope that they may become reconciled."

"Oh dear," Lucy said. "Perhaps it will be more likely now Abby is not there."

"Yes, I think it might be."

"Poor Stephen," she said. "You have had much to bear."

He laughed. "The majority of our servants have proved loyal and trustworthy. Collins and Mrs Hawkins have been with us a long time. They were always kind to me and loved our mother. They only remained because she had begged them to take care of us as much as they could." He squeezed her hand. "When you are ready to return, Lucy, you will be welcomed warmly. I understand that it might be difficult for you but believe me when I say that the best way to eradicate unhappy memories is to make happy ones to chase them out."

"We shall see." She changed the subject. "This house is not quite what I expected. Are the other rooms decorated in so feminine a style?"

"Only the drawing room and one of the bedchambers," Abby said, coming into the room.

Lucy smiled wanly. "Perhaps Father initially expected to bring Mama to Town with him."

A dry laugh escaped Abby. "It was not done for Mama's benefit, his mis—"

"A Miss Huntley was housekeeper here for some years," Stephen interpolated. "It was she who had a hand in decorating those rooms."

"I do not think Lucy needs shielding from—"

"Abby." Stephen spoke in such stern tones that Lucy jumped.

"What is it I do not need shielding from?" she asked.

"It is nothing," Stephen said. "Merely that I am considering selling this house, and so I am glad that a few of the rooms have a woman's touch."

"Oh," Lucy said. "You were not quite truthful when you said you had come about earlier." She groaned. "And the remainder of my new gowns are to be delivered this morning, but I would never have allowed myself to be so extravagant if I had known—"

"Nonsense," he said brusquely. "I do not like the situation of this house, that is all. Whilst we are on the subject of houses, I may as well tell you that I am seeing my man of business today and instructing him to find a tenant for Glasbury Heights. I felt certain neither of you would be overly keen to visit it any time in the near future."

"I never wish to set eyes on it." Abby's voice was iron. She took a breath, and said more gently, "Now, if

I am to come to you this afternoon, Lucy, I must oversee the packing of my trunks."

Lucy moved as if to follow her, but Stephen forestalled her. "You did not get the chance to play for me last evening, would you do so now?"

She smiled. "Of course."

He praised her extravagantly for her efforts and then showed her to her sister's room. She saw her maid was present.

"I hope you don't mind, miss," Dolly said, "but I thought I'd give Pascoe a hand, and she'll return the favour afterwards."

"No, not at all."

"It appears," Abby said, "that I am surplus to requirements. As Stephen is to be out most of the day, I may as well return with you now."

Stephen saw them out himself and they walked away arm in arm.

"I must say, sister," Abby said, "your Mr Ashton is growing in my esteem."

Lucy blushed. "He is not my Mr Ashton."

"I am pleased to hear it, for however pleasant a gentleman, I am not at all sure him capable of offering you sufficient protection. It really should have been he who gave me a set down last evening, not his aunt."

"He is too much the gentleman," Lucy said, "and besides, did you not say only this morning that I do not need to be protected?"

"Do not twist my words, sister. I meant only that you did not need to be shielded from such things as… well, monetary matters. There are many other things you might need protection from."

It appeared that this part of Town was inhabited by those who did not have the means or desire to go anywhere else, for carts, carriages, and pedestrians made their way along the street. The twins were so engrossed in their conversation that they did not notice the curricle that had drawn up on the opposite side of the street.

Their brother, who still stood at the top of the steps, was not so distracted. He knew very little of Bevis, having met him only once before, years ago, at his father's house, but there was something about him that he had not cared for. Perhaps it was the cold look in his eyes or his arrogant air. He was surprised he had agreed to marry a woman he had never before set eyes on. He had not struck Stephen as a man who would be overly swayed by filial duty.

Bevis descended from his curricle, handed the reins to his groom, and sauntered towards him.

"Good morning, Talbot," he said. "Could you spare me a few minutes?"

Although he had no wish to oblige him, it was time Bevis understood his position.

"Very well, but it must only be a few minutes for I have an appointment with my man of business."

He led him to the small study at the back of the house, sending Peter, who stood statue-like in the hall, a meaningful glance. "May I offer you something to drink? A glass of wine, perhaps?"

"Certainly," he said. "It is never too early for a good wine."

Stephen had no idea whether the wine he poured was good or not and nor did he much care. For form's sake he also poured himself a glass, although he did not intend to touch it.

"What can I do for you?" he said, passing the wine to his visitor and indicating a seat.

The earl gave a mirthless laugh as he sat, carelessly crossing his legs. "Come now, Talbot, let us not beat around the bush. I have been more than patient. I have allowed Miss Drucilla Talbot a year to mourn, but it is time I staked my claim."

Stephen leant against his desk and crossed his arms. "As far as I am concerned, you have no claim."

Bevis tossed off the wine. "Have you really so little respect for your father's wishes?"

The baron gave a mirthless laugh. "I had very little respect for them when he was living, and so it is most unlikely that I should do so now that he is dead. My sisters shall have some say in who they marry."

Lord Bevis's smile did not reach his calculating eyes. "Then you might at least offer me an introduction. By not doing so, you are giving Miss Drucilla no choice at all. It may be that she takes a liking to me."

He pretended to consider this. His words set off an uncomfortable echo in his mind. His father had once used a similar argument when he had insisted he meet the earl's sister.

"You will have an opportunity to meet her during the season."

Lord Bevis's eyes narrowed. "And so will everyone else. I had no idea your sisters were such beauties, and I have no wish to see my promised bride fawned over by every lecherous bachelor in Town."

Stephen stiffened. "You may be sure my sister will be closely chaperoned. Now, I must ask you to leave.

We are to return to Herefordshire in the morning, and I have much to do."

He had no intention of informing Bevis of his sisters' trip into Derbyshire, for he had remembered that he also lived in that county, although he was unsure of his precise direction. As his knowledge of the geography of Derbyshire was rather hazy, he would probably have been none the wiser.

His visitor sneered. "I find it interesting that whilst you are reluctant to introduce me to your fair sisters, it appears you have not been so reticent with that idiot Ashton."

Stephen was surprised by the vehemence of his words. He cocked an eyebrow.

"I take it he is not a friend of yours?"

"A friend," the earl scoffed, "hardly, he is an imbecile. Our families have nothing to do with each other."

This reassured the baron. "It was not I who made the introduction, but I see nothing to object to. How is it you know of their slight acquaintance?"

"I saw him walking with your sisters in the park, not that I was sure it was them at the time. I would have enquired as to their names, but they turned and walked away, their noses in the air."

As they would hardly have done so if Mr Ashton had been with them, Stephen deduced that Bevis had intended to speak with them whilst they were alone. This did not please him.

"Their strict upbringing would have ensured they would have done so before allowing a stranger to address them, as yours should have prevented you from making the attempt." He moved to the door, opened it, and raised his voice slightly. "Now, if you will excuse me, my footman will show you out."

Peter had been hovering nearby ready for the summons, but Lord Bevis pushed past both of them, throwing over his shoulder, "I know the way. You have not heard the last of this, Talbot."

"Peter," he said softly, "if memory serves me correctly, Bevis has a house in Half Moon Street. Watch it and inform me of his comings and goings for the remainder of the day."

"Certainly, sir."

"Wait," he said, as the footman headed for the door. "You will stand out like a sore thumb in your livery, have you some other clothes?"

The footman grinned. "Yes, my lord, for my days off. Don't you worry, I'll not be seen."

The baron slipped him a few coins. "Good man. If you need to take a hackney to follow him, do so."

His opinion of Bevis had plummeted even further, and he was left with an uneasy feeling that was still with him when he returned home, having completed his business. He frowned as Peter opened the door.

"You are back earlier than I expected."

"He's gone, sir," the footman said. "And by the quantity of baggage strapped to his carriage, he won't be coming back any time soon."

The baron breathed a sigh of relief. It seemed his words had been nothing but hot air.

"Did you follow him?"

"I didn't need to, sir. A maid came up from the basement almost the moment he left, and I fell into conversation with her."

The baron's lips twitched. "Pretty, was she?"

Peter grinned. "As a picture. He's gone home to his place in Derbyshire, sir. According to Kate… I mean the maid, he was in a pelter. She said he should have gone days ago as he is hosting a shooting party, and now he'll barely arrive before his guests."

He relaxed. Bevis was in a hurry, and his sisters would not leave until the morrow. A convoy that included an enceinte lady and two older matrons was unlikely to travel quickly, and so it was extremely unlikely their paths would cross on the journey. And yet, he could not feel quite easy. Should he go? It seemed something of an overreaction and how would he explain his change of heart? He truly did have pressing matters to attend to. Besides, his sisters had been shackled enough, and he did not wish to smother them.

Abby frequently told him he overthought things and was a worrier like his sister. If he were totally honest, he would be relieved to be rid of her for a few weeks. He was fond of her, but her instinct was to rule, and having invited her to become involved in estate matters, it was proving difficult to extract her from them. It was not that he did not value her opinion, but if he was to fully grow into his role, he must be allowed to make his own decisions. Besides, both Ashton and Kirkby would be with them, as well as their footmen he presumed. He glanced at Peter. He trusted him completely. He was the son of his gamekeeper and was intelligent.

"How would you like a trip into Derbyshire, Peter?"

He grinned. "Never you fear, my lord, I'll keep the ladies safe."

Stephen did not doubt it but resolved to send a note to Viscount Kirkby that very evening. He need not give him all the details, merely tell him that Bevis had shown an undesirable interest in his sisters and ask him to keep them out of his way if their paths should cross.

CHAPTER 14

They started the journey in high spirits, wiling away the time playing charades, this being one of the few games Miss Wardle had deemed suitable for exercising a lady's mind. When that palled, Lady Frampton taught them to play a variety of card games including commerce, loo, and cassino. The notion of gambling was new to both the sisters and added spice to the games, even if their currency was only buttons retrieved from Lady Frampton's sewing basket. Once she heard of this, Lady Kirkby often joined them in the carriage, although she claimed it was a wish to escape Jacko that motivated her.

"He will not be still," she complained. "But as he cannot travel in the servants' carriage with Thomas as Jasper is with him, my only chance of relief is to spend part of each day with you. No wonder Robert wished to travel in his curricle. Please say that I may. Freddie will happily take my place; he is the most obliging of brothers."

Lucy was not sorry when Abby used this opportunity to casually extract information about Mr Ashton. She had felt a little uneasy for the last few days. Their acquaintance was new and therefore superficial she knew, and yet their interactions had felt more than that, especially when he had come to dinner at her godmother's house. He had all but begged her to come, but since then, he had seemed a little distant. It was true that she had seen him only at dinner, the ladies tending to breakfast in their rooms in preparation for an early start. There had been little opportunity for conversation with him even then, as Lady Wirksworth, Lady Frampton, and Lady Kirkby all wished to retire soon afterwards, pleading fatigue, and Abby and Lucy had had little choice but to follow suit. She could not help feeling, however, that he had somehow withdrawn from her. What she could not fathom was why. She had thought him her friend, and she was dismayed to think she might have been mistaken.

She told herself that she was being oversensitive, something Abby had told her often enough, and concentrated instead on learning more of him from his sister. She felt a twinge of envy when Lady Kirkby described the freedom they had enjoyed growing up, and Abby sighed when she mentioned the friends who had been welcomed to stay at any time.

"It sounds idyllic," Abby said.

Lady Kirkby laughed. "Well, I think we were fortunate, and Freddie's friends certainly enjoyed coming to Wirksworth very much, but I must admit that most of mine did not know quite what to make of it. Uncle Lionel often forgot to change for dinner, and it would not be unusual for him to have a smudge of soil on his face." She smiled ruefully. "Aunt Seraphina would quiz them on their opinions on a host of things. As they had not been brought up to have opinions on anything much, it discomposed them. And then there were the animals. There were more of them then, including several bad-tempered cats and a fox."

"A fox? In the house?" Abby gasped.

"We found Jerome when he was a kit," she explained. "The poor thing's leg had been mangled in a trap, and of course he had to come back with us. My aunt refused to release him when he recovered because he could not possibly run from the hunt." She wrinkled her nose. "I am afraid he never became quite house-trained, and he would only allow Freddie to pet him."

The biggest shock, however, came when she mentioned quite casually that her parents had been murdered by housebreakers at Ashton Manor. Lucy and Abby both stared mutely at her.

"Oh, did not Lady Frampton tell you of it?"

"I did not," that lady said. "I did not wish the girls to fashion any ghoulish notions about the house. I believe it is quite ancient, and so I thought it a distinct possibility."

"Oh, I would not worry about that," Lady Kirkby said. "It has been leased all this time and now the son of the old tenant wants to purchase it, something he would hardly wish to do if there was anything at all untoward with the property such as ghosts roaming the corridors. Perhaps you think me heartless that I can speak of it so calmly, but I was only three months old, you see, and Aunt Seraphina and Uncle Lionel were the only parents I ever knew. It affected Freddie far more, I think, for although he remembers very little, he has suffered nightmares all his life. Well, until recently, at least. We are, like you, strangers to Ashton Manor. Only my aunt has memories of it. I look forward to exploring it together."

Lady Frampton cleared her throat and shifted a little as if she were uncomfortable. "I will admit that I may have been a little hard on Frederick in the past. But now Seraphina has told me something of these nightmares, I realise that he had some excuse for his odd behaviour."

Lucy's heart ached for Mr Ashton. She had been plagued by nightmares for months after arriving at Ashwick Hall, and her lack of sleep had only made her melancholy worse. He had been plagued by them his whole life, poor man. She could not fathom how he had remained so cheerful.

By the fifth day of travel, even cards and chatter palled, and Lucy was relieved when it was decided that they would break their journey in Bakewell. They had hoped to reach Ashton Manor that evening, but it was growing dark, and they had been travelling through rain and mist for the past several hours. She had not been able to see much from the window of the carriage, but judging by the ascents and descents, they had entered hilly country.

The carriage came to a halt in front of The Rutland Arms. It was a large, impressive building with a pleasing symmetry and an eye-catching achievement of arms depicting two unicorns over the door. She exchanged a relieved smile with Abby. As they had hoped to finish their journey that day, they had not bespoke rooms, but surely such a sizeable inn would be able to accommodate them? It was not as if Bakewell was on one of the busier coaching routes, after all. She had not heard another carriage pass for the last half an hour, at least.

"I do hope they have room," Lady Frampton said wearily. "For I vow I cannot go another mile."

They entered a spacious hall with a wide, carpeted staircase ahead. A man hurried from a room to their right, introduced himself as William Greaves, the landlord, and soon put any such fears to rest.

"There will be no problem with rooms. We've only a few coaching services using the inn as yet, but that will soon change as I've secured some new contracts. In the summer, we had many visitors, who wished to explore the High Peak, stay with us, but the weather can become unpredictable at this time of year, and the roads, such as they are, treacherous. Now, if you had come two nights ago, I would have had to disappoint you. Owing to the ball we held – we have a very gracious ballroom, you know – the inn was as full as it could hold, why, we even had to turn away Lord Bevis. He was not best pleased when he had to go on for the rain was falling thick and fast."

Lucy and Abby exchanged a surprised glance as the landlord continued, "You may be sure our rooms are comfortably appointed, the sheets well aired, and as the stables are across the road – an unusual but felicitous arrangement – you'll get a good night's sleep."

"However aired your sheets are," Lady Frampton said, "I will use my own."

"As you wish…" The landlord's amiability faltered

at the sight of Mr Ashton striding through the door carrying Jacko.

"Sir! This is a respectable establishment, and I am not sure that we can cater—"

"Nonsense!" Lady Frampton snapped, apparently forgetting her dislike of the monkey. "Unless you wish to dispense with the custom of a viscount and his wife, the widows of a baronet and an earl, the daughters of a baron, and"— she waved a hand towards Freddie— "Mr Ashton, who owns Ashton Manor, a considerable property near here."

The landlord appeared stunned, but as his eyes had become fixed on Mr Ashton and his jaw had dropped, it did not appear that it was the irascible Lady Frampton who was responsible. He recovered himself in a moment.

"Bless my soul," he said. "People hereabouts still talk of… what happened all those years ago. We've never had such a scandal before or since. Can it be that you are returning home, at last, sir?"

"No, no," he said. "Just paying a visit."

A plump, dark-haired lady appeared at the far end of the corridor. "William, what are you about keeping these good people standing about in the hall?"

She ushered three maids out from behind her. "My girls will see to your rooms, immediately." She glanced at Abby and Lucy. "I hope you don't mind sharing; we do have a few guests, you see, who must be up early to catch the Nottingham stage, and we are expecting another gentleman shortly."

"Not at all," Abby said promptly. "We have shared a room the entire journey. We like it."

"Ann," the landlord said portentously, "It is Mr Ashton and his aunt."

The landlady's glance passed over Lady Frampton, settled for a moment on Mr Ashton and Lady Kirkby, and then moved on to Lady Wirksworth. She sank into a curtsy, saying calmly, "I am pleased to see you again, my lady. I was one of those waiting outside the church in Castleton to wish you well when you married, and my cousin was a young maid at the manor."

"What was her name?" Lady Wirksworth asked.

"Emma," she said.

Lady Wirksworth's tone softened. "I remember her. Her hair was always escaping her cap and she often had a smudge of smut on her cheek from cleaning out the grates."

"That sounds about right, my lady. She's Mrs Cooper now and has been housekeeper at the manor for some years. I'm sure she'll be delighted to see you again." Her eyes turned towards Mr Ashton. "She always had a soft spot for you, sir, when she was a girl."

"Did she?" he said, surprised. "I am gratified, of course, but I remember very little of my time there."

Lord Kirkby strolled in and glanced at Mr Greaves. "Are you the landlord?"

"I am, sir."

"Viscount Kirkby. I wish to compliment you on the stables. Not only are they spacious and well designed, but I see you have a separate taproom across from them, an excellent arrangement."

Mr Greaves looked gratified. "I can't take the credit, sir. It is His Grace, The Duke of Rutland, who should do that. We also have a separate entrance and coffee room for those who come on the stage," he said proudly. "I hope I value all of my customers as I should, but I don't see why the quality should rub shoulders with anyone that they wouldn't otherwhere."

The viscount nodded, his eyes sweeping around the company. "Is there any particular reason we are congregating here? I, for one, am rather sharp set."

"Take our guests into the parlour to warm themselves by the fire," Mrs Greaves said, "and I'll send some light refreshments whilst the servants prepare the rooms and I advise cook on the numbers for dinner."

Lucy turned her head as Dolly let out an undignified shriek.

"Jane!"

One of the maids on the stairs turned. Lucy saw the resemblance between them immediately. Jane was a little older and her face thinner and warier, but the large hazel eyes and chestnut hair were the same.

"Bell!" Lady Frampton said sternly. "Whatever do you mean by—"

"It is quite all right," Lucy said quickly. "Jane is Bell's long-lost sister. The shock of seeing her here caused the outburst, which I am sure is quite understandable."

"Well, this is a day for surprises," Mrs Greaves said. "And if Miss Bell would like to come along to the kitchen to await your hot water, ma'am, Jane can see her once she has done her duty."

They were shown into a large, high-ceilinged room which more resembled a comfortable withdrawing room in a country house than the parlour of an inn. It boasted sofas, chairs, and a large round dining table. A welcoming fire flickered in the grate.

"You are too soft on that girl," Lady Frampton said, sinking into a chair. "Perhaps I should have chosen another to be your maid."

"Oh, do not say so," Lucy said. "She suits me very well, and how can I begrudge her being a little overwhelmed by seeing her sister again when I have so recently been similarly affected myself?"

"Well said, Miss Drucilla," Freddie said, admiration sparking in his eyes. "Your compassion does you credit."

She felt herself warm from the inside at his praise.

"Her compassion will lead to her being taken advantage of," Lady Frampton said dryly.

Lucy pushed away her pleasure, remembering that Flora and Anne had warned her whilst at Ashwick Hall that her desire for praise might cloud her judgement of a person's character or intentions. Mr Ashton was merely being kind.

"Tell me of this long-lost sister," Lady Wirksworth said.

"Jane came to London a few years before Dolly… I mean Bell, and the family never heard of her again."

"I do not see anything so surprising in that," Lady Frampton said. "Not all maids can write, after all."

"No, but I believe they both can read and write, and so she became worried about her."

"I should hope she can read and write," Lady Wirksworth said. "For no lady's maid worth the name cannot."

"Never mind your maid," Abby said. "Did you hear that Lord Bevis was here but two nights ago?

Does it not seem strange that he too should come to so out-of-the-way a place?"

"It is not strange at all," Lady Wirksworth said. "His estate lies on the other side of Castleton which is not far from here."

"Oh," Lucy said. "Then you are well acquainted with the family?" Her eyes darted to Mr Ashton who calmed a chattering Jacko as, with a half-hearted bark, an apparently weary Jasper passed him and trotted towards his mistress. "It is just that I had the impression that Mr Ashton and Lord Bevis were not the best of friends."

"We are not," he said, passing the monkey to Thomas, who promptly left the room. "But do not let it trouble you."

"We used to be well acquainted with the family," Lady Wirksworth said, "but there was a falling out many years ago, long before my nephew was born, and we have had very little to do with each other since. Do you mind if I ask how you know Lord Bevis?"

"We do not know him at all," Abby said. "We have seen him but twice and both times he made an unfavourable impression, but we have never spoken to him."

"Think yourselves fortunate," Lady Kirkby said. "He has a sneering way about him."

"I had forgotten that you were present when he played his joke on Bond Street," Lady Wirksworth said, putting a hand to her head.

"If it was a joke, it was a very poor one," Lucy said with unusual heat.

"Undoubtedly," she said. "Where are those refreshments?"

"Are you all right, Seraphina?" Lady Frampton said.

Lady Wirksworth bent, picked up Jasper, and began to stroke him. It seemed to soothe her. "Thank you, Honora, I am weary, that is all, as I am sure you are."

A waiter came into the room carrying a tea tray and a plate heaped high with cakes. Mr Greaves followed him with wine and brandy.

Lucy glanced at Lady Kirkby, and seeing she looked quite exhausted, went to the tea tray.

"How much farther is Ashton Manor?" Abby asked.

"Some seventeen miles," Lady Wirksworth said, sighing. "But it may as well be thirty for the roads are not at all good."

Mr Greaves added another log to the fire and turned his head. "Mr Ramsey has improved the road down into the dale. As it turns back on itself several times, it's not as steep as it could be, but your coachmen will still have to make frequent use of a drag-shaft and shoe. It is the sharp turns that will require the most skill, however. We make deliveries to the Old Nag's Head in Edale twice a month weather permitting, and we've a wagon going in the morning. I can send a man with your lead coach if you wish. The others can follow his example, and Ned can come back with the wagon."

"Is it that difficult?" Lord Kirkby asked, frowning.

"Not if you know the way of it," Mr Greaves said.

"Ned'll see you down safe enough. What time would you like your dinner served, sir?"

"As soon as it can be ready," Lord Kirkby said swiftly.

"Shall we say an hour then? Mrs Greaves always has something in hand for unexpected visitors."

"As long as it is not the leftovers from the ball," Lady Wirksworth said sharply. "I have a delicate stomach."

Mr Greaves looked affronted. "We are not that sort of an inn, my lady."

"Then that will do very well," she said, seemingly oblivious to his offended tone. "I do not intend to change for dinner. As a matter of fact, I do not intend to stir from here until I have supped, and then I shall seek my bed. I would be grateful, however, if you would send in a bowl of water so that I may wash my hands before I eat."

"As you wish, my lady," the landlord said and beat a hasty retreat.

"Although it pains me to say it, I am of the same mind as you, Seraphina," Lady Frampton said. "I will keep you company whilst the others refresh themselves."

Lucy handed out the tea and cakes and was not surprised when Mr Ashton came to receive a cup. Even at dinner, he drank very little wine. His hair was once more rather wild, his curls springing from his head in disordered clusters. Although she knew it odd of her, she preferred it to the more restrained, glossy style his valet created, no doubt with a generous application of pomade. She felt that this was more like the Mr Ashton she had first encountered, and this reassured her so much that she found herself able to speak to him quite naturally.

"I hope, Mr Ashton, that Jacko was not too restless today? It has been our longest day on the road. It is no wonder that Lady Wirksworth is so fatigued."

"He does not like to be cooped up for hours at a time, it is true, but I took him up on the box seat for an hour or two before the rain started in earnest."

Ah, that explained his dishevelled locks. A soft gleam of amusement came into her eyes. "That must have startled passers-by."

He grinned. "One gentleman nearly drove his gig off the road, but it delighted the children in several of the villages we passed through. They ran alongside the coach waving. I would have stopped and introduced him if we had not had so far to go."

"Jacko is not a circus animal to be paraded," Lady Wirksworth said, but her tone lacked force.

"No, no, of course not," Mr Ashton said soothingly. "But it would have done no harm and brought them a great deal of pleasure, I am sure."

"Or it might have brought a great deal of displeasure down on their heads for failing to execute whatever errand they had been sent upon in a timely manner," Abby said tartly.

"Then it is as well we did not stop," he said, "for I would not have had that happen for the world."

"Whilst you made an excellent point, Miss Talbot," Lady Wirksworth said frostily, "might I suggest that your anger would be better directed at those who would deliver such retribution on a child rather than on one who wishes only to provide a moment's pleasurable distraction?"

Lady Kirkby sent her brother a sympathetic smile. "Poor Freddie, to be so snapped at for nothing more than an altruistic impulse. You will make a splendid uncle and ruin my children with indulgence, I am certain."

The words of both Lady Wirksworth and her niece seemed to make an impression on Abby. She coloured. "Forgive me, Mr Ashton. My fatigue does not excuse my poor manners."

He laughed. "You are feeling rolled up, Miss Talbot, to apologise for such a trifle. I would go and lie down if I were you."

She smiled, amusement chasing the chagrin from her eyes. "Has anyone ever been able to prick your good temper, Mr Ashton?"

He glanced at Lord Kirkby who was regarding him with a wry smile. "I cannot call any instances to mind, but I am sure when I was a boy someone must have."

"You dressed Robert down when we were children for saying something horrid to me," his sister said. "I believe it came to fisticuffs."

The viscount laughed. "You knocked me down and bloodied my nose, Freddie."

"I know," he said. "I was not going to mention it, however, not before the ladies."

"I deserved it," the viscount said. "I think we were thirteen, just the age when a boy does not wish an eight-year-old girl trailing about after him." He threw a smiling glance at his wife. "Most boys, anyway. You, my friend, never objected to Lucinda tagging along. And if you are honest, you will acknowledge that I was taken off guard by such an unprecedented bout of anger, and my fall was caused by me stumbling over a tree root."

"I admit it freely," he said.

"I am glad you got your deserts," Lady Wirksworth said dryly.

"Yes," Lord Kirkby said, an amused grin touching his lips. "You said so at the time."

Lucy's eyes went to her sister. "Are you ready to go up, Abby?" She took her arm as they left the room. "I was impressed with your apology."

An odd smile touched her sister's lips. "In one way, Mr Ashton reminds me of our brother."

Lucy looked bemused. She could not discern any likeness between them. "What do you mean? Our brother is quiet and serious, Mr Ashton lively and cheerful."

"That is true, but like Stephen, he does not take umbrage at my unguarded comments."

"Unguarded?" Lucy said. "You have intentionally had a little dig at him every evening."

"Yes," she agreed. "But only in the mildest of ways, but today's comment was not calculated."

Lucy squeezed her arm. "You were thinking of our punishments if we displeased Miss Wardle."

"Yes," Abby admitted. "Things must be far worse for children who are poor and forced to work as soon as they are able, but I should not have spoken so to Mr Ashton. It was very good of him to turn my apology off so lightly and with such humour."

"Perhaps he is becoming accustomed to you."

Abby looked thoughtful. "Yes, perhaps he is."

Lucy smiled. "I am happy you are beginning to

appreciate him, for I was not happy with your remarks, however mild."

"It was just an experiment, a game if you will. I wished to see if his gentlemanly manners might crack under the strain of fending off my comments." She laughed. "At first, I thought him too stupid to notice, but I was mistaken. He is merely impervious to them."

A maid awaited them in the hall and the opportunity for further conversation was lost. They followed her up the stairs, Lucy's steps a little faster than her sister's. She was eager to hear Dolly's news and was disappointed to find only Abby's maid in the room.

"Bell brought your water up, Miss Drucilla," she said. "And I hope you don't think it too much of a liberty, but I sent her off again seeing as how I can give you any assistance you need. Bell said that I was to fetch her immediately if there was any objection."

Lucy smiled. How could she begrudge her a little longer with her sister just to satisfy her curiosity?

"That won't be necessary."

CHAPTER 15

Freddie and Lord Kirkby bowed as they left the room and moved a little apart.

"Miss Talbot must be softening towards you, Freddie," Lord Kirkby said with a faint smile. "She appeared to be genuinely sorry for snapping your nose off."

"Oh, she means nothing by it. Her nature is prickly like my aunt's."

The viscount chuckled. "I would not make the comparison in Miss Talbot's hearing, my friend. No beautiful young lady likes to be compared to an elderly matron."

"I am not that much of a gudgeon, Robert. I hope she will curb her tongue, however. Not for my sake but for her sister's. Miss Drucilla does not like it when she cuts at me."

"No, I had noticed," the viscount said in a soft drawl. "I think that she might like you more than Jacko, after all. Her eyes shone quite delightfully when you praised her for her thoughtfulness towards her maid." His gaze became intent. "And yet, you have hardly spoken to her these past few days, indeed, you have engaged more with her sister."

"Nonsense, there has barely been any opportunity. She is naturally quiet and can hardly get a word in at the dinner table. I like her very well, but…"

Lord Kirkby raised an eyebrow as he broke off, flushing. "But?"

Freddie eyed him a little resentfully. "You make something out of nothing. I hardly know the girl, after all."

His friend regarded him steadily. "And nor will you if you carry on in this vein, which might prove awkward as she is to be a guest in your house."

Freddie frowned. "You do not understand, Robert, and you know I always make a hash of it when I try to explain things."

"Then perhaps I can help you," his friend said gently. "You do not think yourself worthy of her, which is, of course, nonsense."

It seemed he had struck a nerve, for Freddie's gaze sharpened and he took a step closer.

"Is it? You say Miss Drucilla likes me, and perhaps she does, a little. I have seen it with injured animals. They often bond with the first person they feel comfortable with, and as it appears I was the first gentleman in Town to make her acquaintance, that person is me. Miss Drucilla is like a dove; gentle and peace-loving, and she needs to feel safe and protected. She should feel safe and protected, but I do not think I am the man to do it.

"She likes me because I do not alarm her, because we both like animals, and because she feels a little sorry for me, I think, as she feels compassion for Jacko, Jasper, or her maid. But I draw the sort of attention she would not like, and the sort of comments that would make her uncomfortable, some far worse than any her sister can fashion. When she sees that I am regarded as an idiot by much of the *ton*, when I fall asleep at the dinner table and forget what we were speaking of only a few minutes before, she will not like me. It is better that I do not encourage her affection."

Once the viscount had recovered from this very lucid explanation of his friend's feelings, he put his hand on Freddie's shoulder. "Do you honestly think so little of yourself, my friend? I thought that you did not care for the ill-mannered jests aimed at you."

Freddie attempted to run a hand through his hair, wincing when it became embedded in a knot of snarled curls. "I did not... I do not, but she will, and it would make her miserable. If ever anyone deserves to be happy, it is Miss Drucilla."

The viscount smiled wryly. "I cannot disagree with you there. Even the sharp-tongued Miss Talbot deserves to be happy. What sort of father sends his daughters away after their mother dies to be brought up on a remote country estate with only their sour-faced governess for company?"

"It was deuced odd."

"Was it not?"

"Perhaps the fellow did not like females, in which case, I daresay they were better off."

The viscount laughed softly. "I sometimes envy your ability to find the bright side in any situation."

"You should try it some time. I do not envy your habit of questioning every little thing. It is enough to give a man a headache. I will admit I am drawn to Miss Drucilla, but it will not do. Although she is twenty, she is as naïve and innocent as a chit just out of the schoolroom. She needs a man who can help her navigate the complexities of the *ton*. She needs someone like you, Robert. Someone who is respected, intelligent, and who can silence a man or woman with a well-chosen word or a lift of his eyebrow. I am not that man."

The viscount sighed. "Very well, you must make your own decisions. I would not have broached the subject if I had not thought that perhaps you liked her but did not know how to go on. But consider this, my friend. I have spent several evenings in Miss Drucilla's company, and unlike you, I have tried to draw her out. Unsuccessfully, I might add. You might think she needs a man like me, but I do not think she would agree with you."

Freddie put a hand to his brow. "That headache is growing worse by the second."

Lord Kirkby laughed. "Talking of headaches, it is a pity Bevis has decided to come home just at this moment. He is bound to discover sooner or later that you have returned and have guests."

Freddie shrugged. "What if he does? We are here only for a few weeks, and he is unlikely to pay us a visit."

"I would not be so sure of that," the viscount said. "Talbot sent me a most unsatisfactory note before we left. He mentioned that Bevis had shown an interest in his sisters and asked me to keep them out of his way."

"An understandable sentiment."

The viscount frowned. "It is understandable to us

because our acquaintance with him is of long standing, but what can Talbot know of him? He is several years younger, has rarely come to Town, and lives in Herefordshire. Their paths can hardly have crossed."

"I dare say he saw him in Town and did not like the cut of his jib," Freddie said. "I thought him a sensible fellow."

"I hope that is all there is to it," the viscount said.

Freddie shook his head. "There you are again, worrying at things like a dog with a bone. If a problem arises with Bevis, I will deal with him."

A lopsided grin tilted the viscount's lips. "Do you know, I rather think you will. Now, I think I will take Lucinda up to our chamber; she should rest before dinner. You should do the same." His eyes rested on Freddie's hair. "It will take some time for your valet to deal with that bird's nest."

~

At dinner, Abby seemed determined to please.

"I have heard something of your childhood at Wirksworth Hall, Mr Ashton. Would you mind telling me a little of the house itself?"

"Certainly. The original Jacobean manor burned down in 1730, which is a pity for many Wirksworth family heirlooms were lost. However, it was replaced with a handsome house in the Palladian style which is no doubt far more comfortable than the original."

"Is comfort important to you, sir?" Abby asked.

"What an odd question," he said. "Of course it is. Who wishes to be beset by draughts, smoking chimneys, and receive their dinner cold because the dining room is so far from the kitchens?"

Lucy held her breath, sure that Abby would punish him for suggesting her question an odd one. But she merely smiled.

"Very true," Lady Wirksworth said. "I felt I was drowning in luxury when first I went to Wirksworth although the house is not at all ostentatious, merely well appointed. You will discover the truth of my nephew's words when we arrive at Ashton Manor, Miss Talbot. The lower courtyard is surrounded by the medieval wings, and the upper by later Tudor additions."

"It sounds interesting," Lucy said cautiously, determined to make more of an effort to join in the conversation this evening. "Surely it cannot be that uncomfortable if the same tenant lived in it all those years?"

Lady Wirksworth laughed dryly. "Perhaps my memory is faulty, but I do not think so. I have known of families who own several estates who have either abandoned such an inconvenient property or knocked it down and started again. We did not own another property, however, and it would not have mattered if we had. My father would never have voluntarily left the manor, nor would he hear of removing a single stone. Particularly the one in the eastern wing of the lower courtyard, which we believe to have once been part of a curtain wall before it became incorporated into the house."

"What is so important about that stone?" Lucy asked.

"It is carved with the date 1078 and as the original

dwelling within would most likely have been wooden and is long gone, it is the only proof of the existence of a house at the time the conqueror ruled England. We seem to have escaped his survey. It is hardly definitive proof, however, as it might have come from anywhere. It is not unusual for stones to be taken from a ruin to be used in another building.

"But in answer to your previous question, Freddie's tenant, Mr Ramsey, was a wealthy wool merchant, and such a person might compensate for his lack of pedigree by acquiring a property that reeks of history, however inconvenient. There was the added advantage that the estate is awash with sheep, the land being fit for little else apart from mining, and so a good source of wool for his mills and factories. It has been a mutually beneficial relationship, and one I hope will continue with his son even if Freddie decides not to sell to him."

"I should think that it must bring a very good price with the added value of the sheep," Abby said. "Although once that interest is sold, you will lose the steady income that they must bring you. It is something you will need to weigh carefully, Mr Ashton."

As Freddie looked rather startled and had at that moment a mouthful of beef, it was Lord Kirkby who answered her. "How true, Miss Talbot, and how surprising that you should think of such a thing."

She regarded him coolly. "Because I am a mere female?"

Lady Wirksworth gave a crack of laughter. "Good gal."

The viscount was unperturbed by her arch tone. "Because it is my experience that someone of your sex and age would know little of such things or wish to do so."

She raised her chin. "I have not spent the last two years sitting by the fire sewing, Lord Kirkby, but have been taking an interest in my brother's affairs."

"How fortunate Lord Talbot is."

His tone was bland but the slight lift of his eyebrow provocative. Lucy saw her sister's lips tighten and tried to catch her eye, but Abby's gaze remained fixed on the viscount. Lucy let out a low breath when her eyes suddenly brightened with amusement and a puff of laughter escaped her.

"Well done, Miss Talbot," Lady Kirkby said. "It is the only way to deal with him when he becomes odious."

"Odious, my love?" he said, a teasing light in his eyes.

"Most definitely," she said. "Stop baiting Miss Talbot. I am sure she has been a great help to her brother."

"He has said as much," Lucy said, "but my brother was inexperienced in such matters and needed some support for a time." She sent Freddie a smile. "Mr Ashton, on the other hand, has had charge of his affairs for years. I am sure he will know just what needs to be done."

Her eyes widened in concern as, after staring at her a moment, he started to cough, a morsel of food apparently becoming lodged in his throat. The viscount stood, leant over and began to pat him sharply on the back.

"You should chew your food properly, Frederick," Lady Frampton said. "And you should not eat so much. The rest of us finished our meal some five minutes since."

"Thank you, Robert," he gasped, "you may leave off pummelling me now." He wiped his streaming eyes and took a gulp of his wine.

Lady Wirksworth rose to her feet. "I am for bed."

"As am I," Lady Frampton said.

"Yes," Lady Kirkby agreed. "I feel as if I could sleep for a week."

Lucy felt a little disconsolate as she and Abby followed them from the room. Mr Ashton seemed more comfortable talking with Abby than her. She was beginning to wonder if she had been right when she had suspected that he had smartened himself up for her sake, and if his admission that he would be disappointed if she did not come had been because her sister could hardly come without her.

∾

When the door closed behind the ladies, Lord Kirkby and Freddie took their glasses and settled themselves in the armchairs by the fire.

The viscount grinned. "Was it Miss Drucilla's blind faith in you or her rather sweet smile that made you choke, my friend?"

Freddie sighed. "Both. But I have done nothing for her to have such faith in me."

"If it worries you so much, perhaps you should do something to shake it."

Freddie's eyes widened. "Upset her, you mean?"

"If it becomes necessary, and only for her own good, of course."

Freddie looked shocked. "Is that what you did to rid yourself of unwanted admirers? Not that Miss Drucilla is unwanted or an admirer, precisely. It seems a dashed hard-hearted thing to do."

The viscount's eyes narrowed. "And closing your eyes and folding your arms at a ball just as a young lady is about to fall into them is not?"

Freddie looked hurt. "Robert! You know I could not help it."

The viscount's eyebrow lifted. "Could you not? I know, of course, that your trouble sleeping is real, but I have sometimes wondered if you did not use your habit of falling asleep anywhere to your advantage on occasion."

Freddie stared at him in astonishment. The creak of the door opening dropped into the silence, but he could not turn his eyes away from his brother-in-law's interrogative stare.

"You may clear the table," the viscount said.

"I might, of course, but I can't think why I should."

The flash of surprise in Lord Kirkby's eyes released Freddie, and he peered around the wing of his armchair. Just inside the door stood a man of impressive height. Rain dripped from the brim of his hat and the many capes of his driving coat. He swept off his beaver hat, revealing closely cropped chestnut hair, and grinned.

"How are you, Robert?"

The viscount gave a surprised shout of laughter, jumped to his feet, and hastily crossed the room. "Captain Anthony Fairbrass as I live and breathe!

Have you finally finished your wanderings and come home at last?"

The newcomer shook his hand, smiling wryly. "As you see."

His eyes moved to Freddie as he stood and crossed the room. A small frown hovered in them for a moment before the light of recognition brightened them. "Ashton!" He held out his hand. "I hardly recognised you!"

Freddie took the proffered hand. "Fairbrass. Was I really such a shagrag before?"

"Not at all! You must remember that I have not seen you since we left Eton, and we were all little more than scrubby schoolboys. You did not attend university with us."

Freddie smiled ruefully. "There would have been little point. It was a relief to leave my schooling behind and concentrate on learning more practical things such as estate affairs."

Their acquaintance's lips twisted. "Something I avoided for years." He glanced at Robert. "By rights, I am now Captain, Sir Anthony Fairbrass, although I prefer not to use my military rank. I left it behind with the war."

The viscount put a hand on his shoulder. "I did not know. I must have missed the notice of your father's death."

"I can hardly blame you for that; I did myself. It took some time for the news to reach me as I never stayed in the same place for very long. It caught up with me in Venice. I have been at Walthamstow these past two months trying to get a grip on things."

"Sir? May I take your coat?"

He stepped aside, revealing a slender man with striped trousers and a thin, curling moustache.

"Ah, there you are, Rigatoli," he said, shrugging it off and handing it and his hat to him. "I hope your journey was more pleasant than mine?"

"I arrived before the rain set in, sir. Should I have your dinner brought here?"

"Certainly, you should. I have had the good fortune to run into two old friends."

"Very well, sir."

He raised an eyebrow. "You will not mind me in all my dirt?"

"Do not be a fool," Lord Kirkby said. "Come and warm yourself by the fire and have a glass of wine."

Two waiters and a maidservant came into the room, making short work of clearing the table. When they had left, the viscount said, "Why are you here of all places? Derbyshire is some distance from Sussex."

"So it is." He smiled ruefully. "I am afraid I have bolted. Both of my sisters descended on me, their husbands in tow."

"You do not get along with them?" Freddie asked.

"Not when they spent the first week of their visit berating me for my self-indulgence and lack of filial feeling, and the second urging me to get leg-shackled. They are much older than I and must always think they know best. Just when my patience was at an end, I received an invitation to a shooting party."

"Oh? Where?" Lord Kirkby asked.

"Gaines Park."

The viscount's eyebrows shot up. "I did not think you a particular friend of Bevis."

Sir Anthony laughed dryly. "You know I am not,

but I needed some excuse to get away and his invitation provided it. I am hoping he has improved with age. I had planned to spend only a couple of days with him before carrying on into Yorkshire to see you."

"And you would have been welcome," Lord Kirkby said. "But we are to visit Freddie's estate, Ashton Manor."

A waiter and maid entered carrying several dishes. Freddie rose to his feet, yawning.

"I don't know how it is, but I am suddenly tired. I will leave you two to catch up. You are welcome to come to us when you have had enough of Bevis. We are only in the next valley, you know."

"That is very kind of you, Ashton. I shall certainly do so. I will make an early start in the morning, so I will say goodnight and goodbye."

As the baronet went to the table to inspect the dishes, the viscount stood and bade Freddie goodnight.

"Goodnight, Robert," he said quietly. "I'd prefer it if you did not mention the Misses Talbot to Fairbrass."

He frowned. "I know you do not know him as well as I, but you can trust Anthony. He will meet them if he pays us a visit anyway."

"Of course, but he will no longer be staying with Bevis. He would not be the first man to be indiscreet after a glass or two, and the claret always flows freely at these occasions."

The viscount gave his lopsided smile. "Very well, Freddie."

CHAPTER 16

When the twins entered their bedchamber, Pascoe was laying out their night things.

"Has Bell not yet returned?" Lucy said.

"No, but—"

Abby interrupted her. "Our godmother was right; she is taking advantage of your good nature. She has had more than enough time to catch up with all her sister's news."

"She was here, miss," the maid said. "But then her sister appeared at the door sobbing her heart out."

"What has happened?" Lucy asked.

"All I know is that her sister has been dismissed."

Lucy's eyes widened. Had Mrs Greaves deemed that Jane had spent too long away from her duties? Surely not. She had seemed such a reasonable woman.

"Where are they now?"

Jane looked up towards the ceiling. "In her sister's room in the attic."

"Then I will go to them. If my maid's sister is in

trouble because I allowed Dolly to keep her too long, then this is partly my fault. I must set it right, but I will not approach Mrs Greaves before I know precisely what has happened."

"I will accompany you," Abby said.

Lucy hesitated. Once, she would have welcomed her sister's support, depended on it, and it had taken her a long time to accustom herself to the lack of it. It would be easy to fall back into old ways, but she would not do it.

"Thank you, but no, sister. If Jane is so distressed, she will hardly wish for an audience."

Abby opened her mouth as if she would protest but then closed it again and nodded. "Very well, but take Pascoe. You should not be wandering around the inn on your own, and she may show you the way."

Lucy followed the maid to the end of the corridor. It appeared to be a dead end, but Pascoe turned the handle of a door Lucy had assumed to be a bedchamber revealing a narrow staircase. The servants' stairs. She followed her up several flights until they emerged into a long corridor. A door halfway along was slightly ajar, and the sound of stifled sobs came to Lucy's ears.

"You may wait for me here, Pascoe."

"As you wish, ma'am."

As she approached, she heard Dolly's voice.

"Of course they won't. Our sisters will love you whatever you have done."

She knocked on the door and pushed it open. The room was small, barely wide enough to fit two narrow beds and a rather battered set of drawers. Jane lay curled in a ball, her head resting on her sister's lap whilst Dolly stroked her hair as if she were a mother comforting her child. Jane's red puffy eyes widened when she saw Lucy and she sat up quickly, her hands going to automatically pat down her hair. Dolly rose hastily, her expression anxious.

"I'm sorry, miss. I meant to be there when you came up to bed, but Jane was in such a state."

"I told you to go back down," Jane said. "Please, my lady, do not turn my sister off."

"You may be sure I won't," Lucy said. "But I would very much like to know why *you* have been turned off."

The sisters looked at each other, alarm in one face, hesitation in the other.

Jane wrung her hands. "Please don't make me tell you."

"I cannot make you," Lucy said, "but I would like to help you if I can."

The maid shook her head. "There's nothing you can do."

That was a very real possibility, but she was determined to try. "Then I will speak with Mrs Greaves. I had meant to anyway, but I would have liked to know what it is I am dealing with."

Jane wrapped her arms around herself.

"Tell her," Dolly said gently.

The maid squeezed her eyes shut. "But my disgrace will reflect badly on you, Dolly."

"I believe my mistress to be fair."

"Thank you," Lucy said. "Now, sit down, both of you."

The sisters sat side by side on one bed, and Lucy on the other.

Jane wiped her eyes on her apron. "I slipped outside with Dolly and told her what had happened to me after I went to Lunnon. I thought we were alone, but Mrs Greaves had come out for a breath of air and overheard us."

"What did happen to you?" Lucy asked gently. "Tell me the whole."

"There was a customer at our inn who kept bothering me. I told Ma, but she said he was a good customer, and we couldn't afford to make him angry. The night I left she was drunk, and she told me that I should let him have his way and stop pestering her. It was the last straw, and so I went to Lunnun. I thought it would be easy to find a position and then get Dolly one before he started on her."

"But it was not?"

Jane shook her head. "I was an idiot. When I got down from the stage and looked about me, I felt afraid. It was so noisy, so busy, and I didn't know a soul or how to go about finding a position. Then a woman approached me. She seemed kind and told me that she had a room in her house where I might stay until I found my feet. She said she would not charge me for the first week or two." A sob escaped her. "She sent me to a registry office, and they charged me a fee that took most of my remaining money, but they didn't find me a position. Then Mrs Lardy said I owed her money, and I would be sent to debtors' prison if I didn't pay up. She said I could work it off."

"How?" Lucy said.

Colour infused Jane's cheeks. "By pleasing her customers."

"Oh, did she have a shop of some sort?"

A bitter little laugh escaped the girl. "The sort where the women are the merchandise, miss."

Lucy gasped.

"When I said I wouldn't, she dosed me with laudanum and locked me in my room with a man and it happened anyway. She made me a whore and took most of my earnings for clothes, board, and lodging so I couldn't even pay off the debt I owed her."

Lucy recoiled as if she had been struck. A hand flew to her mouth and her eyes filled with tears. "That is… is…"

"That is what happens to gullible girls from the country who turn up without a position," Jane said, her voice hard. "There were other girls there, although I never saw them until after I had become one of them."

"That's why she didn't write to me," Dolly said. "She couldn't have if she wanted to, and later she was too ashamed."

"How did you escape?" Lucy asked, her eyes round and her voice barely more than a whisper.

Jane pulled up her sleeve. A long oval patch, darker than the rest of her skin, almost covered her forearm. "There was a fire, and I managed to escape in the chaos. I jumped on the first available coach. It went to Nottingham, and I got a job in a coaching inn there. I didn't like it much because I was back where I started, always fighting off the customers, but it was better than being a harlot. It was there I met Mr Greaves. He has his own coach, and he's not too proud to drive it if he's short-handed. He offered me the position here and promised I would not be molested." Tears once more welled up. "And I haven't been. It's a first-rate establishment, and I felt safe here… at least until…"

"Jane," Lucy said, "none of what happened was your fault, and I will tell Mrs Greaves so."

Jane shook her head. "It won't make no difference."

Lucy stood. "We shall see. Where might I find her at this hour?"

"She has a little parlour at the back of the house on the ground floor. I expect she'll be making out the orders for tomorrow."

Lucy went out. "Pascoe, you may go back to my sister."

The maid frowned. "But, Miss Drucilla—"

Lucy raised her eyebrows as Flora often had, and the maid nodded, dropped a curtsy, and hurried away. Lucy made her way down the servants' stairs, counting the landings so she would know when she had reached the ground floor. When she opened the door and stepped into the hall, she was relieved to see Mrs Greaves coming out of a room opposite.

"Are you lost, ma'am?" she asked. "Those stairs are for the staff only."

There was disapproval in her voice and Lucy had to fight the impulse to apologise.

"No, not at all, but I thought this might be the most direct route to find you, Mrs Greaves. I am Miss Talbot, one of Mr Ashton's party. I wonder if I might have a word with you?"

A flash of recognition entered the woman's eyes, and her disapproval was replaced by wariness.

"Ah, yes. You are Miss Bell's mistress. I suspect I know what it is you wish to say."

"Mrs Greaves," she said, "what happened to Jane was despicable and tragic, but it was not her fault."

The landlady sighed. "Perhaps not. I believe such women as Mrs Lardy wait for incoming coaches bringing innocent girls from the country and lure them to their bawdy houses."

Lucy was appalled but also relieved. It did not appear that Mrs Greaves was going to be difficult.

"And is Jane a good worker?"

"She is."

"Well, then. I am sure you must have been shocked, but now that you have had time to reflect—"

Mrs Greaves shook her head. "I have not changed my mind. I feel sorry for Jane, but you must consider my position, Miss Talbot. This inn is known to be a superior establishment. We attract the quality, and who is to say that someone might not recognise her?"

Lucy blinked. "Do you mean that *gentlemen* frequent… such places as Mrs Lardy's establishment?"

An amused but kindly smile touched the landlady's lips. "You are an innocent, Miss Talbot, and I am sorry that you have had such a rude awakening to the ways of the world. Not all gentlemen would frequent the kind of establishment Mrs Lardy runs, but those less discerning, might."

"But surely it is unlikely that—?" she began, unwilling to give it up.

Mrs Greaves sighed. "It has already happened, I believe, although it seems unlikely the man in question saw Jane for he was here but a few moments, the inn being full." She indicated the door that separated this part of the house from the customer's domain. "Two evenings ago, Jane came hurtling through that door, her cap pulled down over her eyes, and her hands shaking so much the dishes on the tray she carried rattled. Very odd behaviour for one who is generally calm and efficient. I asked her why for I will not allow any of my staff to be mistreated, but she insisted she was merely in a hurry as we were so busy."

Lucy's heart sank.

"And what is more, that gentleman lives not many miles from here and so he is likely to come again. If he saw her and spread the word that we were the type of inn that hired fallen women, it would ruin the good name we have worked so hard to establish."

Lucy's mouth drooped. "I see, but surely there is something we can do for her?"

"I've done what I can. She shall have a reference, what wages are owing, and a seat on the Nottingham stage. I can do no more."

"That is very good of you," Lucy said, her throat tight.

She turned and pushed the door to the servants' stairs open. She stumbled up them, tears blinding her as she thought of Jane's plight and that of others like her.

She had forgotten to count the landings and pushed open a door to see where she was. A blurred figure walked towards her. She tensed, wiping at her eyes. Relief flooded through her as the form coalesced into the figure of Mr Ashton. His brows drew together.

"Miss Drucilla! You are distressed. Here, take this."

She took the proffered handkerchief and dabbed at her cheeks. "Thank you. I am quite all right now."

He looked at her intently, his blue eyes full of concern and dismay. "What is it?" he said gently. "How can I serve you?"

She gave him a wan, watery smile. "There is nothing, sir. It is just that I have discovered some things this night that have shocked and saddened me."

His eyes darkened with something very like anger and she took a half step away from him.

"Miss Drucilla," he said. "If someone has offered you some insult but tell me who, and I will make him sorry for it."

She shook her head. "The injury is not of recent date, and it was not I that suffered it." She drew in a breath, her eyes suddenly sparkling with indignation. "Are you aware, sir, that innocent girls are lured to houses of ill repute and forced into a life of degradation?"

His eyes shot open. "I know there are such places, of course, and that circumstances can lead some women to choose—"

"Choose?" she said, colour rising in her cheeks. "Whether they were forced by circumstance or an unscrupulous person into such a place, there was no choice in the matter! And *gentlemen* frequent such places. Who will make *them* sorry for the insult given to these women?"

He regarded her in awed fascination. "Yes… well… things are not quite as simple—"

"It should be illegal to run a house for such infamous purposes!"

"Such places are not publicly approved of," he said, "but a blind eye is generally turned if the establishment is discreet, unless there is a public disturbance, or some other crime connected to the house." He ran a hand through his hair. "Your sentiments are admirable and your distress understandable, Miss Drucilla, but your innocent ears should not have been sullied with such knowledge. Where did you come by it?"

"It matters not, I have heard it, and I cannot unhear it." She drew a hand across her brow. "Forgive me, sir. I am a little overwrought. I must go. Goodnight."

"Allow me to escort you to your door," Freddie said. "You should not be wandering the corridors on your own."

As there was something she wished to collect from her room, she accepted his escort. When they reached her door, he bowed, his eyes troubled.

"Goodnight, Miss Drucilla. Please do not dwell on things that you can do nothing about, and which might trouble your sleep."

She merely nodded and entered her room. It was empty. A flicker of annoyance flashed in her eyes. Abby had gone against her wishes. She only hoped she did not judge Jane too harshly. She hurried over to her portmanteau, retrieved a leather pouch her brother had given her, and made her way back to the attic. She might not be able to do anything on a large scale, but she could help ensure that Jane was not forced into such a position again before she could find some sort of decent employment. Pascoe waited in the narrow corridor and merely shrugged when Lucy sent her an exasperated glance.

"You may go," she said.

Abby looked up guiltily when she entered Jane's room and smiled wryly.

"I am sorry, Lucy, but when you were so long, I worried for you."

She was relieved to see that Jane was no more upset than before.

"I understand now why Mrs Greaves cannot keep you," Lucy said. "Although I am sorry for it, perhaps it would not be comfortable for you to remain. You would be anxious lest the gentleman that you recognised two nights ago returned."

Jane nodded. "I thought Mrs Greaves might have worked it out; she is a knowing one."

Abby's eyes widened. "Who was he?"

Jane shrugged. "I don't know. He had a thatch of red hair, a hooked nose, and a temper is all I remember."

Lucy and Abby exchanged a shocked, knowing glance.

"I've persuaded Jane to go to our sister Rebecca," Dolly said. "She could do with some help on the farm and with the children, and she won't turn Jane away whatever she thinks."

Lucy smiled and held out the purse. "Good. Please, take this, Jane. If there are any problems this should keep you safe until you find your feet."

The girl shook her head.

"I insist," Lucy said. "I only wish I could do the

same for every other poor young woman who is forced to sell herself."

"That wouldn't do no good," Jane said. "They don't all come to it like me, and some make much more than they would on a maid's wage. The likelihood is they would take your purse and continue in the trade."

Lucy gasped.

"It's the way of the world, miss," Jane said. "And some of the gentlemen are none so bad once you get used to them, but it weren't the life for me."

"Oh, I see."

Which was a patent lie for Lucy did not see at all. She again held out the purse, but Jane again shook her head.

"Your sister has already been very generous, not that I wanted to take her money."

Abby rose to her feet. "It is time for bed, sister."

Once they were tucked up for the night, Lucy said softly, "Thank you, Abby, for your kindness. I must ask your forgiveness once again. I thought you were just interfering, trying to manage everything, and I was afraid you would be unsympathetic to Jane's plight."

Abby found her hand and squeezed it. "I did interfere, just a little. It is sometimes hard to remember that you do not need me to watch over you. As for poor Jane, I would be hard-hearted indeed not to feel for her, but I am not surprised you thought it. When we were at Glasbury, I sometimes spoke to you quite harshly, but I was always sorry for it afterwards." She laughed softly. "I am not sure I would dare criticise you now, sister. You would not stand for it."

Lucy smiled in the darkness but then bit her lip. Mr Ashton's face swam before her wearing the startled expression that had crossed it when she had railed about the fate of fallen women. She had been so immoderate in her speech, and on a subject ladies were not supposed to know or talk about. What must he think of her? She closed her eyes. He had tried to tell her things were not so simple as she supposed, and Jane had only confirmed that. He must think her a simpleton.

CHAPTER 17

She need not have worried. Much against his will, Freddie was quite enamoured with her. Lucy's empathy for those of her sex in a less fortunate position than herself provoked his admiration. Her impassioned speech had lit up her eyes and animated her face in a way that had stopped his breath. It was not the first time he had glimpsed the spirit that lurked underneath her quiet exterior. It only seemed to emerge when her sense of injustice was aroused, and it was entrancing.

It was not the thing for young ladies to know or talk of such things, of course, and certainly not to a gentleman they were unrelated to. It was another example of her blind faith in him, a trust he neither felt he deserved nor was necessarily capable of carrying the burden of.

He had been walking back to his room whilst these things went through his mind, but he paused with his hand on the door handle. He frowned as he wondered again who had imparted such knowledge to Miss

Drucilla, distressing her in a way that was unforgivable. He would very much like to have a word with that person.

Turning away, he retraced his steps to where he had first seen her. Pushing the door she had come through open, he saw the servants' stairs. He stood back and held the door for Miss Talbot's maid who appeared around the bend. She curtsied and murmured her thanks.

He watched her disappear from view and then mounted the stairs until he came to the attics which he assumed housed the servants' quarters. A door was ajar about halfway down. He walked towards it, pausing outside when he heard a voice. Miss Drucilla's voice. She should not be up here. He put out his hand to push open the door further but then her words registered.

Please, take this, Jane. If there are any problems this should keep you safe until you find your feet. There was a brief pause and then, *I insist. I only wish I could do the same for every other poor young woman who is forced to sell herself.*

He listened to the girl's answer and retracted his hand. *That wouldn't do no good. They don't all come to it like me, and some make much more than they would on a maid's wage. The likelihood is they would take your purse and continue in the trade."*

He closed his eyes. Jane was the name Bell had called out, and she was her sister. The maid's voice was flat and rather defeated, and she had just added a little more to Miss Drucilla's education. His anger deflated. He could hardly take the girl to task, and at least Miss Drucilla must now realise that she could not help everyone who sold their bodies to survive, not least because they did not all wish to be rescued.

For a moment he had had an image of her walking the streets or worse, going to houses of ill repute handing out money to every fallen woman she came across. It would have been both pointless and dangerous. When he heard her sister's voice suggesting they retire, he withdrew with all haste.

He lay awake for some time, his thoughts scattering, but then they formed into a coherent whole, and a slow smile stretched his lips. He had told Robert that Miss Drucilla needed to and should be protected, and that had been his first instinct when he had seen her distraught face earlier. His heart had clenched at the unhappy bewilderment in her eyes, and he would have done anything to wipe it from her face. In truth, for the first time in his life, he had known the desire to sweep a woman into his arms and tell her everything would be all right.

It was perhaps fortunate that she had rallied quickly, and her inner strength had shone through. *And gentlemen frequent such places. Who will make them sorry for the insult given to these women?* He chuckled. Her understanding had been imperfect but her indignation heartfelt.

She had soon recovered her equilibrium. When he had heard her insisting that the maid take her money, she had been calm, collected, and compassionate. She did need protecting but not because she would be blown over by every ill wind, but because once her compassion was aroused, she was naïve and impulsive. But surely that was something that time and a gentle, guiding hand would rectify? He sighed. That did not mean he was the man to do it, however. Or was he? She trusted him and would listen to him he felt sure.

After some time arguing with himself in this manner, his thoughts drifted to the morrow. He would see Ashton Manor for the first time in almost twenty-five years. He scrutinised his feelings, searching for signs of anticipation or excitement, but he felt nothing. Until he fell asleep, and his dream returned.

He was in the dark, his heart beating uncomfortably fast as he tried to reach the door and the faint light beyond. This time he got closer than ever before and managed to reach out and touch the door handle. Instead of the door receding, however, he felt himself pulled away from it by an invisible force.

He woke, sweat sheening his brow. He frowned, confused, the fog of sleep still enveloping him. He had been sure that his dream had been telling him to return home, but now it seemed to suggest that he should not. He laughed wryly. He was an idiot. Dreams did not dictate a man's actions. He had enjoyed a brief respite from them but the notion that they would never return had been wildly optimistic. Ah, well. Within a few days, he would be sleeping anywhere, his concentration would become sporadic, and Miss Drucilla would see him as he truly was. It was, perhaps, for the best. He winced. Miss Talbot would enjoy herself immensely at his expense. That too would perhaps be for the best. If his shortcomings were brought repeatedly to Miss Drucilla's attention, then she could be left in no doubt that he was unworthy of admiration.

They congregated outside the inn the following day, waiting for the carriages to be brought round.

Freddie preferred Robert's curricle to a closed carriage, but as the morning was fine and they were nearing the end of their travels, Lucinda claimed the privilege of accompanying her husband.

Lord Kirkby lifted her hand to his lips. "The privilege is all mine, my love. Besides, if the terrain is to become as interesting as the landlord suggested, I would rather have you near."

"You may come with me, Freddie," Lady Wirksworth said. "And there will be no entertaining the passers-by, children or otherwise, for Thomas has Jacko. I shall take Jasper in the carriage today." She looked around. "Where is Miss Drucilla? She took him for a walk some half an hour ago."

"Not on her own, I hope?" Freddie said.

"Of course not," Lady Wirksworth said. "Her maid and footman went with her, although why Lord Talbot thought it necessary to send him, I do not know."

Abby sent Freddie a wry look. "I am sure Mr Ashton approves. When he found us walking in Hyde Park with only our maids, he suggested we should have at the very least a footman to accompany us."

He smiled wryly. "So I did, and I am sure it must be comfortable for you to have him with you."

Abby laughed, glancing across the square. "Not if Peter is to dog my every step as he does Lucy's."

Freddie followed her gaze and saw her sister coming towards them. Jasper trotted between her and Bell, his tongue lolling from one side of his mouth, and the footman brought up the rear.

"By Jove, I do not believe I have ever seen Jasper move so fast."

As Dolly and Peter turned towards the stables to take their places in the servants' carriage, Lucy came hurrying up to them. "I am sorry if I have kept you waiting. The town is charming and the area about the river so picturesque that I lost track of time."

"You are just in time," Lady Wirksworth said. "I take it Jasper gave you no trouble?"

Lucy laughed, bent to pat the pug, and after unwrapping her handkerchief, offered him a small morsel of sausage. "Not at all. My ankles are unmolested, and I believe he enjoyed himself very much."

"But not without bribery, I see," Lord Kirkby said dryly.

"It is not bribery," Lucy said firmly, "but rather a reward for good behaviour."

He raised an eyebrow. "Exactly how many sausages were in your now empty handkerchief?"

Her smile was rather impish, Freddie thought. He liked it.

"I shall say only that he has been *very* good."

Lady Wirksworth nodded approvingly. "As you seem a favourite with him, might I suggest you join me and Freddie in our carriage today?" She glanced over at Lady Frampton. "You do not object, Honora?"

"Not at all," she said. "Abby will be company enough. I have a niggling headache and would prefer the girls not to be chattering about me." Her glance went to Lucy. "There is no need for concern; it is very slight."

A laden wagon just then left the stables across the road, followed by Lord Kirkby's curricle and the carriages. Freddie helped his aunt into the first one, before turning to aid Lucy. She took his outstretched hand and looked up at him confidingly. Her cheeks were already pink from her walk, but he thought the shade deepened slightly. He had to bend his head to catch her softly spoken words.

"Can we please forget our conversation of last evening, Mr Ashton?"

"I cannot think of what you speak, Miss Drucilla." He grinned. "My lamentable memory, you know."

He was rewarded with such a blinding smile that for a moment his mind went blank, and he just stared at her like a moonling. She still held Jasper's leash, and it was he jumping onto the step that recalled him to his duty. He took the leash from her so that the dog would not pull her in after him and handed her into the vehicle.

The town was charming, the view from the window offering him glimpses of narrow streets and low thatched cottages. An ancient five-arched bridge led them across the river, and then they began to climb away from the town. The countryside was rolling and pleasant, with green fields and patches of woodland, streams often burbling through the valleys. He gave the appearance of being absorbed in the view, allowing his aunt and Miss Drucilla to make light conversation. For all his aunt's apparent disinterest in the population at large, she was eagle-eyed and astute where those dear to her were concerned, and he had no desire to give her any reason to suspect his liking for Miss Drucilla was anything above the ordinary.

The gently rolling hills soon became steeper, and expanses of moorland and heath covered by long grasses, heather, and bilberry shrubs became more dominant. Freddie turned his head as Miss Drucilla suddenly gasped and edged along the seat opposite to peer out of the window. He saw awe and wonder in her eyes and smiled. They had mountains enough in Yorkshire and he had forgotten the impact they could have when first viewed. To the left of the road, the land now fell steeply to a deep ravine, rising precipitously again on the other side. Scrubby trees hung from its side, and rocks jutted from a thin covering of grass or moss.

"It is as if some god had gouged it out with a giant axe," she said. Her eyes followed the ravine, taking in the high hills beyond. "I could see mountains in the distance at Glasbury Heights, but I never got a sense of what a still and solemn power they possess."

His eyes widened. "Could it be that you have read Shelley's poem, *Mont Blanc*, Miss Drucilla?"

She glanced towards him. "No, I have not. What made you think so?"

A slight tinge of colour touched his cheeks as he said, "*Mont Blanc yet gleams on high:— the power is there, The still and solemn power of many sights, And many sounds, and much of life and death….*"

Lucy suddenly giggled, and his colour deepened.

"Forgive me," he said, unusually stiff. "Perhaps you do not enjoy poetry."

"I thought it very good, Freddie," Lady Wirksworth said consolingly. "I am glad all that nocturnal reading has not been for nothing."

Lucy's eyes widened and her own cheeks flamed. "Oh no… please do not think I was laughing at you. I promise you; I was not. It was myself I was laughing at. I could never remember the words when my governess asked me to learn and recite by heart some part of a dry old text or a horribly long poem, and I certainly failed miserably when asked to compose one. So, you see, it struck me as funny that I had inadvertently referred to the mountains as a poet had. I think it very clever of you to remember it, and I thank you for sharing it with me."

He remembered something she had said on their second meeting. *It is much more difficult to learn when your teacher is impatient or tries to rule you by fear.* He now felt certain to whom she had been referring.

"Your governess sounds like a rum old stick," he said.

The colour quickly left Lucy's cheeks and she stroked the back of her hand. His chest tightened as the notion that this tartar of a governess might have struck her there entered his head.

"She was in a difficult position, I suppose," she murmured.

"It does not sound as if she should have been in any position," he said.

She merely smiled, her eyes a little sad. He wished to banish the look.

"I have the volume of poetry with me… well, in my baggage, at any rate. Would you like to borrow it so that you might read the rest of the poem?"

Her eyes brightened. "Thank you, Mr Ashton. I would like that very much."

They stopped soon afterwards for refreshments at The Cross Daggers in Hope, a small village in a pretty vale. Lady Frampton professed herself to be feeling much better, and Lady Wirksworth suggested that Lucy now join her in her carriage.

"Yes, of course," she said, anxiety clouding her eyes. "I hope I have done nothing—"

Lady Wirksworth patted her cheek. "Of course not, you foolish child. I have enjoyed your company; it is refreshingly undemanding. But I think you and your sister should enjoy the final part of the journey together." She smiled. "And perhaps you would take Jasper with you. He will insist on lying on my feet until they become quite numb."

"Oh, yes, of course…" She looked anxiously at Lady Frampton, but that lady seemed to be in an unusually mellow mood.

"It is quite all right as I believe there are only a handful of miles to go."

The road onward was winding, leading them upwards. It was sometimes hemmed in by soaring walls of rock, at others edged by patches of woodland or plains of scrubby grass. At last, they looked down into a valley, a swathe of green cutting between the hills on either side. Clouds now scudded across the sky, but the sun appeared long enough to glint on water hinting at the stream that ran through it. The small village of Edale nestled far below, the houses looking like they may have been made from a child's building blocks.

The steepness of the descent was ameliorated by the winding nature of the road, bending back on itself in a series of turns that revealed differing views and details of the scenic vale. It was after one of these turns that a prickle of awareness at the back of his neck made Freddie suddenly lean forwards, his eyes scanning the valley below. Heaped conical mounds of grass-covered rock and earth at first obscured his view, but then he saw the grey stone turreted walls and towers of Ashton Manor, nestled under a rising hill bent at the top like a horse's saddle. He supposed it must be an imposing edifice up close, but the hill behind dwarfed it.

An image flashed into his mind of him looking down on the same view as a boy although he had been going in an upward direction. He had been leaving his home. A sudden rush of sadness gripped him and to his horror, he felt his eyes growing moist. He blinked rapidly and felt the touch of a cool hand on his.

When his aunt had suggested Miss Drucilla change carriages, he had been sorry because she had looked so mortified and yet relieved because the impulse to stare at her lovely countenance had been almost irresistible at such close quarters. Now, he was grateful. He turned his head and saw rare tears also sheening his aunt's eyes.

"You remember," she said. "For a moment you looked just as you did that day."

He could not speak and so he nodded.

She gripped his hand harder. "This visit may be more difficult than you imagine, my dear. Lucinda will have no memories, but yours may resurface. It is why I wished you to return. I have seen you staring at your parents' portrait and the rather worried look you wear when you turn away. I hope that you will remember them. Why should you not? We both know that animals never forget the cruelty they have suffered. Jasper is, in general, the most indolent of animals, but Thomas knows that he must be vigilant, for if a boy with the kindliest of intentions throws a stick for him, he will be in danger of being bitten."

Freddie frowned. "But, Aunt, I may not remember my parents, but I am certain they were never cruel."

"No, of course not. I expressed myself poorly. I meant only that if animals can remember things that have happened years before if something prompts them, then so can you. I think your dreams are trying to help you remember, but something within you prevents them. Being in the house may make it easier for you somehow, but those memories may bring you pain."

Freddie had long since given up trying to work out the way his aunt's mind worked, but he wondered for the first time why she had invited their guests. His worst enemies had never seen him cry, but he had very nearly done so just now, and his aunt had not seemed at all surprised. Surely, she would not wish any but their closest family members to witness such a show of weakness.

"If you knew that my memories might return and cause me some distress, why did you invite the Misses Talbot and Lady Frampton?"

She sighed. "Freddie, if you are to remember anything, I wish those memories to come naturally. I did not wish you to be trying to force them and to have guests to entertain seemed a good way to distract you. To distract all of us if I am honest. My history with the house has not always been happy as you now know, and although Lucinda is not a squeamish girl, since she has been with child, she has become more sentimental. I did not want her to have time to dwell on things that she has paid scant attention to before."

Before they reached the village, they turned onto a track that wound through the vale. The clouds were now a dark mass above them, and a cold wind had begun to blow, fingers of it creeping around the edges of the carriage window. A flock of sheep huddled together, standing perfectly still beneath a stand of trees, patiently waiting for the rain that was surely to come. Freddie could only be grateful that it had waited until they had arrived, for he imagined the road they had just travelled would become quite treacherous in a downpour.

CHAPTER 18

Lucy looked into the valley, her eyes fixed on the house below. House? It looked more like a castle; the high crenellated walls and turrets designed to repel enemies. A wall enclosed the property and gardens, finishing at an imposing gatehouse. As the clouds covered the sun it looked rather gloomy and forbidding, but as none of the gothic novels so popular in society had ever come her way, she did not allow this to trouble her. What property would not look forbidding when in the shadow of a mountain and with a black curtain drawn over it?

"So that is Ashton Manor," Lady Frampton said, her tone suggesting that she was not impressed with what she saw. "I am glad I brought my warmest shawls."

"Judging by the profusion of chimneys, you will not lack a fire," Lucy said, unwilling to denigrate Mr Ashton's home.

"No doubt they will all smoke," her godmother said with a sniff.

Abby chuckled. "Even a merchant with a penchant for historic buildings would surely not allow the chimneys to smoke?"

They were descending only at a walk, and as they approached yet another bend, they came to a halt whilst Mr Ashton's vehicle completed the turn. For a moment, Lucy had a clear view of his carriage window, and through it his face turned towards his aunt. Her breath caught in her throat. The carefree and cheerful demeanour that he habitually assumed was entirely absent. His expression was pensive and sad. She turned away, feeling as if she were intruding on a very private moment. She now understood why Lady Wirksworth had not wished her to remain in the carriage. She should have guessed. However little he remembered, seeing the house where his poor parents were murdered could not but provoke such a reaction.

"We shall explore every nook and cranny," Abby said brightly. "And if we do not discover at least one ghost with a clanking chain, I shall be disappointed."

"I beg you will not say so," Lucy said. "What ghosts would there be apart from those of Mr Ashton's parents?"

Abby's smile faded. "You are right. I had forgotten the nature of their death." Her brow wrinkled. "Does it not seem odd to you that there might be housebreakers in so isolated a spot?"

"Perhaps that is why it was chosen," Lady Frampton said. "But I must admit that it does not appear to be the easiest of properties to target."

They turned onto a track that led through the vale and soon came to the gatehouse. Two huge iron-studded wooden doors stood open to allow them through. The carriageway was edged on one side by trees and rough pasture on the other where more sheep grazed. They crossed a small bridge over a fast-flowing stream and saw the house on slightly higher ground ahead. There were a series of steep stone steps to a doorway at the bottom of a square tower. Lucy was relieved they did not approach it but turned away from the house; it would be difficult for the older members of the party to enter that way. They travelled through a stand of trees, then passed a stable block, and drew up on a gravelled turning circle. A dozen shallow steps lead to a huge arched doorway large enough to drive the carriage through. It was also set into the bottom of a square tower, although this one was wider, deeper, and taller.

The housekeeper, a middle-aged woman of neat aspect, stood on the bottom step. She could not keep a smile from her face as they approached. Next to her stood a white-haired butler who also wore a smile, if a rather vague one. Behind them were a few maids and two poker-faced footmen. Lucy reflected that it was just as well Lord Kirkby had sent his home with his butler, or they would be awash with footmen with very few errands to run.

The housekeeper dropped into a respectful curtsy as they approached.

"Mrs Cooper, I believe," Lady Wirksworth said, a small smile touching her lips. "Although I knew you as Emma."

The housekeeper's eyes widened. "To think you'd remember me, my lady."

Mr Ashton inclined his head. "Mrs Cooper."

She sighed. "Oh, sir, how happy I am to see you."

Lady Kirkby murmured a greeting, and the housekeeper laughed softly.

"Oh, my lady, you turned out like your brother, after all, and yet you had such a mop of dark hair when you were born."

Lady Kirkby seemed not at all put out at this familiarity but smiled. "So I believe. It apparently all fell out, leaving me quite bald. I can only be grateful that I have no recollection of such a mortifying event. When it grew back it was blonde as you see."

"I trust you have accustomed yourself to Tinsley?" Lady Wirksworth said. "He has no doubt informed you of how I like things to be done?"

The housekeeper smiled. "Quite accustomed, my lady. I will admit I was not sorry when Mr Thomson sought another appointment after Mr Ramsey left us because he was as starched up as Mr Ashton's shirt points. Mr Tinsley and I go along very nicely."

"I am pleased to hear it." Lady Wirksworth turned to the butler. "I hope your journey was not too irksome?"

"No, no," he said, his eyes looking past her at nothing in particular.

"And you brought Mrs Godley?"

"I did, my lady."

"And how glad I was to see her," Mrs Cooper said. "We had one of those French man cooks but he up and left before Mr Ramsey was cold. I was glad to see the back of him for he was always complaining, and I don't hold with covering good meat with outlandish sauces."

Lord Kirkby cleared his throat. "While this is all very interesting, Mrs Cooper, might I suggest we move out of this sharp wind? My wife is, after all, with child."

The housekeeper looked dismayed. "Oh dear, and here I've been rattling on. You can't tell beneath that cloak she's wearing."

"Very interesting manners for a housekeeper," Lady Frampton murmured as they followed her into the house. "And there is something odd about that butler."

They entered a vestibule, the floor made of worn, uneven stone flags. There was a door on the other side similar to the one they had just come through, presumably leading to the upper courtyard, and a smaller one to their right, doubtless leading into the tower. They turned to their left and entered a high-ceilinged entrance hall. A carpet partially covered the flags, and there was a huge blazing fire at one end with several chairs placed around it. Wooden stairs flanked by suits of armour led from it to a balustraded landing, and a large, small-paned window allowed what light there was to enter.

"I think it would be best if we went straight to our rooms, Mrs Cooper," Lady Wirksworth said, regarding a long case clock set against the wall. "Dinner will be served within the hour, I expect."

"Very well, ma'am," she said. "Fanny, you can show Lady Frampton, Miss Talbot, and Miss Drucilla Talbot to their rooms."

The maid had been hovering at the back of the group but now came forward, dipping into a brief curtsy before leading the way up the stairs. They passed several chambers before coming to a few rounded stone steps leading into an antechamber that had space only for two chairs and a small table. This corner room gave onto a long gallery that jutted at a right angle to the main house. It must have been some hundred feet long and possessed a huge window the width of the room at one end. Lucy noted two inviting alcoves with window seats, marking them as the perfect place to escape with a book. On a bright day, this room must have been warm and airy. The maid led them across the room into a corridor, off which lay Lady Frampton's chamber.

That lady sighed. "I see I will have earned my dinner before I ever reach the dining room."

The maid indicated a door at the end of the corridor. "There's a parlour in there for guests in this part of the house. The young ladies' chambers are on the other side. The stairs outside the parlour go down to the old banqueting hall. You can get to the upper courtyard from there. It'll bring you back to the great hall. It's the quickest way. Only mind yourself on the cobbles, ma'am. If it rains, they can be treacherously slippy."

Lucy stifled a giggle as her godmother was rendered momentarily speechless.

"Thank you, Fanny," Abby said. "Lead on."

The parlour was dark and chilly. One wall was panelled and another had old tapestries hanging from it. The ceiling was low with wooden beams running across. There was a fireplace, and small-paned windows at one end. The chintz-covered chairs looked old but comfortable. They went into another corner anteroom with curved worn stone steps that led to a small landing.

The maid gestured at a wide spiral stone staircase

leading downwards. "That's the one I spoke of." She opened the door in front of them. "I'm afraid your rooms lead one into the other, but we thought as you were sisters, you wouldn't mind."

"We do not," Abby said.

"There's no dressing rooms, I'm afraid."

It was not a problem in this room at least, for there was a tallboy, armoire, and a large chest at the end of the four-poster bed. They seemed to be in the medieval part of the house for although there were two windows, one looking over the lower courtyard, and one over the upper, they were small, and the room dim. The skittering sound of raindrops bouncing off glass announced the storm.

"You have this room, Abby," Lucy said. "I will have the next."

It proved to be identical, except for a small door in the corner of the room. Intrigued, she went to it and pulled at the handle. It was locked.

"Where does this lead, Fanny?" she asked.

Abby had followed and said teasingly, "Let us swap rooms immediately, sister. If there is to be a secret stair, I would not have you lying awake at night wondering who might come up it."

A shiver ran down Lucy's spine, but she ignored it. Such a notion was ridiculous.

"No, Abby. I am quite happy with the room. Besides, if it is locked, no one can get in."

"There is no secret stair, my lady," Fanny said. "It's a small storage cupboard, I believe, but the key was lost years ago, well before I came here."

"So you say," Abby said. "But your explanation seems far too mundane for so ancient a house."

"It is true, nonetheless," Mrs Cooper said, coming into the room. "I've been here since I was a girl, and I hope I know every corner and crevice of this house." She gave each sister a large key. "I've oiled the locks to your rooms so they should turn easily."

Lucy put it in the lock and then opened the door to see what was on the other side. There was only a corridor at the end of which was an ancient wooden door decorated with curling iron scrollwork.

"That leads to the chapel tower, my lady," Mrs Cooper said. "So named because there's a door into the chapel at the bottom." She turned at the sound of footsteps. "Ah, here are your things."

Peter and one of the footmen she had seen earlier entered the room carrying her trunk, and Dolly followed behind them carrying a pitcher of steaming water.

"I'll leave you to get ready," Mrs Cooper said. "Welcome to Ashton Manor and if there is anything you need, anything at all, just let me know."

She and the footman left the room the way they had come, but Peter went out through the other door.

"What are you doing?" Lucy asked the footman.

He looked over his shoulder. "Just getting the lay of the land, Miss Drucilla."

Dolly opened the trunk and shook out a dress of pale blue muslin. "Well, this is a warren of a place," she said.

"Where have they put you, Dolly?"

"There's rooms a plenty for servants on the far side of the lower courtyard, ma'am."

Lucy frowned. "If it is inconvenient, I could ask for a truckle bed to be set up in here."

"There's no need miss, unless this place has given you the frights and you want me near?"

Lucy smiled. "It has not yet, but I will let you know if that changes."

"I don't suppose it will, my lady. It seems to me you're one as can cope with anything. It's not always the loudest who is the bravest."

She laughed. "Oh, I do not think I am at all brave, Dolly."

The maid began to help her out of her travelling dress. "It took some courage to stand up for my Jane, and there's not many fine ladies who would have done it."

"That was only right," she said gently.

"Doing what is right can take courage too," the maid said. "It is often easier to look the other way."

Lucy smiled. "I can see that you are determined to champion me and will say no more."

"Best not, my lady, or you'll be late. Now, where did I put the rose cashmere shawl? It will complement your dress nicely and keep off the chill."

She was grateful for it when she and Abby joined the rest of the party in the great hall. The warmth of the huge fire did not seem to emanate very far into the room. No doubt the high ceiling and thick stone walls were responsible. Mr Ashton came to greet them and Lucy was pleased to see he was his usual smiling self.

"I hope you found your rooms comfortable," he said.

"We are very well situated," Lucy said. Ignoring Lady Frampton's snort, she continued, "I look forward to exploring a little tomorrow."

"I am determined to find a secret stair although I

have been informed that there is none," Abby said. She opened her eyes wide. "Please tell me it is not true, Mr Ashton."

Lucy was a little taken aback at her purring tone. Was her sister flirting?

"There is not a *secret* stair," Lady Wirksworth said. "But there are one or two hidden ones."

Abby laughed delighted. "Well, they are secret to us."

"As they are to me," Lady Kirkby said. "Do not tell us, Aunt. We can search for them tomorrow. It will be fun."

"You should be resting," Lord Kirkby said sternly.

She rolled her eyes. "I am enceinte, not ill."

"But you have been."

She sighed. "Very well. If I feel at all tired, I will stop and rest."

"I shall come with you," he said.

She laughed. "Robert! You cannot wish to go hunting for secret stairs!"

"No," he agreed, "but I do wish to ensure that you navigate the many stairs you will no doubt traipse up and down safely, and that you will rest if you need to."

"Spoken like a sensible man," Freddie said. "I shall also come. It will be as good a way as any to reacquaint myself with the house."

Abby laid her hand on his sleeve and gave him a dazzling smile. "Oh, yes, please do. Your company must always be acceptable."

A soft gasp escaped Lucy. Abby was most definitely flirting. Glancing at Mr Ashton, she saw the compliment had amused rather than flattered him.

He chuckled. "I will remind you of that the next time I provoke your sharp tongue, Miss Talbot."

"I am determined it shall remain perfectly blunt."

Lady Wirksworth made a noise somewhere between a snort and a snicker.

"So, it is decided," Lady Kirkby said. "After breakfast, we shall scour the house for the secret stairs."

"I hope I am not left sitting in this draughty hall or that dark little parlour we have been assigned," Lady Frampton said.

"There is a perfectly comfortable drawing room, Honora," Lady Wirksworth said. "Mrs Cooper had the fire lit soon after we arrived, and we shall retire there after dinner."

The butler came into the hall and hit a brass gong suspended from a wooden frame. Its sonorous sound filled the room.

Lady Frampton winced. "Was that really necessary? A simple announcement that dinner was ready would have sufficed."

"It is how dinner is always announced at home," Lady Wirksworth said. "Lionel could hear it from the shrubbery and I from anywhere in the house. Besides, Tinsley likes using the gong."

Lucy glanced at the butler and saw the truth of this assertion. His eyes were closed, and a wide smile stretched his lips.

"Seraphina! Do you mean you asked your butler to bring that thing with him?"

She raised an eyebrow. "And why should I not?" A mischievous glint came into her eyes. "I also asked him to bring Juniper."

Lady Frampton waved a hand. "I do not need to know what servants you have brought."

"No, of course not. Shall we go in?"

Lucy turned to Freddie, laughter in her eyes. "Mr Ashton," she murmured, "am I to believe your aunt asked Tinsley to bring the one-legged popinjay who says things that are not fit for a lady's ears?"

He grinned. "It would appear so."

"Where do you think she has put him?" she asked.

He chuckled softly. "In the drawing room, I expect. I have half a mind to forgo the port so that I might hear what he says in Lady Frampton's presence." A slight frown puckered his brow. "That was unworthy of me. I do not wish any lady who is my guest to become distressed."

Lucy nodded. "I do not think you need worry, Mr Ashton. She might be outraged, but I doubt she will be distressed."

"That is what I thought," he said. "And neither do I think you will be, but you should not be exposed to his language, you know. Although, I must say, he rarely falls into his old ways these days."

Lucy's eyes danced. "To tell you the truth, I am looking forward to it. Juniper cannot be blamed for merely repeating what he has heard, after all."

CHAPTER 19

Freddie's wish was to be granted. When Lady Wirksworth stood at the end of a well-received meal, which if not piping hot by the time it reached the table, was at least agreed to be tasty, Lord Kirkby glanced at Freddie.

"Shall we go in with the ladies? I think we are all a little tired from our journey, and I see no reason to prolong the evening."

As Freddie had twice turned away to stifle a yawn, he could not disagree. "A splendid idea."

The dining room led directly into the drawing room. It was long and low ceilinged, the wooden panelling and beams seemingly a theme of the house, but it was pleasant enough. Red velvet curtains were drawn across the windows, tapestries with blue and gold thread hung from the walls, and a fire blazed in the grate. Jasper already lay curled up before it.

Here the hand of Mr Ramsey could be seen. The furnishings were modern. Pale green silk covered gilt-legged sofas and chairs were placed near the fire and others surrounded a well-polished round rosewood table near the window.

Freddie's eyes went to a tall stand in the corner of the room. A dome-shaped object covered by a dark muslin cloth sat atop it, although it must be barely discernible to anyone who did not know to look for it. The light from the single candelabra and the fire hardly penetrated that far. He glanced at Lucy and saw her eyes scanning the room. They paused for a moment and then turned to meet his. They exchanged a smile.

Lady Wirksworth sat down on a sofa near the fire and ran her fingers over the covering. "Mr Ramsey had good taste, but it is fortunate I do not allow Jasper on the furniture. The silk is extravagantly fine and would easily rip."

"I will admit this room is better than I looked for, Seraphina," Lady Frampton said. "I apologise if I was a little irritable earlier. It has been a tiring few days."

"That is quite all right, Honora," she said. "I know how incommodious this house can appear to one who is not yet accustomed to it."

As they all settled themselves near to the fire, Mrs Cooper came into the room carrying a tea tray. She placed it on the round table. The butler followed her in. He carried a tray holding three glasses and two decanters: one of port and one of brandy.

"Port or brandy, anyone?" he said, as if he were the host speaking to his guests. The gentlemen declined.

"I would like a glass of port, Tinsley," Lady Wirksworth said.

"A port or a brandy, that's the dandy!"

Tinsley's lips quirked into a poignant smile as he set the tray down.

"Good grief," Lady Frampton said.

"It is Juniper," Lady Wirksworth said. "I tried to tell you of him earlier."

Lady Frampton did not appear to be annoyed, but rather stunned. "Seraphina, it has been many years since I saw Sir Lionel, but——"

"You are perfectly correct," she said. "Juniper does not merely repeat words or phrases but mimics voices. That was one of Lionel's sayings. She sulks if I am parted from her for too long and so I asked Tinsley to bring her here."

"I quite understand," Lady Frampton said. "I am almost envious. I would so like to have a popinjay who could mimic Anthony."

"Shall I make the tea, ma'am?" Mrs Cooper asked.

"That is not necessary," Lady Wirksworth said. "Miss Drucilla will do it; she knows just how we like it. But you may light the other candelabra. Now that Juniper has awoken there is no need for it to be quite so dark."

Lucy obediently went to the table, but her hand paused as she reached for the tea canister.

"It's dark. Freddie doesn't like the dark. Light a candle for him."

This, in a fair imitation of Lady Wirksworth's voice. Feeling his cheeks warm, Freddie suddenly laughed ruefully and sent Lucy a look that said *I have my just deserts*. He crossed to her side.

"It is true that I do not particularly like the dark, but I hope I am no longer afraid of it."

"There is no need for you to be embarrassed," she said, spooning tea into the pot. "Who does like the dark, after all? At least Juniper has said nothing to put the ladies of the party to the blush."

"Oh, may I see?" Abby said.

"Certainly," Lady Wirksworth said.

Abby took the candelabra the housekeeper had just lit and carried it to the corner of the room, illuminating the muslin cloth covering the cage. Holding up the candles, she removed it, revealing a bird with silvery grey feathers, a white face, and a red tail.

"Good evening, Juniper. I expected you to be more colourful, but I admit your silver feathers are handsome and your scarlet tail very pretty," she said.

"You're a saucy piece!"

This was said in a rough, raspy way that made Abby gasp and step back. "I certainly am not!"

Freddie took his cup of tea from Lucy, their eyes reflecting a moment's shared amusement before he retreated to a chair set a little back from the fire. The popinjay hopped on its one leg along the perch towards Abby and tilted its head.

"A shilling for your favours!"

She gasped again and threw the muslin back over the cage.

"Do not be distressed, my dear," Lady Wirksworth said. "He was once owned by a sailor. He is often prompted by a word. I suspect handsome and pretty set him off."

Freddie glanced at Lady Frampton, but she seemed fascinated rather than offended. Her lips twitched as if she were trying to repress a smile. "Oh, Seraphina. If it is not just like you to have a talking popinjay, but I wonder if perhaps it is unsuitable to be in company with young ladies."

"I am not offended," Lucy said, bringing her a cup of tea.

"That is probably because you did not understand his words," she said dryly.

"I did understand," she said quietly. "You told me once that I knew nothing of the world and that I could not form opinions on anything until I stepped into it. I expect what you meant was that I should learn only the pleasanter aspects of life, such as enjoying the attentions of respectable gentlemen, shopping, dancing, and gossiping about it all with other ladies."

"Precisely. I wished you to enjoy yourself."

"And I have," she said, "for the most part."

"But other than shopping, you have not done those things as yet."

The viscount and Freddie exchanged amused glances at the implied suggestion that they were not included amongst the ranks of respectable gentlemen she might meet.

Lucy sighed. "You know I do not care for them and do not wish for a season. Yet I have learned things, not least about myself." Her eyes went to Abby. "I have been guilty of self-indulgent pity, of judging others rather than considering my own actions and character, of wishing to hide rather than face painful truths." Her eyes returned to her godmother. "I hope I am no longer quite so guilty of those faults, but it is the less pleasant aspects of life that have opened my eyes, not going to balls and parties. I do not wish to be shielded from them, for how can I have any serious opinions on anything if I prefer ignorance to knowledge?"

"Bravo, my dear," Lady Wirksworth said. "I knew you were a good gal the moment I set eyes on you."

Lucy smiled self-consciously. "I am still very ignorant, I know."

The popinjay spoke again. "Can't put a wise head on young shoulders."

Lady Kirkby laughed. "That is another of my uncle's sayings, and I am afraid it was generally directed at me."

"I always thought him uncommonly sensible," her husband murmured.

She choked. "Why… you… you fibster!"

Abby went to the table and offered to take the teacups from her sister. "I am proud of you, sister," she murmured. "Although you are far too critical of yourself."

"No," she said gently. "I was far too critical of you."

A small smile twitched her sister's lips. "Do I take it that as you can forgive that ridiculous popinjay's unruly tongue so you will forgive mine from now on?"

Lucy chuckled. "The popinjay only repeats what it has heard, Abby, and cannot help it."

Freddie rested his cup on his knee, his head still full of Lucy's earlier words. She did not wish for a season; therefore, she did not need someone to help her navigate it. He thought of the secret smile they had exchanged, their shared amusement at Juniper startling the company with a sudden outburst and hope took root in his heart. Apart from his doubt that any female could or should put up with his foibles, he had always known that any bride of his must be able to like his aunt and accept with kindness whatever animal was brought into the house. It had seemed an unlikely prospect. Could it be that Miss Drucilla was the perfect bride for him, after all? He yawned, his eyes growing heavy as his disturbed night caught up with him. He would just close them for a brief moment.

He awoke with a start as he felt a gentle hand on his shoulder and warm breath tickling his ear.

"Mr Ashton."

His eyes sprang open to find Lucy crouched in front of him. Her eyes were warm and her smile understanding. She held his cup in her hand, and he noticed tea had spilled into the saucer. She straightened, saying in a businesslike fashion, "I see you have finished your tea, sir. Let me take your cup."

"Oh, yes, thank you."

He was thankful that his aunt's and Lady Frampton's backs were towards him. His sister was in conversation with Miss Talbot, but his brother-in-law met his gaze squarely. He lifted an eyebrow but said nothing. He did not need to; his eyes conveyed his message clearly. *See, she is not shocked or disgusted by your lapse of decorum.* That flare of hope once more rose in his breast, but he reminded himself that it was the first time she had witnessed it. It would not do to get ahead of himself.

The party broke up soon afterwards. They filed out of the drawing room, crossed the dining room, and came once more to the great hall. Freddie strode to the table at the foot of the stairs and handed out the candles that had been placed there, wishing each of his family and guests goodnight as he did so. Miss Drucilla glanced up at him shyly from beneath her lashes. How had he not realised how long they were before?

"Goodnight, Mr Ashton. I hope you enjoy a restful night's sleep."

He hoped so too. He had been allocated the only chamber to the left of the staircase. The room his parents had shared according to the housekeeper. He stood in front of it for some moments but did not attempt to enter, instead staring at the door set into the wall at the end of the corridor. There was only one place it could lead: into the tower above the level of the main entrance to the house. A vision of himself running through that door burst into his mind, and he heard a tinkling laugh. His mother's laugh. He suddenly knew he would find the nursery within. He walked towards the door, hesitating before it.

He jumped back startled as it suddenly opened, wincing as a few drops of candle wax fell onto his hand. "Lipton!"

"I'm sorry, sir," his valet said. "Let me see to that immediately."

He shepherded him into his chamber and across to the basin of cold water that stood in the corner. Freddie plunged his hand in.

"I didn't expect you up quite so soon, sir, and Mrs Cooper and Mr Tinsley wished to offer me some hospitality."

"That is quite all right, Lipton. You startled me, that is all. I did not expect anyone to come from the nursery."

"No, sir. I quite understand. But as the tower abuts the nursery wing, it was the quickest route back."

The butler removed his hand and gently pressed a towel to it. "I'll just put some salve on those burns."

Freddie glanced at the three small red marks on his hand. "That is hardly necessary—"

"I beg to differ, sir," the valet said. "They can turn nasty. I'll put some salve on, and we'll see how they fare in the morning."

Suddenly feeling extremely weary, Freddie capitulated.

"I am confused, Lipton. You said you came from the nursery wing, but the nursery was in the tower."

The valet glanced up. "Perhaps it was in your day, sir. It would have been a deal safer, as the kitchens aren't below."

And it would have been nearer to his parents. He somehow knew that his mother had wished her children close by her.

"It was dark and so I couldn't really see what it's used for now. There, all done. Let me help you off with your coat."

Freddie lay in the dark for some time. He had a feeling he had been in this bed before, wedged between his parents. He closed his eyes and could almost feel the solid weight of their bodies on either side of him. At last, he slipped into a deep sleep.

Was the wail he had heard real or part of a dream? It was probably his baby sister. He vaguely recalled that Mama had brought him from the nursery as he was unwell.

"There is nothing to worry about, my dear. But we

would not like your little sister to become ill, would we?"

He had mutely shaken his head, and she had carried him to her room and laid him on a cot in her dressing room. She had given him a drink of barley water and then tucked the blankets in.

"I shall enjoy having you to myself for a few days, my little darling. And I promise you will feel better soon."

He shivered under the blankets, wondering how he could feel so cold when his head felt so hot. His small body was suddenly wracked by coughs, and his nose began to run. He could not breathe. As the coughing fit subsided, he sat up, gulping in the cool air.

"Mama," he called, the words emerging in barely more than a whisper as they rasped across his sore throat. "Mama."

When she did not come, he struggled out of bed, his legs feeling weak and wobbly beneath him. He looked about the room until he saw the thin sliver of light beneath the door. As he walked towards it, the door opened. A man with light brown hair, blue eyes, and a fond smile came into the room carrying a candle.

"Papa!"

"Back to bed with you, Freddie. Your mother needs some rest."

He gave him another drink of barley water and tucked him in. He left the room, leaving the door ajar.

Freddie woke. His eyes smarted and his hand went to his chest as if by pressing it he might subdue the ache that pulsed there. He remembered them. Their kind eyes, their gentle words, his mother's light fragrant scent, and his father's earthier one; roses and sandalwood. Their time together had been short, but it had been filled with tenderness, laughter, and love. Why had he not been able to recall any of this before? He sighed. It did not matter; he remembered now, and he was glad.

His racing heart calmed, and his lips curved into a bittersweet smile. He looked forward to the morrow, feeling sure that other memories would resurface as they searched the house.

CHAPTER 20

The drapes had been pulled across her windows when Lucy returned to her chamber, but they did little to muffle the sound of rain skittering across the panes.

"Have you had a pleasant evening, ma'am?" Dolly said.

"Yes, thank you." She frowned. "I hope you won't have to cross the courtyard to get to your room."

"No, ma'am. I can go through the tower at the end of the corridor. It's the long way around, but at least it is dry."

She smiled. "I am glad. How was your evening?"

Dolly laughed. "It was better than Thomas's."

"Lady Wirksworth's footman?"

"The very same, ma'am. Lady Wirksworth said he must take Jacko all over the house to get his bearings, but he slipped his leash and he's had to go chasing him up and down the towers and through all the rooms. Fortunately, Mr Tinsley had prepared the servants for his arrival and told them just what to do if he appeared, or I dread to think what chaos he would have caused."

"And what are they to do if he appears?" Lucy asked.

"He told them on no account were they to scream, but they should greet him calmly using his name and offer him some nuts if he approached. They've all to keep some about them. If he doesn't approach them, they're to ignore him but let Mr Tinsley, Thomas, or Mr Ashton know where he is."

"That sounds sensible. At least they won't be afraid of him now."

The maid giggled. "No, they won't be, ma'am, because he's made them all laugh. It seems he likes an audience. They were having a bite of supper in the servants' hall when he came in, Thomas puffing and panting behind him. They all said, *Good evening, Jacko,* and he jumped on the table and bowed! Thomas lunged for him and he—"

"Took his wig?" Lucy ventured.

"That's it, ma'am. He snatched it off his head and put it on his own. Of course, he couldn't rightly see as it was too big for him, and Thomas managed to slip his leash on."

"Oh dear," Lucy said. "I hope that poor footman was not made a laughing stock."

"Oh, no, ma'am. He might have been if he had appeared embarrassed, I suppose, but he just grinned, replaced his wig, and picked up a tankard of ale from the table saying as how he had earned it. Jacko clapped his hands as if he agreed, and then went with him as quiet as a lamb."

Lucy had disrobed and now slipped on her nightgown. The maid pulled back the covers and removed the warming pan. Lucy climbed in and wriggled into the warm sheets.

"The trouble is, everyone laughing at his antics only encourages him."

"I don't see the harm," Dolly said. "Would you like me to blow out your candle, miss?"

"Yes," she said sleepily. "Goodnight, Dolly."

She pulled the cover up to her chin and tried not to think about the cupboard in the corner. It was locked, she told herself. And just a cupboard. The housekeeper had no reason to lie to her, but she had to admit that a house that possessed hidden stairs made her feel a little uncomfortable. Particularly a house where the servants seemed to be so far away.

Determined not to dwell on such thoughts, she allowed her mind to drift to Mr Ashton. Her lips curved at the thought of him. She thought of their shared amusement that evening and her heart warmed. It melted completely when she thought of him asleep in his chair. She had been about to join the circle about the fire when she had glanced at him. He had been half in shadow, but she had seen that his head lolled to one side. Her eyes had darted about the rest of the group, and she had been grateful that Lady Frampton's back had been to him. Abby had been laughing softly at something Lady Kirkby had said to her, and her husband had been gazing at his wife, a gentle smile on his lips.

Wishing to alert Mr Ashton without drawing attention to him, she had sauntered casually about the room looking at the rather unremarkable paintings before approaching him. His saucer and teacup had begun to slide from his thigh, and she had grasped it quickly, wincing as the cup had rattled against the saucer. She had held her breath, waiting for some comment to be made. It had not come. She had gazed into his face and thought how peaceful, handsome, and vulnerable he looked. The urge to brush the curl from his forehead had been almost irresistible. The thought had shocked her into motion, and she had leant forward to whisper in his ear.

She nibbled her lip. She had hoped Mr Ashton was her friend, but was it possible that she wanted more? Was she falling in love with him? Is that why she had been so disappointed when she had suspected he might favour Abby over her? It had not seemed that way tonight. She frowned as she recalled Abby's coquettishness. Had her sister set her sights on him? She had only once discussed love with Abby, and she had been dismayed by her requirements for a husband. *You see how hopeless my case is. I wish for a man who does not love me and yet is kind and will not dictate to me or object to my flaws. Such a man does not exist.*

She drew in a sharp breath. If her sister could somehow persuade Mr Ashton to favour her, there was every possibility he might become that man. The thought made her stomach sink. She wished Abby to be happy, and whilst she believed Mr Ashton would do everything in his power to please his wife, Abby would attempt to lead him by the nose. She could not help it. She liked to have her way. *And you want him for yourself.* Did she? Were her own selfish desires clouding her judgement? Was she once again guilty of maligning her sister?

She rolled onto her side, tucking her hand under

her cheek. She might be reading far too much into it, falling back into old habits of worrying about every little thing. Abby's behaviour had struck an odd chord, but perhaps she was merely trying to make amends for her previous rudeness.

Despite her concerns, Lucy slept well, not waking until Dolly brought her water. She smiled sleepily as the maid drew back her curtains. Weak sunshine sent diamond patterns dancing on the bedspread as she sat up. She shivered, her breath puffing into a white cloud before her. The air was cool, and the fire had not been lit.

"Choose something with long sleeves, Dolly," she said. "And I shall need my pelisse and half-boots. I wish to see if I can find my way to the gardens before breakfast."

"I can show you the way, miss," the maid said. "The quickest way is through Miss Talbot's room, but as Pascoe is still waiting for her water, I don't think she'll be up yet."

"Then we shall not disturb her."

Once she was dressed, Dolly led her down the corridor to the tower. The door opened onto a large square room. It was empty apart from a worn leather armchair set before a fireplace, a desk, and a tall, narrow, cupboard. A door was set into the wall opposite and a narrow wooden staircase led up to the next level or down to the ground floor.

"I admit I am tempted to explore," Lucy said. "But I shall wait until after breakfast. Do you know, Dolly, that there are hidden staircases somewhere in the house?"

The maid shuddered. "I don't like the sound of

that. Why, anyone might spy on you without you knowing it."

"I admit I will feel better when I know precisely where they are," Lucy said. "We are to search for them this morning."

"You be sure to tell me what you find, Miss Drucilla."

Lucy tensed as she heard footsteps on the stairs somewhere above her. Her eyes went to them, and she let out a relieved gasp when Peter's amiable face came into view.

"Peter! You gave me a fright."

"My apologies, ma'am," he said. "As his lordship requested I watch over you, I thought it best I have quarters nearby." He regarded her pelisse. "Are you going out, ma'am?"

"Yes, Dolly is showing me the way."

"I'll do that, ma'am. I'm sure Miss Bell has other things to do."

"That's true enough," the maid said. "I've not even tidied your things away, ma'am."

"Very well."

The staircase led down to a door that opened onto a vestibule. There were two other doors which Peter informed her led to the lower courtyard and the chapel. They passed through an open arch that led into a large room with a fireplace set into a panelled wall. The panels above it were darker, stained by years of soot and smoke. Several stags' heads with huge antlers were hung on the walls around the room, as were shields set either side of crossed swords or axes. There was a long table on a raised stone dais at one end of the room, and another running almost the length of it. Glancing up she saw a minstrels' gallery. The room was cold and had the musty smell of disuse.

"The banqueting hall, miss," Peter said.

Lucy felt certain that no banquet had been held there for many a year. They walked the length of the room, passing the curving staircase towards the far end that led to her and Abby's bedchambers. Beyond it was the dais and a door that led into a long corridor with a host of mismatched chairs ranged along stone walls.

"Here we are," Peter said, nodding to a squat door.

Judging by this underwhelming portal and the rather dusty table that stood by it, with two baskets and a trowel upon it, Lucy judged that this was not the main entrance to the gardens. She turned the handle and pushed, but the door only groaned.

"Allow me, ma'am," Peter said, setting his shoulder to it. It opened, creaking as it did so. "I think it has swollen because of the rain."

It gave onto a flight of stone steps that hugged the building leading to the gardens below.

"Thank you, Peter," she said. "That will be all."

"Very well, ma'am. I'll just see you safely down these steps; they're a little worn."

She accepted his hand, still a little unused to such solicitude.

He nodded towards the wall to their right. "That's the kitchen garden, ma'am, but if you follow the path through that hedge, you will discover several smaller gardens, and a set of steps that lead up to a terrace. There is a door just past the corner of the house which will take you into a parlour, but it is shielded by a hedge, so you'll miss it if you don't look for it. If you prefer, you can go on until you come to the main entrance."

She smiled. "You have discovered much in the short time we have been here."

"But not everything according to what you told Miss Bell."

"No, not everything," she agreed. "Good morning, Peter."

She took the path, emerging in a garden with symmetrically laid out beds edged with clipped low hedges and gravel paths. She was struck at once by its formal design which was in stark contrast to the roughhewn hills dusted with mauve rising behind them. It was as if a little bit of civilisation had been dropped in the wilderness and it felt incongruent somehow. It was not at its best, however. Many of the flowers had lost their blooms and their stems had been flattened by the wind and rain of the previous evening.

The path led her through an arch into a rose garden. Lucy imagined it was very pretty in the summer, but it felt a little melancholy as the many bushes were bare of flowers. Passing through the other side she saw the steps Peter had spoken of. She glanced at the house and saw that a part of the building that was almost entirely covered by windows jutted at a right angle to the main house. She smiled, beginning to get her bearings. That must be the far end of the long gallery. The steps led to a large rectangular grassy area, bordered on all sides by a gravel path. She walked around it to a high stone wall on the other side. It was a sheltered spot, and flowers still bloomed in the bed below, their bright white, red, and yellow petals adding a much-needed dash of colour to the garden. She bent to inhale their sweet, musky scent, the crunching of footsteps on gravel warning her of someone approaching. She did not look up, some instinct informing her of who it was.

"Good morning, Miss Drucilla."

She hesitated before standing, a slow smile curving her lips. "You have a habit of coming upon me whilst I am smelling flowers, Mr Ashton."

"It would appear so," he agreed. "Which is your favourite?"

She bent again, her fingers brushing feathery leaves as she reached for a white flower with a yellow centre. "This one; it has a sweet smell."

"*Cosmos bipinnatus*," he said. "That is the sweetest smelling of the three. The butterflies and bees are very fond of them." He touched a finger to a red, daisy like flower. "*Dahlia pinnata*, pretty but without much scent."

Lucy reached for a bright yellow flower with a conical brown centre. "And this—"

Freddie had also moved his hand towards the flower, and they touched. Both drew back, smiling bashfully.

"It is *Rudbeckia* or Black-eyed Susan in common parlance. Its scent is stronger when the flower petals drop," he said softly.

"It is very pretty," she murmured.

His eyes roamed her face, pausing for a moment on her lips before rising again. "It cannot hold a—"

"Lucy!"

It was Abby's voice, but Lucy found it strangely difficult to withdraw her gaze from Mr Ashton's. She could not help thinking that if there had been a flower the colour of his eyes in the border it would have been immeasurably superior to any other.

"I saw you from the window in the long gallery," Abby said, breathing a little heavily. "It is as well I did. You should not be strolling about unchaperoned with Mr Ashton."

The light censure in her voice broke the spell and Lucy turned her head. She noticed that Abby wore neither pelisse, cloak, nor bonnet, and her hair, generally so neat, had been bundled into a knot and was already escaping its pins. She had left the house in such a hurry that she did not even carry her reticule. This struck Lucy as curious for Abby seemed inordinately attached to it. She even slept with it under her pillow.

"I met Mr Ashton quite by accident."

Abby turned an arch look in his direction. "You, sir, should not have approached my sister when she was alone."

His eyes widened. "By Jupiter! You are correct, Miss Talbot. It completely slipped my mind." He bowed. "I will leave you to—"

Abby smiled. "There is no need for that now that I am here. It is a little cold, however. Shall we return to the house? I am sure breakfast will be ready, and I am famished."

Lucy thought she heard a sigh escape Mr Ashton, but he offered each of them an arm.

"Certainly. I would not wish you to catch a chill."

He led them unerringly to the door of the parlour, which had been obscured from the path not only by a hedge, but a large bay window. Lucy looked up at him.

"Mr Ashton, is this the way you came?"

"No," he said. "I came by way of the main entrance."

Her lips curved into a smile. "Then how did you know it was here?"

He chuckled. "I have no idea."

Lucy patted his arm. "How wonderful."

Abby looked perplexed. "Why is it so wonderful?"

"Because Mr Ashton's memories are returning. We lived with our mama until we were twelve years of age, and yet we have so few recollections of her. How much more difficult must it be for Mr Ashton who left his home before he was six years of age?" Her heart thumped and mortification swept through her. "Oh, Mr Ashton. I am so sorry. How insensitive of me to remind you."

He now patted her arm. "Do not fret, Miss Drucilla. I have always known what happened to my parents. You are right when you suggest it is wonderful that I am beginning to remember things. Perhaps when we explore the house, I will recall more."

When they entered the room, Tinsley stood watching the footmen laying a round table, a faint frown between his eyes.

"Move that fork a little to the left, Samuel," he said gently.

The footman cast him a resentful glance that the butler did not deign to notice. "Very good." He dipped his long, slender fingers into his fob pocket and pulled out a watch. He deftly flicked open the silver casing and regarded it. "You may tell Mrs Cooper that breakfast may be served in ten minutes."

"Very good, sir," he said sullenly.

He looked at the second footman. "Charles, you may take Miss Drucilla's hat and pelisse, and take them up to her maid."

As Charles hurried to carry out this instruction, the butler acknowledged his master for the first time.

"Good morning, sir. Mrs Cooper tells me that Mr Ramsey preferred to take all his meals in the dining room, but she mentioned that this room was used as the breakfast room in your day. I trust you have no objection?"

A slight frown puckered his brow. "None at all, Tinsley, what I object to is the insolence of that footman. Samuel, is it?"

"It is, sir. As her ladyship had not asked me to bring Matthew, I assumed there were already footmen employed at the manor. When I arrived, however, there were none. It is hard to keep good footmen in so out of a way place, I am afraid. Mrs Cooper put the word out and Samuel and Charles were the only ones who applied for the position. I believe Samuel was previously employed as a stable hand and so I have given him the benefit of the doubt, but if his attitude does not improve, you may sure I shall send him on his way. He disappeared for several hours shortly after your arrival yesterday and if the Miss Talbot's footman had not stepped in to help with dinner, we would have been short-handed."

"He went out in all that rain?" Freddie said.

"It appears so," the butler said. "I admit, I did wonder if he had gone for good, but he was here again this morning, saying he had gone for a walk and got lost."

"It seems an odd thing to do," Freddie said, "but I suppose it is possible."

"Ah, very good, Tinsley," Lady Wirksworth said coming into the room. "I had meant to make it clear that I wished breakfast to be served in the garden room, but as usual you have anticipated my needs." She glanced at Freddie. "Having thought on it, I am in agreement with Robert; Lucinda is likely to be quite exhausted by your little game. Therefore, I will direct you where to search. The long gallery, the chapel tower, and Miss Drucilla's chamber."

Abby laughed. "Do you wish to exchange rooms, now, sister?"

Lucy put up her chin. "Certainly not. Once I know where it is, I shall be quite comfortable."

CHAPTER 21

They went first to the long gallery. As the others tapped on panels and peeked behind tapestries, Freddie sat on a chair set against the wall, his eyes casually skimming over the room. His eyes drifted shut as he heard laughter echoing in his mind. He smiled as a vision of a small, blond-haired boy running the length of the room came to him. He crawled under a table and closed his eyes, convinced that would make him invisible. He put his hands to his mouth to stop a giggle escaping as he heard the long, measured stride of his father. It escaped when a finger tickled his ribs. He crawled out and was lifted onto his shoulders. He smiled down at a woman with silken blonde hair and amused blue eyes.

"If you do not wish to be caught, my darling, you must find a better hiding place." The baby in her arms gave a little cry and she smiled ruefully. "I shall take her back to the nursery." She raised a hand and stroked his cheek with a finger. "Do you wish to come, Freddie?"

He shook his head. "I wish to find another place to hide."

His father swung him down. "I have something to show you that I think you will like."

"Come along, Mr Ashton. This is supposed to be fun and here you are sleeping!"

His eyes snapped open. A face hovered in front of his. He had gazed into an almost identical visage at such close quarters only the evening before, and yet his reaction was far different. Miss Drucilla's warm, understanding gaze had made him want to lean forward and press his lips to hers. He had known the same urge this morning in the garden.

Miss Talbot's expression hovered between amusement and pique, and he somehow knew that in time pique would win. As she straightened, he glanced past her and met Lucy's eyes. They smiled, although a hint of anxiety lurked there. Only a hint, however, and she did not jump to his defence. Good. He rose so swiftly to his feet that Abby took a step back.

"I was not sleeping," he said, his eyes still on Lucy. Her lips tilted. She knew what he was about to say. "I was remembering. Do you all give up?"

Lord Kirkby appeared already to have done so. He sat on the window seat, whispering something in his wife's ear, but at this he drew back. "We most certainly do."

The heavy rectangular table he had hidden under as a child was still in the room, but it had been moved to stand against the wall to the left of the fireplace. Freddie strode to it, grasped one end, and lifted, turning it at right angles to the wall so the panelling was revealed. He regarded it closely for several seconds, knelt, and pressed his finger to one corner of a panel. There was a faint clicking sound and three sections of panel swung open.

"Let me see," Lady Kirkby said.

Freddie stood back and she peeked into the opening.

"It is the hidden staircase," she said.

Her husband moved her gently to one side and knelt to get a better view. "So it is, but you will not attempt to use it. Not only is it steep, dark, and narrow, but the second stair looks rotten."

"Where does it lead?" Abby asked, coming forward to peek into the darkness.

"To a small door that leads to the garden," Freddie said.

"I did not see one this morning," Lucy said. "But there is ivy covering the wall beneath here."

"Another thing to search for," Abby said.

"Yes," Lucy agreed. "It would be as well to ensure it is locked."

Freddie sent her a reassuring smile. "If it will ease your mind, we shall certainly look for it. But let us first examine your chamber and the chapel."

Dolly sat sewing in a corner. She smiled as her mistress entered the room and jerked her head towards the cupboard in the corner.

Lucy gasped. "Mr Ashton! You have had the door to the cupboard removed."

He smiled ruefully. "I asked your footman if he would try to force it open. He was happy to oblige. I did not request him to remove it, however."

"He damaged it beyond repair," Dolly said. "I'm making a curtain to hang there until it can be replaced. But you may be certain that there is nothing in there, ma'am. Peter searched it thoroughly."

Lucy and Lady Kirkby went to inspect it anyway. Abby peeked in the wardrobe and even in the drawers, seemingly determined to discover something. Lord Kirkby examined the floorboards. As this room was not panelled, there was nowhere else to search. Freddie looked around the room, his eyes coming to rest on the fireplace. No fire had been set although the blackened bricks suggested that it had been lit many times. Another memory came to him.

"Freddie! We have not yet finished. Where are you?"

It was his mother's voice. She had been trying to teach him his letters when the nursemaid had asked her to take a look at the baby. He had felt resentful, although he could not have named the emotion then, and so he had fled the nursery.

"Freddie!"

He had been standing in front of the fireplace in this room. There had been no grate, and he had grabbed a stool, put it underneath the chimney, and stood on it. His only thought had been to hide, but he had banged his hand on something hard. He had explored it by touch and realised it was a ladder. The bottom rung had been level with his chest. He had tried to pull himself up, but he had slipped back down grazing his leg on a brick that jutted from the chimney. Planting his foot there, he had managed to haul himself up far enough to place his knee on the bottom rung. He had climbed, counting each step. There had been only seven rungs and then he had felt an opening before him. He had heard the scrape of wood on stone and then his mother's voice beneath him.

"Do not try to climb into the priest's hole, Freddie. You will fall and hurt yourself. Your papa will show you if you finish your lessons."

"Very well, we give in," Abby said, her exasperation clear.

Lucy followed his gaze and moved to the fireplace. "Is it here?"

He grinned. "Yes. I discovered it when I was five. The bricks are painted. It is not a real chimney. There is a ladder that leads to a space just large enough to hide a man. No one can enter your room that way." He went to her, picked up the tinderbox that lay on the mantle, and lit a candle. He passed it to her. "Take a look."

She bent and twisted awkwardly, holding the candle up. "Yes, I see the ladder."

She straightened and returned the candle. "Thank you."

"If you are uncomfortable—"

She shook her head. "I am not. If no one can enter my room, there is nothing to fear."

"May I look?" Abby said.

Freddie handed the candle to her. She bent almost double and stepped into the fireplace before straightening. After a few moments, she bent again and stepped out.

"What a clever ruse," she said, passing the candle to her host and smiling radiantly up at him. "How clever of you to have discovered it and at such a young age. I am sure I would never have thought of it."

"You surprise me," Lord Kirkby said, raising his

eyebrow. "I had begun to think your talents had no end."

A faint bloom of colour touched her cheeks. "And I that yours had no beginning."

Lady Kirkby gasped. "That, Miss Talbot, was both unwarranted and unfair. What do you know of my husband, after all?"

"That he likes to prod and poke me whenever he may," she snapped.

Lord Kirkby smiled. "At least I am consistent."

Freddie glanced at Lucy, concerned lest this exchange might upset her, but he was surprised to see her biting her lip as if suppressing a smile. So, she had noticed her sister's change in demeanour towards him. The gossips of the *ton* might think that he was not aware of the lures thrown his way, but they were mistaken. Miss Talbot had decided to cultivate him, and there were only two reasons he could fathom. She wished for a husband who was both wealthy and biddable, as had some ladies before her. Robert had, he felt sure, divined this, but that did not mean he would allow him to treat Miss Talbot with anything other than respect in his house. He looked directly at his brother-in-law, remembering how he had teased his sister when they were boys, exasperated that she would follow them everywhere.

"Shall we move on to the chapel tower? It seems this game has made some of us regress to childish tendencies."

Robert's stunned expression gave Freddie a momentary spurt of satisfaction. He had been on the receiving end of his tongue many times, but rarely had he repaid him in kind.

"Very well," he said, smiling wryly. He glanced at Abby. "Forgive me, Miss Talbot. I shall attempt to guard my tongue."

She nodded stiffly. "As will I."

They went to the chapel tower.

"Shall we start at the top and work our way down?" Abby suggested.

Lord Kirkby glanced at the stairs, and then the sparsely furnished room they were standing in. "My wife and I will search this room."

"Yes," Lady Kirkby agreed. "I will admit that I am beginning to tire, and although it seems nonsensical, I am already hungry again."

Her attentive husband led her to the armchair before the fireplace and reached into his coat, producing a slightly squashed cake.

"Oh, Robert," she sighed. "I never thought you would turn into such a considerate husband."

Abby mumbled something under her breath and started up the stairs. Freddie gestured for Lucy to go ahead of him. There were two floors above. The first had a narrow bed pushed against the wall, a wash stand, and a small set of drawers. As the floor and wall were made of stone and there was only a very small fireplace, it took only a few minutes to scour the room. The second had only two chests and a door set into the wall. Beyond it a short flight of stairs led onto a flat roof with a low balustrade enclosing it.

"Well," Lucy said, wrapping her arms about herself as the chill breeze whipped about her. "Although our search has yielded nothing, at least the view is lovely."

Freddie turned in a circle, eyeing the dark clouds

gathering behind the hills. He frowned as he saw something moving along the track through the valley.

"Are you expecting visitors?" Lucy asked, her eyes clearly better than his.

He saw it now. It was a carriage. "I did proffer an invitation to a friend of Robert's who came to The Rutland Arms whilst we were there." He smiled ruefully as a few drops of rain began to fall. "I fear you must put off your search for the door beneath the long gallery. Judging by the dark clouds bubbling up, this shower is the precursor to another downpour."

"I think I have had quite enough excitement for one day," Lucy said. "And you must greet your visitor."

Freddie chuckled as he saw Lord Kirkby quickly withdraw his hand from Lucinda's stomach as he came down the stairs. "Have you made *any* attempt to search this room?"

The viscount shrugged. "I find my wife far more interesting."

Freddie glanced at Abby, curious to see if she would keep her word to guard her tongue. What he saw surprised him. Her lips were pressed together, but he did not think it was to stop acidic words escaping them. Her eyes were melancholy, and in the few seconds it took her to blink, sheened with moisture.

"That is as it should be," Lucy said.

At that moment, the door of the tall, narrow cupboard set against the wall creaked open. All eyes swivelled towards it. Jacko sprang through it, spotted Freddie, and hurried towards him. It appeared he would climb up his legs, but Freddie held out his hand, palm upwards, and the monkey obediently sat.

"Have you been leading Thomas a merry dance?" he said sternly.

The monkey brought its arm up to cover his eyes.

"That is all very well," Freddie said. "But…" He paused. "I suppose I cannot blame you for hiding; it was a penchant of mine when I was a boy."

Whether the monkey responded to his words or tone was unclear, but he dropped his arm and bared his teeth in an approximation of a grin.

All eyes turned back to the cupboard as the door creaked again. Thomas's head peeked around it and then withdrew. The cupboard was too narrow for him to do anything but come out sideways, and even then, it was a squeeze. His wig was askew and the knees of his breeches dirty.

"Good Lord," Freddie said. "Where did you come from?"

Thomas grimaced. "The chapel, sir. Lady Wirksworth said I must allow Jacko to pick a place he felt comfortable and let him explore. I closed the doors and thought it would be safe to take my eye off him for a moment, and when I looked for him again, he was nowhere to be seen." He sighed, straightening his wig. "I swear, sir, he will be the death of me."

"Nonsense," Freddie said. "You know you are fond of him."

Jacko went to Thomas and took his hand, looking up at him and gibbering.

The footman's lips twitched. "You pesky varmint."

Lucy hunched down in front of the monkey, although she did not attempt to touch him. "So, there is another secret stair, and you found it. You are really very clever, Jacko." She reached into her reticule, produced a slice of apple, and put it in her palm. "I think you deserve a reward."

The monkey glanced up at Freddie, and when he nodded, took the fruit.

Lucy rose to her feet. "Was the way very difficult to find?"

"Yes, ma'am. I searched everywhere for Jacko, and then I saw it. I could hardly believe my eyes. There's a stone coffin, richly decorated on the side. A piece of it had opened and there was nothing beyond it but darkness." He shivered. "I didn't want to go in there in case it was full of bones, and so I called Jacko, but when he didn't come there was nothing for it. There wasn't anything there but a short tunnel leading to a staircase that comes to the cupboard. The back middle section slides back."

"I do not remember it," Freddie said, striding towards the cupboard. The door had swung almost closed again. He reached to open it, but hesitated, gooseflesh rising on his arms and the back of his neck. He shivered, suddenly cold, and then jumped back, a strangled sound leaving his throat.

Peter stepped out of the cupboard. "Sorry, sir, I didn't mean to give you a fright. This is a queer old place."

Freddie gave a shaky chuckle. "You must not blame any of us for the house's oddities, Peter. They were created centuries ago."

The footman frowned. "Be that as it may, sir, and meaning no disrespect, it don't sit right with me."

"Perhaps you should keep your opinions to yourself, Peter," Lucy said gently. "And as I doubt any of us wishes to find ourselves in a coffin, empty or otherwise, perhaps you would return the way you came and make sure the way is closed again."

He bowed and disappeared once more into the cupboard.

Freddie glanced at Thomas, his heart still beating a little fast. "I think it might be best if you put Jacko in my aunt's room for half an hour. He has had quite enough excitement and will no doubt be ready for a rest." His gaze moved on to the viscount. "We saw a carriage approaching, Robert. I suspect it may be Fairbrass."

A sardonic smile twisted Lord Kirkby's lips. "I am not at all surprised. I strongly doubted he would remain under Bevis's roof for more than a night."

"No!"

All eyes turned to Abby. Her face was ashen and her eyes wide. "You must not let him in."

"Miss Talbot?" Freddie said.

She did not respond, her eyes fixed on her sister. Lucy had clasped her hand over her mouth.

"Can it be that you are acquainted with Sir Anthony?" Lord Kirkby said, frowning. "I find it unlikely as he has only recently returned from abroad. Unless you met him during your time in France, Miss Drucilla?"

Lucy shook her head.

"We are not acquainted, and neither do we intend to become acquainted," Abby snapped. "If he stays, we must go."

"But why?" the viscount said. "He is a very good fellow, I assure you."

"Because he has come to claim me, and I will not have him!" Abby said, before turning and running from the room.

"Come to claim someone he has never met and who he does not even know is here?" Freddie said bemused. Lucy's hand had dropped to her chest which rose and fell rapidly. "Miss Drucilla? Are you quite all right? Do you need to sit down?"

She attempted a smile but only achieved a grimace. "No, thank you. It was just the shock, you understand."

"Well, no," Freddie said apologetically. "I am probably being dreadfully dim-witted, but I am afraid I don't. Can you explain?"

She sighed, her hand going to her forehead as she tried to gather her thoughts. "Forgive me. It is not you who is being dim-witted, but I. Of course you do not understand. If Sir Anthony does not know we are here, it must be a horrible coincidence."

As Freddie looked on still mystified but apparently unwilling to press her further, the viscount cleared his throat.

"What is a horrible coincidence, Miss Talbot, and what did your sister mean when she said Fairbrass had come to claim her?"

She smiled wanly. "Oh dear, I am not making a great deal of sense, am I? When we returned to Talbot Hall, my father told us that he had arranged marriages for us, that they had been planned for us since we were infants. Abby was to marry Anthony Fairbrass."

"Good Lord!" Lord Kirkby said. "No wonder he remained abroad so long."

Fire suddenly sparked in Lucy's eyes. "This is no time to poke fun at my sister, sir."

"I was not doing so," he said calmly. "As Anthony

has never met your sister, he can have no opinion of her. He is here because his sisters were hinting he should wed, and he will not be pushed into doing anything he does not wish to. Neither, I am sure, would he ever agree to be promised to a girl he had never met."

Colour flooded her cheeks. "I am sorry if I misunderstood. Are you sure he would not?"

"Absolutely sure. He was a captain in the army, a leader of men, more suited to giving orders than taking them. Has he ever approached your sister or your brother before or since your father's demise?"

"No," she admitted. "But if he has been abroad…"

"He has been in England for some months, long enough to make enquiries if he wished to. I suspect that once he learns of your sister's presence, he will be as eager to leave as she is."

"Oh, I see," she said faintly.

A rather unpleasant notion entered Freddie's head. "Who were you promised to?"

Lucy gulped. "Viscount Gaines. He was supposed to visit us but my father suffered a stroke and so he was put off."

"Bevis!" Lady Kirkby gasped. "Oh, no. That would never do!"

Lucy blinked. "I said Gaines, not Bevis."

"They are one and the same," the viscount explained. "Gaines is the family name, Bevis the title he inherited last year."

Lucy's eyes widened in disbelief. "That horrid man who almost ran Mr Ashton down and then stared at me in such an odious way in the park is the man I was supposed to marry?" Her voice shook with indignation rather than fear. "Then it is as well my brother will not uphold my father's plans because I could never marry such a man."

Freddie's eyes turned icy. "Most certainly you could not. I would not stand for it! I would run him through rather than allow him to come within speaking distance of you."

CHAPTER 22

⨯

Lucy found nothing to object to in Mr Ashton's vehement statement. In truth, she was rather impressed and thrilled by it. The ice in his eyes melted into concern.

"I cannot in all good conscience turn Sir Anthony away," he said, glancing at the window, through which could be seen a rapidly darkening sky, "but neither do I wish you to… your party to leave."

Neither did she. Indeed, she was determined they would not. "Abby was taken by surprise and understandably upset. I think her words an empty threat, however. I hardly think our godmother would agree to another journey quite so soon. I will go to my sister and inform her of what Lord Kirkby has told me. I am sure once she understands the situation, she will calm down. Her temper generally burns out as quickly as it fires up."

In the minute or so it took her to reach her bedchamber, the rain was once more skittering against the windows.

"Miss Drucilla," Dolly said in relief. "Miss Talbot flew through here looking quite wild and said I should pack your things. Am I to do so?"

"No, Dolly," she said firmly.

She found her sister's maid laying out dresses on Abby's bed. "Wait until you have further word, Pascoe, or you may have to unpack everything. Where has my sister gone?"

"She went to find Lady Frampton, ma'am."

Lucy could hear Abby's irate tones before she reached her godmother's room. She did not knock, being certain no one would hear. Abby paced up and down the room, her cheeks flushed, but she came to an abrupt halt the moment she saw her sister.

"Lucy! Aunt Honora insists she will not leave in this rainstorm, but you must persuade her. I would rather be stuck in mud halfway up the mountain than remain here another moment."

"You need not waste your breath, dear," Lady Frampton said, briefly closing her eyes. "Nothing would make me leave whatever the weather."

"No, of course it would not," Lucy said gently. "I can see that you are still a little fatigued from our journey here."

Abby was never at her best when vexed, and she turned on her. "Of course you do not wish to leave. You are too busy simpering and making sheep's eyes at Mr Ashton, and you do not have Viscount Gaines coming to call."

Lucy raised her chin but spoke quietly. "It is you who have been guilty of trying to ensnare Mr Ashton, Abby, and I wish you would stop. You have no true affection for him but only wish for a kind, biddable husband. He is not as biddable as you think, however, and is, I am sure, fully aware of what you are about. As for Viscount Gaines, he is now Lord Bevis, and although he may not have called, he lives only in the next valley."

Abby's eyes widened. "Bevis? Good grief."

"Precisely," Lucy said. "And yet I am not quaking in my slippers, and nor would I, even if he came to call."

"Neither am I quaking," Abby protested. "Sir Anthony cannot make me marry him, after all, but I have no desire to meet him."

"Then you are in accord," Lucy said. "For I have been reliably informed that not only is he unaware of your presence here, but that he is likely to wish to leave when he discovers it. He is, apparently, not the man to marry on command, being used to command himself. Indeed, he left his home because his sisters have been trying to persuade him to find a wife."

Abby blinked. "He did not know of my presence? He has not come to claim me?"

"He has not," Lucy said.

Abby slumped on the bed. "I assumed Lord Kirkby or Mr Ashton had mentioned us at the inn, and that is why he came." Her spine straightened. "However, even if all is as you say, we have suffered much indignity because of him and Lord Bevis. How can I bear to meet him? How can you? I would have expected you to be quite overset at the prospect."

"Perhaps you do not remember all that happened that day perfectly," she said. "It was only the current Lord Bevis's father who requested the examination, and our father's pride and prejudice ensured he permitted it. It is not right to hold Sir Anthony to account for something that was not his fault."

"You speak a great deal of sense, Lucy," Lady Frampton said. "I have been trying to tell you for several minutes, Abigail, that you have nothing to fear. I would never allow you to be importuned in any way."

"And neither would Mr Ashton," Lucy said with conviction.

"What would he do to protect me?" Abby scoffed. "Tell his friend that he was being ungentlemanly with that irritating chuckle of his?"

"I told you that you did not hold him in affection," Lucy said. "As your case is so very different to mine, Lord Bevis being an enemy of Mr Ashton, not to mention a detestable person, and Sir Anthony being a friend of Lord Kirkby, and by all accounts, a very good fellow, I do not know what he would do. I am certain, however, it would be something far more effective than that."

Abby regarded her intently, her eyes narrowing. "Has Mr Ashton said what he would do if Lord Bevis importuned you?"

"Certainly," Lucy said, not quite able to keep the satisfaction from her voice. "He said he would run him through if he came within speaking distance of me."

"Really?" Lady Frampton said. "I must say, Frederick has improved much of late."

Abby suddenly laughed. "I wonder if he *can* fence?" She shook her head as Lucy regarded her quite fiercely. "No, no, Lucy. What a lioness Mr Ashton has turned you into, but it is quite unnecessary for you to tell me that you are sure he is capable of anything. What is more, I will quite give him up, for I see that he is not as unworthy of you as I had first supposed."

Lady Frampton had been leaning wearily against her pillows, but she sat up at this. "Lucy? Is there something between you and Frederick?"

She felt her cheeks heat, but said truthfully, "I think there might be, but I am not entirely certain if he means anything by it."

"By what, precisely?" her godmother asked.

"It is difficult to explain," Lucy said. "He has not said anything of his feelings, although I think he was about to pay me a very pretty compliment in the garden this morning when Abby interrupted us. But once or twice he has looked at me in such a way… in a warm way that has quite taken my breath away."

"Well," Lady Frampton said, "he is certainly an eligible match. Many caps have been set at him."

"I am not setting my cap at him," Lucy protested. "And as I am so inexperienced, it may be that I am imagining things."

"I do not think you are," Abby said.

Lady Frampton gasped and spoke sharply. "And yet you knowingly tried to cut your sister out?"

Abby coloured. "I had my reasons. Lucy does not wear her heart on her sleeve, and I had thought him altogether the wrong sort of man for her, and perhaps the only sort of man for me. I will admit I may have been wrong. I will also admit that I may have overreacted to Sir Anthony Fairbrass's visit." She stood and shook out her skirts. "And to prove I am not quaking in my slippers, I shall not hide away, but go down to the drawing room."

Judging it best not to disturb the Misses Talbot, Freddie led his sister and brother-in-law down to the chapel. It bore the rather solemn atmosphere of most places of worship, but also bore the traces of disuse. The pews bore a smattering of dust, a few of the flags were cracked, and the altar was bare of any ornament.

"I cannot help but feel it was inappropriate to allow Jacko in here," Lord Kirkby said.

"Animals are also God's creatures," Freddie said. "Although it would not do to allow him in during a service. It does not look as if any service has been held here for quite some time, however. I believe Mrs Cooper said that a church has been built in the village since we left. Mr Ramsey may have preferred to go there."

Lucinda went to a sarcophagus with a marble effigy of a child. "How sad that he died so young," she said, laying her hand for a moment on the boy's.

Freddie felt the hairs on his arms and neck rise. "Let us go. Fairbrass will arrive at any moment."

The door at the end of the chapel led them to the west wing of the upper courtyard. They passed through a study, a billiard room, and a well-stocked library, before coming to a door that led either up into the nursery tower or into the vestibule of the main entrance. Tinsley and the surly footman he had met earlier stood waiting to greet their visitor.

"Tinsley," Freddie said. "I gather you saw our visitor approaching."

"No, sir, it was Peter who did that. He warned me a few moments ago."

Freddie raised his eyebrows. "That fellow might be footman to the sisters, but he seems to make himself busy elsewhere most of the time as far as I can see."

"I have met him several times in various parts of the manor," the butler conceded. "He tells me he likes to know every nook and cranny of any house he is in."

Robert murmured something in his ear, and he nodded.

"Tinsley, you may expect Sir Anthony Fairbrass. Show him into the library, if you will."

"Yes, sir. You may have seen the fire has been lit. I thought you gentlemen might wish to retire there at some point today. I will put Sir Anthony in the green room above the library if that is acceptable."

As Freddie had not had the leisure to fully explore, he had no idea if it was or not, but he had learned to trust his butler's judgement.

"That is all very well," Lady Kirkby said. "But do not hide away for hours." Mischief danced in her eyes. "Although I am, of course, sorry that Miss Talbot is so disturbed at Sir Anthony's arrival, I must admit I am agog to see them meet. I will go and bring Aunt Seraphina up to date on all that has occurred."

"Yes, but do put your feet up and rest, my dear," the viscount said, turning to re-enter the library. "I rather think this is the best room in the house," he said, walking over to a desk and pouring some wine.

Freddie glanced at the book-laden shelves, the well-polished tables of varying heights and sizes, the clusters of chairs and sofas made for comfort rather than to present an elegant appearance, and absently agreed with him, his mind still grappling with the knowledge that Bevis had hoped to make Miss Drucilla his wife. He did not doubt that he had. That is why he had asked questions about her in the park and then approached her brother. Talbot's brief note to Robert now made sense. The thought appalled him. The thought that she should marry anyone but himself suddenly appalled him. Tinsley's voice recalled him to his duties.

"Sir Anthony Fairbrass."

He strode forward to shake his hand. "Welcome, Sir Anthony."

Lord Kirkby grinned, shook his hand, and clapped him on the shoulder. "I thought we might see you sooner than later. Sit down and I will bring you a glass of wine."

The large man settled himself in a wingchair by the fire. "Thank you. My hope that Bevis had improved with time was misplaced. I always thought he had a screw loose but now I am inclined to think him quite mad."

"Freddie would agree with you; he almost ran him down on Bond Street not so long ago."

"And do not forget he pushed that fellow out of the window at Harrow, and his father tried to hang my aunt's cat."

Sir Anthony looked bemused. "His father tried to hang your aunt's cat?"

"It is a long story," Freddie said, "but that was undoubtedly the act of the madman."

"What excuse did you give for your early departure?" Lord Kirkby asked.

"I merely said that as the weather seemed set to

remain inclement and I have a strong dislike of being out in the rain, I would call it a day."

"Your coming has caused quite a stir," the viscount said. "One of our guests threatened to leave."

Sir Anthony smiled wryly. "You set my mind at rest. I had feared I might be about to disappoint Miss Talbot's expectations."

Freddie and the viscount stared at him.

"Bevis invited me to his party to discuss the Talbot sisters. He did not get the opportunity until his other guests retired, however, and he was three sheets in the wind." He grimaced. "He thought I would be as eager as he to bring to fruition our fathers' ridiculous plans."

"How did he take it when you told him you were not?" Lord Kirkby asked.

"I did not tell him anything," Sir Anthony said. "He has that irksome habit of only being interested in the sound of his own voice when he is disguised. I learned long ago never to try to argue with someone in that condition; it is both tiresome and fruitless.

He was under the misapprehension that because our fathers thought of themselves as the *Companions of the Conqueror* – a misguided and wholly unproved assumption in my view – that we must also do so. I do not believe for an instant that he either believes or cares about it, but rather that he has for so long considered Miss Drucilla Talbot his that he is reluctant to relinquish the idea, especially now he has seen how very beautiful she is." He paused, raising an eyebrow. "Are the sisters so beautiful?"

"Diamonds of the first water," the viscount said. "Although they have not been brought up to value themselves greatly. They were sent away after their mother died and from the ages of twelve to eighteen were brought up by a glumpish governess on an isolated estate in Wales."

"Good God!" he said. "With the exception of Ashton, perhaps all of our fathers were mad." He frowned. "Perhaps Talbot thought that they would meekly accept his dictates if they were starved of company."

The viscount laughed. "Miss Talbot is not at all meek, Miss Drucilla more so."

"Perhaps she once was," Freddie said, "but she is far more resilient than I gave her credit for. There is a quiet strength and a growing confidence in Miss Drucilla that is—" He broke off. "Anyway, she is a pleasant young lady."

"Ah," Sir Anthony said, "I thought Bevis's ramblings were due to the unnatural animosity he has always felt towards you, Ashton, and his jealousy that you had the sisters under your roof, but I see his fear that you would snatch Miss Drucilla from under his nose was not wholly unfounded."

"Snatch her?" Freddie said. "She is not a prize to be snatched or stolen, and she is not and never has been his, nor will she ever be."

"Very true," Sir Anthony said, "but that does not change the fact that Bevis believes her to be his by right."

"How did he discover the girls were here so quickly?" the viscount asked.

Sir Anthony smiled grimly. "I have a habit of keeping my wits about me; the vigilance I developed in the army cannot be shed with my uniform. Bevis was playing cards when his butler came in and whispered something in his ear. When he slipped rather furtively from the room, I attempted to follow him. Unfortunately, his butler was in the hall and so I could not. I returned to the room and took up station on a window seat there, and some fifteen minutes later, I saw a bedraggled figure pass by the window in the livery of a footman." He looked at Freddie. "You, Ashton, have a very large rat in your house who has just taken my baggage up to my room."

Freddie's eyes widened and he rose to his feet, his jaw mulish. "Samuel! I knew there was something off about him. Well, I shall send him back to his master with a flea in his ear and a message for Bevis!"

"No, do not do that," Sir Anthony said quietly. "You should never let the enemy know you have rumbled them."

Freddie sat back down, his eyes uncharacteristically sharp. "You think he has something planned? Some mad scheme to… oh, in your words, snatch her?"

Sir Anthony's lips twisted. "If I am to believe his comments were not merely drunken bravado, I have reason to think so"

"Then perhaps it would have been better if you had remained at Gaines Park," Lord Kirkby said frowning. "You might then have watched him closely and perhaps prevented him putting any such plan into action."

"I might have," Sir Anthony acknowledged. "But it was not until I saw the footman come out of this house that I believed him serious. I suggest you put someone on to watch Samuel. I doubt very much Bevis could gain entry to this house without his assistance. Of course, it needs to be someone who has cause to be near him, and who you trust."

"I have the very man!" Freddie said. "Although he is not mine precisely. The Misses Talbot brought their own footman, Peter. He will, I am sure, wish to protect them."

"Very good," Sir Anthony said.

"Yes," Freddie said, "but I do not like the idea of us just sitting here waiting for something to happen, and neither do I wish to frighten Miss Drucilla by telling her of our suspicions."

"As Bevis is not known for his patience, I do not envisage us having to wait very long. And you must certainly not inform anyone apart from Peter and perhaps your butler, if he is to be trusted, of any of this. We cannot risk Samuel overhearing anything that will alert him to the fact that we are on to him, nor must anyone behave any differently about him."

"No, I see that," Freddie said.

"And we must take it upon ourselves to watch the Misses Talbot closely, without the appearance of doing so, of course."

Lord Kirkby rose to his feet. "So, we have a plan. Now, I think we should join the ladies."

"I will see if I can discover where Peter is," Freddie said. "The sooner he knows what is afoot the better. The problem is, he is never where he should be."

But Peter stood in the great hall looking blankly ahead.

CHAPTER 23

Lady Frampton tidied herself whilst Abby went to tell her maid not to pack after all. After tucking a few stray strands of hair back under her cap, shaking out the skirts of her dress, and donning a warm but elegant shawl, she was ready.

"Lucy," she said, sitting in a chair by her dressing table. "Come here, child."

Lucy went to her, sitting on a footstool at her feet. "Yes, Aunt Honora. What is it?"

Lady Frampton smiled ruefully. "Only this. I know I can be irritable at times, but I hope, like Abigail, I can own to my mistakes."

Lucy took her hand. "You are talking of Mr Ashton, are you not?"

"I am. I saw him falling asleep in the oddest of places, talking rather incoherently, and not seeming to care a fig that he was often the butt of some rather unkind jokes. I am afraid I judged him rather harshly. I thought that like many young men he imbibed too freely and was rather stupid. When Seraphina told me that he had suffered nightmares since he was a small child, and that he was more often sleep deprived than foxed, I began to realise my mistake. I have never spent so much time in his company as I have this past week, and I have come to realise that whilst he might not have the sharpest of minds, he is by no means stupid."

"He is far from stupid," Lucy said, smiling fondly. "And neither do I have the sharpest of minds, Aunt Honora."

"There are different kinds of intelligence, Lucy," she said. "I have known people who can absorb and retain all sorts of facts and figures, but who have not the remotest common sense. I have known others who have a sharp wit and mind but who lack the ability to fully understand the effect their words might have on others." She grimaced. "I believe I might be one of them. Apart from the people closest to me, I do not always consider the feelings of others."

"That is not true," Lucy said.

"I am afraid it is, Lucy. You and Frederick are both much better at it than I, and both of you are kind, considerate, and honest." She chuckled. "But you also have backbone. I believe Frederick *would* run Bevis through with his sword, as I believe you would always do what you knew to be right." She smiled. "What I am trying to say is that if Mr Ashton should declare himself at any time, I would be very happy for you." She stood, shook out her skirts again, and said crisply, "Now, where is Abigail? She must have been gone for all of twenty minutes."

"Perhaps she has changed her mind."

Lady Frampton sighed. "Let us go and see."

They found her inspecting herself in the mirror. She had changed into a moss green dress that suited her admirably, donned a pearl necklace and earrings, and had Pascoe arrange her ebony hair so that a few long curling tresses fell over one shoulder.

"You have made a great deal of effort for someone you have no inclination to meet," Lady Frampton said dryly.

Abby's eyes sparkled with challenge. "As I must meet him, I may as well present a good appearance. If Sir Anthony would reject me out of hand, I will show him what he has passed up." She looked at her maid. "The cream shawl please, Pascoe."

Lucy looked bemused. "But why? Surely you do not wish him to change his mind?"

"Certainly, I do not," Abby said. "I would not marry him if he were the last man on earth."

Lady Frampton chuckled. "You wish to punish him a little, but be careful, Abigail. It seems your little game with Mr Ashton did not go unnoticed."

"Oh, I do not mean to try and flirt with him," she said. "I realise I have no aptitude. I shall merely be my natural self."

"I see," Lady Frampton said. "You wish to dazzle him with your beauty, whilst treating him abominably."

"Only if he gives me cause," she said, glancing at Lucy. "I do not do it to make you uncomfortable, and if I do, I am sorry for it."

Lucy sighed. "No, you do it because it is one more rejection. Let us hope that Sir Anthony gives you no cause to snap at him."

As Abby swept from the room, Lady Frampton

murmured in her ear, "Oh, do not spoil all her fun, Lucy. You must remember that Sir Anthony might have written to your father or brother to inform them that he had no intention of marrying her and so relieve her mind, but it seems he did not."

"Oh," Lucy said. "Yes, how true. That really was too bad of him."

"And I think that you rather splendidly illustrated my earlier point. You see things that I do not. It struck me when you said his dismissing her out of hand was one more rejection. Abigail has not dressed only for him, but for herself. It is her armour to give her courage."

Abby's courage seemed to fail her a little as they walked through the dining room. Her step faltered and she paused before the drawing room door.

"Allow me to go in first, my dear," Lady Frampton said. "That way you may have time to take Sir Anthony's measure whilst he greets me."

"Yes," Lucy said, putting her arm through hers. "We will go in together."

Abby smiled wryly. "Thank you, sister. It seems our roles have reversed, and it is you who now bolsters my resolution."

Lucy was struck by what an imposing figure Sir Anthony presented. Lord Kirkby was tall, but Sir Anthony was at least a head taller. Everything about him from his broad shoulders to his square jaw and piercing grey-blue eyes spoke of strength and determination, and yet his clothes were supremely elegant as was his bow.

"He is very handsome," Lucy whispered.

"In a rugged sort of way, I suppose," Abby

murmured. "But you could say the same of the mountain behind the house."

Lucy repressed a giggle as she realised her godmother was speaking.

"Allow me to introduce my goddaughter, Miss Drucilla Talbot."

Lucy walked forwards and dipped into a hasty curtsy as the baronet bowed and murmured something about it being his pleasure.

"I am pleased to make your acquaintance, Sir Anthony," she said, peeping up at him. His eyes seemed to harden and his jaw tighten. Unsettled, she moved away quickly, and Lady Kirkby pulled her down beside her.

"This is going to be very interesting," she murmured. "I do not believe I have ever seen your sister look so dashing. They do make a handsome couple, do they not? What a pity they are both so set against each other."

"And here is my other goddaughter, Miss Talbot," Lady Frampton said, moving a little away.

Abby came forwards in a stately fashion, her chin held high, before sinking into a graceful curtsy. Sir Anthony put out his hand to help her rise.

"Miss Talbot, it is a pleasure to meet you at last."

Lucy leant closer to Lady Kirkby, murmuring, "Oh dear. If only he had stopped at *you*, the *at last* was a mistake."

"Yes," that lady agreed. "I quite see. It touches on a matter best left unaddressed, perhaps."

Abby looked up into his face, one delicately arched eyebrow rising.

"Is it?" she said coolly. "Forgive me if I take leave to doubt that."

Even from her vantage point, Lucy could see his eyes flash in surprise. He had clearly expected her to at least observe the social niceties. If only he had not said at last.

"You could, after all, have met me long before this if you had so desired." She smiled. "Or at least informed me that you had no intention of doing so. That would have put both our minds at rest I should have thought."

She did not give him time to respond but moved away.

"Do you know, she is right. I had not thought of that," Lady Kirkby murmured. "He deserved the reprimand."

Sir Anthony was left standing rather awkwardly alone, but after a moment his lips twitched, and he crossed the room to Lord Kirkby's side. Freddie entered the room, his brow puckered, but it cleared as he saw the gathering.

"Well, you are all in here, after all. It was so quiet I thought you might have removed to the library. Do you know, I think perhaps we should. It seems rather crowded in here and it is dashed gloomy."

"Bring a candle, bring Freddie a candle."

He chuckled. "Thank you, Juniper, but I do not require a candle. It is not time for bed."

"Time for bed! Where's that saucy wench?"

Sir Anthony laughed and walked over to the cage. "Quiet your saucy tongue, popinjay. There are ladies in the room."

Juniper tipped his head and uttered a word that made Lady Frampton gasp and rise hastily to her feet.

"Perhaps we should retire to the library. I have not yet seen it."

Freddie fell into step beside Lucy. "I am sorry you had to hear that. I do not think Juniper appreciated being scolded by a stranger."

Lucy wrinkled her brow. "I did not understand it."

Freddie blew out a breath. "Good, forget it."

She laughed softly. "Was it very rude?"

"Extremely," he said.

"Oh," she breathed as they entered the library. "I like this room, and you were right; it is far more congenial than the drawing room for such a large party. The chairs in there are very elegant, but they are not at all comfortable."

"Feel free to have a good look round," he said. "Or choose a book." He put his hand to his forehead. "Forgive me, Miss Drucilla. I had completely forgotten to give you the book of poetry I promised you."

"Do not give it a thought. There has hardly been time to read any—" She broke off, her gaze fixed on something tucked in one corner of the room. It was covered with a black cloth, but its shape was unmistakeable. "Mr Ashton, you have a pianoforte."

"Do I?"

"Most certainly you do," she said. "May I take a look?"

"Of course," he said, walking with her to the instrument and removing the cover.

She ran her hand over the glossy wood before lifting the lid and pressing a finger gently against one of the keys. "It seems to be in perfect condition," she said.

"I expect it was left here by Mr Ramsey," he said.

She sat down on the stool. "Would you mind very much if I played something? It has been so long, and I used to practise every day."

"Mind?" he said. "Miss Drucilla, I would be honoured to hear you play."

The others had settled themselves in little groups and the quiet murmur of conversation drifted through the room.

"Just a moment," Freddie said. "I will announce the delight in store."

"Do not do that," Lucy said. "They may keep on talking, I will merely provide some background music."

She spread her hands over the keys, her fingers tingling with anticipation. She would play the Haydn sonata Anne had insisted she learn at Ashwick Hall. It encapsulated so many moods within the one piece. Playfulness, calmness and tranquillity, triumph and tragedy, blending sweet notes with discordant ones, so that by its end you had been taken on a journey that encompassed life in its entirety. Or at least that is what she imagined.

As usual, once she began, she was transported to another world, completely unaware of everything other than the music, her fingers moving as if by their own volition, creating a waterfall of notes that flowed one over the other. And as usual, when she finished, she still heard the music thrumming through her body and soul long after the notes died away. She was not given the time she liked to come back to herself before a round of applause more discordant than any note she had played made her eyes spring open.

She blinked. Everyone was on their feet, and Tinsley was openly weeping, even the footmen who were handing out drinks had paused to stare, Peter grinning so proudly that you would have thought her achievement his.

"Miss Drucilla," Freddie said, his voice breaking.

She turned her head and saw him seated but a few feet from her. His eyes were awash with tears and he suddenly lurched upwards only to fall on his knees before her. He took her hands in his. "Miss Drucilla, I have never given much thought to music, but you have opened my eyes. That was wonderful. You are wonderful. You touched something in me that I did not know existed. I am not worthy of you, but if you will consent to be my wife, I will strive every day to become so."

"Oh, Freddie," she said, returning his clasp. "You are more than worthy of me, indeed, any woman must feel herself fortunate indeed to become your wife."

"Drucilla," he said, but then paused, "Or should I call you Lucy?"

She laughed. "I thought I preferred Lucy, that by adopting a different name I could become someone different. But, Freddie, I was always Drucilla, and although I never liked the name, hearing it on your lips has changed my mind."

He got to his feet and pulled her up. "Then, Drucilla, would you do me the honour of becoming my wife?"

"Yes, of course, I will."

And then she was in his arms and his lips touched

hers in the lightest but most delicious of kisses. He pulled her closer, but another round of applause made her lean back. His glazed eyes stared into hers and she put her hand to his cheek. "Dearest Freddie, I think you may have forgotten we have an audience."

He turned his head and then smiled sheepishly. "So we have. Shall I send them away?"

She laughed, her eyes seeking her sister's. Abby came to her, holding out her hands. "Cilla, I am so happy for you."

"I know," she said.

"Congratulations, Miss Drucilla."

Sir Anthony had followed Abby.

"Thank you, sir."

He turned to Freddie and shook his hand. "Your timing was interesting, Ashton, but I am happy for you."

"Interesting?" Abby said. "It was the perfect timing. He saw my sister as she truly is, her inner self revealed to any with the wit to see it, sir. I am not surprised Mr Ashton was literally at her feet."

His eyes turned to Abby, their expression mocking. "Your sister is very talented, Miss Talbot. I wonder if you could match her performance."

Abby's eyes glinted. "Why should I wish to?"

He shrugged. "Are not all young ladies trained to play to impress a prospective bridegroom?"

Lucy blinked. What was he trying to achieve?

"As I am not seeking one, I feel the question is moot."

"Is it that you have no talent, or are you afraid that *you* will reveal something of yourself?"

Abby's eyes were dangerously bright. "I will not

attempt to match Cilla's performance, sir. You are correct in your assumption that I could not."

"We all have our particular talents, Sir Anthony," Lucy said. "You should not assume that because we look so similar they must be the same. I may be able to play well, but Abby outshines me when it comes to singing."

He smiled. "Then perhaps you can play so that your sister may sing."

Abby's eyes narrowed. "I shall sing, sir, but not for you. I will do it to honour Cilla's engagement."

"Thank you," Lucy said. "Shall we begin with *Where the bee sucks, there lurk I*?"

She was proud as her sister's clear voice filled the room. Abby had always loved to sing. She had used to say that it drove her frustration away. Her voice trilled and soared, the ballad simple but charming.

She curtsied and smiled as she received her applause, and then she threw Sir Anthony a challenging glance. He smiled and inclined his head.

"Are you satisfied, sir?"

"My appetite is merely whetted," he said. "I hope you have another song in your repertoire?"

She looked at him scornfully. "It is unlikely that I have but one."

Lucy launched into *The Joys of the Country*, wishing to lighten the mood with Charles Dibdin's comic song of ludicrous contradictions. Abby would enjoy singing such a daring piece, particularly as it poked fun at gentlemen.

Her voice trembled in surprise when halfway through the first line, Sir Anthony joined in. She recovered swiftly however, her chin rising a little. It had to be said that his baritone blended beautifully with Abby's voice. Lucy repressed a wince as Sir Anthony's rich tones briefly overpowered her sister's on the third and fourth lines of the first verse. *Where sweet is the flower that the maybush adorns, And how charming to gather it, but for the thorns.*

Glancing quickly up at her sister, she saw her cheeks were flushed, but her bright eyes sparkled with sudden amusement rather than anger. From that moment on they sang in perfect harmony, and they elicited several chuckles from their audience. The final verse poked fun at gentlemen becoming sotted and Abby's voice took on an ironic tone. Lucy noticed, however, that the singers regarded each other with mutual irony as they sang the lines; *Where in mirth and good fellowship always delighting, We agree, that is when we're not squabbling and fighting.*

When the song came to a close, the round of applause was resounding.

Sir Anthony smiled. "Well, spitfire, shall we cry friends?"

Abby tilted her head very much like Juniper had done earlier and Lucy held her breath.

"Why did you provoke me so?"

He smiled wryly. "I am not perfectly sure, but I did wish to hear you sing or play and my instincts told me that you would not at my request unless I, er, provoked you."

She laughed. "At least you are honest, sir."

"As are you, Miss Talbot. I will admit that you had some cause to be angry. I have been abroad these many years and have only recently returned. I had informed my father what I thought of his plans for us, and as it was he who made the agreement, I assumed he would pass on that knowledge to your father." His lips twisted. "I should not have relied on it, however, as he always was one to delay an unpleasant task. Please accept my apologies."

Abby's lips tilted. "Very well, sir, I accept."

CHAPTER 24

Dinner that evening was a lively, jolly affair. Many toasts were given to the betrothed couple, and Freddie was teased gently about his rather abrupt but heartfelt proposal.

"If it isn't just like you to get an idea in your head and act upon it immediately," Lady Kirkby said.

"But I did not," he protested. "The idea popped into my head at least an hour before."

This caused an outbreak of laughter, which became muted when he gazed at Drucilla, his eyes shining with a combination of love and amazement. "You have made me the happiest man alive. I can still hardly believe it."

Nor could he believe the answering look she gave him, so soft and affectionate, for it was precisely what he had never expected to see. It was how Lucinda gazed at Robert, and Winifred gazed at Oliver.

That night when he gave Drucilla her candle, he had the privilege of kissing her cheek. She smiled up at him, a delicate flush warming her cheeks.

"Goodnight, Freddie. Sleep well."

He had no doubt that he would, and that he would dream of her. As he walked the short distance to his chamber, the door into the nursery tower opened. Thomas appeared with Jacko beside him.

"Mr Ashton, sir, I think there is something you should see."

"Can it not wait until the morning?" he said. Every second wasted, was a moment not thinking of his beloved.

"No, sir. I don't think it can."

"Very well."

The large square room they entered was largely devoid of furniture, but a child-size chair and an old rocking horse spoke of its former use. Jacko climbed onto the horse and set it rocking.

"Over here, sir. Jacko found it."

Thomas went to the wooden stairs that led up to where the night nursery had once been. He climbed to the point where they turned the corner. Freddie suddenly knew what the footman was going to do.

"Wait," he said. "Come down. I will do it."

Thomas turned surprised. "You know of it?"

"I had forgotten, but I remember now."

He had been a mischievous little boy, and even more so after Lucinda had been born. He had not only liked to hide himself, but other things too. Thomas had found his secret hiding place. He had discovered it on the very day his parents had died.

The stair was narrower near the wall as it turned the corner, and the wooden tread was not quite flush. He slipped his finger under it and pushed. The tread slid into the riser above, revealing a hollow space. It was not large enough for a person or even a child, but it was the perfect place to hide things.

He held his candle over it and saw two black cases, one long, thin, and rectangular, the other square. He took them out and pulled the stair tread back into place. A chill raced down his spine, and he turned quickly and ran lightly down the stairs. He scooped Jacko off the horse.

"You go to bed, Thomas. I will take Jacko to my aunt."

He gave two sharp knocks on her door.

"Come in, Thomas. I am ready for Jacko now."

He went in.

"Ah, Freddie. How glad I am it is you. We can have a lovely talk about—" She stopped, registering the tense look on his face. "Freddie, what is it? Do not tell me you have had a falling out already? No, that can't be right. It would be very difficult to fall out with Drucilla, I think."

He placed the two black cases on the bed in front of her before setting Jacko down on his blanket at the end of the bed.

"What are these?" she said, opening the long, slender case first. She gasped and stared, incomprehension writ large on her face. "Freddie? How can this be?" She withdrew a beautiful emerald necklace.

Freddie recognised it from the painting of his parents that hung at Wirksworth Hall. He knew the other box would hold a matching pair of pendant earrings. "I hid them that day. I had found a place under the stairs in the nursery turret and thought it would be a good game."

"Oh, Freddie," she said, opening the square box.

"These were the only items that we thought taken that night."

He sat on the edge of the bed. "I know. Father must have disturbed the thieves before they had a chance to take anything."

Lady Wirksworth put her hand over his. "Well, I am glad you found them, for you will be able to pass them on to Drucilla." She cleared her throat. "Have you remembered anything else of that night?"

He shook his head.

"That is probably for the best. Now, Freddie, you have had a very exciting day. Do not let this surprise spoil it. It changes nothing, after all."

His smile was a little wan. "I will try not to. Goodnight, Aunt Seraphina."

It was easier said than done, for the reminder had taken some of his joy, and a vague feeling of disquiet made him reluctant to close his eyes. He felt certain the dream would come, and he did not wish it to. He wished to dream only of Drucilla. He called her sweet face to mind as his eyes became heavy.

When it came, the dream was very different and far worse than anything that had gone before.

He awoke in the dark, the full moon shining through his window. He wished to close the curtains, but he could not reach them. He went to the archway that separated his room from his sister's. Nurse would be sleeping next to Lucinda's crib. But she was not there, and neither was his baby sister. He went to the stairs. It was pitch black, but he put his hand on the wall and went carefully down. He went to his parents' room, but that too was empty. Fear began to snake through him. Where had everyone gone? He picked up a candle from the bedside and went out onto the landing.

He heard a scream. He hurried to the end of the corridor dropping the candle as he reached the stone steps of the corner antechamber. It went out. Dark surrounded him and his heart thumped in his chest. There was a faint light under the door to the long gallery.

"No!" His mother's voice.

He rushed to the door and opened it, stumbling into the room. A candelabra stood on a chest nearby sending flickering huge shadows over the opposite wall as his father wrestled with a man.

Another with a muffler pulled up over his face pointed a gun at his mother.

"Give the babe to me. I don't want to hurt her."

Freddie rushed to his mother, wrapping his arms about her and hiding his face in her skirts. She backed towards the opposite doorway.

"If you do not wish to hurt her, go away. You will not shoot me. You would be hung for murder."

"Only if I'm caught."

Freddie felt her hand on his head. "At least let my son go."

"I'm not interested in your son, only your daughter."

Her mother suddenly turned, making him stumble backwards. She put a hand on his arm and leant down, whispering, "Freddie, take your sister and hide. Do not come out until I come for you."

She gave him no time to answer, thrusting Lucinda into his arms. The man with the gun roared and Freddie ran, his breath coming in short gasps. Lucinda was strangely quiet in his arms. He had reached the chamber with the false fireplace when he heard the gunshot. He felt something warm trickling down his leg. He knew he could not climb up to the priest's hole with Lucinda in his arms. She was already so heavy. The sound of pounding feet on floorboards had him moving again. He entered the chapel tower and raced to the wardrobe. His hand trembled as he found the small knob that would make the panel slide. He had barely closed it before he heard the wardrobe door creak open. He held his breath, trying to stop the sob that threatened.

After a few minutes, he descended the stairs on his bottom and huddled at their base. It was cold and dark. Lucinda gave a faint cry and he put his crooked finger in her mouth for her to suck as he had seen his mama do.

His eyes snapped open. He was drenched in sweat. He sat up his eyes wide. The thieves had come to steal Lucinda. Fury gripped him, and he leapt from the bed, donned his dressing gown, and without pausing to light a candle, went to his aunt's room. She would be able to tell him if the thoughts racing through his mind were completely insane or not.

She was awake reading, as she so often was in the middle of the night. She put down the book and opened her arms.

"Oh, Freddie. You have remembered something. Come here and tell me all about it."

He sat on the bed and allowed her arms to envelop him. His anger made the words come out too fast, tumbling over each other, and it took some time for his aunt to grasp the fundamentals of his dream. He sat up, wiping at his eyes. Her face had gone grey, and he wondered if he should not have told her of it.

"It could only have been Roger Gaines who plotted such a heinous thing. I told you that he had come when Lucinda was but a few weeks old and asked that she be promised to his son. I had come for the birth, and so I was here at that time. I went back to Wirksworth a few weeks later."

"That was my thought," Freddie said. "But I could hardly credit it. It was a ridiculous plan. Why, anyone who sees us must know that we are siblings. How did they think they would get away with it?"

Lady Wirksworth wiped a tear from her cheek. "You must remember that at that time Lucinda had a shock of black hair and did not look at all like you."

"But to murder my parents!" he said. "Someone should pay! Bevis should pay!"

His aunt sighed. "But the current earl could have had nothing to do with it, Freddie. He was but a babe himself, and I do not think the men he sent meant murder.

"I have purposely never told you any details of that day because the doctor advised me against it. He thought that you might have seen something, and that if your brain chose to forget, it was better not to prompt any memories. But your nightmares have blighted your life to a certain extent, and when you decided to come here, I thought perhaps you might remember, and they would stop forever. But I never expected them to reveal this."

"Tell me the details now," Freddie said. "Where was our nurse?"

She patted the bed. "Come and lie down beside me and I will tell you all I know."

"Wait a moment," he said, returning to his room and pouring two measures of brandy.

"A very good idea," she said when he returned, taking the glass.

He tossed his off and settled beside her. "Go on."

"I was told that your mother had discovered nurse had given Lucinda a measure of laudanum because she was fractious, and she thought she might be teething, and it was not the first time she had done so. She sent her to the servants' wing and told her she must leave the next day.

"It was not uncommon for your mother to pace the long gallery when she was agitated. She was concerned that Lucinda was so still and quiet and had sent to Castleton for the doctor. Of course it took some time for him to arrive. He had barely stepped foot into the house when the shot was heard. By the time he reached the long gallery, your parents were dead, and the thieves had fled down the hidden stair. The servants were roused but they were nowhere to be found, and anyone who knows the paths and pack-horse trails through these hills would be able to easily escape detection.

"Your mother's dress was ripped, It appeared she had struggled with someone. It must have been the man you saw holding a gun. I imagine she was trying to give you time to hide, and it is entirely possible that the gun went off by accident. Your father had a nasty gash to the back of his head. He had fallen and hit it on a large chest. So, it seems his death may also have been an accident.

"You were found by Emma, Mrs Cooper as she is now. She knew of all your hiding places. It was assumed that you had been with them in the long gallery and hid to protect you both, and when the jewellery was found missing by your mother's maid, the whole was assumed to be a bungled robbery."

Freddie brought his knees up and rested his arms on them. "So they died just so the current earl could marry Lucinda. It seems so farfetched."

"It is, but I know how obsessed my father was, Freddie. I thought he had accepted that I would never marry Roger Gaines, but I was wrong. He said I must tell him myself and sent us for a walk. Roger tried to force himself on me."

"God's teeth! Do not say so!"

"But I do say so, and what is more, he would have succeeded if there had not been a large stone to hand for me to hit him over the head with. What is more, my father knew what he intended. They thought that if I were deflowered, I must agree. They were wrong, of course. I would have rather died in a ditch."

A sharp knocking came on the door.

"Come," Lady Wirksworth said.

The door opened to reveal Peter. "Thank heavens I've found you, Mr Ashton. I'm as sorry as I can be, but Miss Drucilla is gone!"

Panic clutched at Freddie's heart, and he pushed the footman out of the way and sprinted down the corridor. He did not hesitate to throw open Miss Talbot's door and tore through her room into Drucilla's chamber.

"Drucilla!" he cried.

When he discovered her bed empty, all rational

thought fled, and he went to the chimney and called her name again.

"Freddie?"

He whirled about and saw her standing in the doorway of her sister's room, rubbing her eyes. He flew to her and pulled her tightly against his chest.

"You are safe!"

"Why would I not be safe?"

"You were not in your bed!"

"No, I shared Abby's bed tonight, but I have a vague recollection of her getting out." She smiled bashfully. "I remember now, she said she would sleep in my bed because I kept saying your name in my sleep and she could stomach no more of it."

Freddie had not brought a candle, so the bed was in darkness.

"Abby?" she said, walking to it. "How can you sleep through Freddie's shouting?" She gasped. "She is not here."

A bobbing light came into view. Peter came in breathing heavily.

"Sir, I have woken Lord Kirkby and Sir Anthony. They are getting dressed and will meet you in the library."

"Where would she go?" Drucilla said. "She seemed to have accepted Sir Anthony."

"Do not worry, my love," Freddie said. "We will find her." Turning to Peter, he said, "I will dress immediately and then hear what you have to say for yourself."

By the time he arrived in the library, everyone was assembled, including all the ladies of the house.

Drucilla's skin was alabaster, and Lady Frampton held her hand.

"As there was no help for it, we have told them of our suspicions," Lord Kirkby said.

"You should have told us of them before," Lady Wirksworth snapped. "Did it never occur to you that we might have some ideas of our own on how to deal with this situation? No one knows better than I what that family is capable of."

"This is pointless," Sir Anthony said. "There is no time for recriminations. Peter, tell us what you know."

"I've kept an eye on Samuel as you said, sir. He's done nothing suspicious, and he has certainly not left the house. He wanted to take the letters to The Stag's Head in Edale this afternoon, but Mr Tinsley said Charles must go."

Sir Anthony looked around the room. "Have any of you written letters today?"

"I wrote one to a young friend of mine, Adrian Emmit, this morning," Freddie said.

"And I wrote to two of my friends before breakfast this morning," Lady Kirkby said.

"I also wrote to an old friend this morning," Lady Frampton said.

"I wrote to my brother," Drucilla said.

"So, it is entirely possible Samuel may have been able to send a communication of his own," Sir Anthony mused. "I doubt Charles would have examined all the missives. I assume Samuel is missing?"

"Yes," Peter said.

"Then I also assume he has somehow spirited Miss Talbot away. But how?"

"I don't know," Peter said. "I've set myself up in

the chapel tower to be near to Miss Drucilla, and not only did I make sure her door was locked before I turned in, but I locked the doors to the chapel tower so no one could come that way."

"What alerted you that something was amiss?" Sir Anthony asked.

"It was a bat, sir. I'd left my window open, and it flew right in. Anyway, as I was awake, I thought I'd check Samuel was where he should be. When he wasn't in his room, I came to check on Miss Drucilla. Her door was unlocked, and she was nowhere to be seen. So I sounded the alarm."

Sir Anthony frowned. "Was the door to the chapel tower still locked?"

Peter scratched his head. "Now you mention it, sir, it was. I had to unlock it to get to Miss Drucilla's room."

"So he could not leave that way."

"Miss Talbot's room was also unlocked," Freddie said.

"I locked it when we went to bed," Drucilla said quietly. "I am sure of that."

"So, it was unlocked from the inside. How did he get into Miss Drucilla's room?" Sir Anthony said.

"The priest hole in the chimney!" Freddie said. "He must have hidden there. All he had to do was wait until she was asleep and then come down."

Sir Anthony groaned. "Why on earth was I not told of it?" He shook his head. "It does not matter." He glanced at Drucilla. "Your sister is spirited; she would not have gone willingly. Did you hear anything? He must have had to go through your room to leave."

He grimaced when Drucilla shook her head.

"Once Abby left me, I fell into a very deep sleep."

Tinsley came into the room, his face grave. "I've checked the stables, and a carriage horse is missing. One of the coachmen thought he heard scratching noises about an hour ago, but he thought it was rats. Mr Brown at the gatehouse says the gates have been closed and barred all night. Nothing has passed that way."

Sir Anthony nodded. "Am I right in assuming there are trails in the hills behind the house that could take you over the mountain and down towards Castleton?"

"Yes," Lady Wirksworth said. "But even though there is a full moon, you would have to know the way very well."

"He is mad! Stark raving mad!" Freddie said. "He must know we will come after him."

Sir Anthony's jaw clenched. "I imagine he will have claimed his prize by then and thinks that will ensure Miss Talbot will marry him."

"But it is me he wants," Drucilla said. "Surely she will tell him he has made a mistake?"

"He won't believe her, and if he did, I am not sure he would care." He pressed his hands together in thought. "I have ridden through the mountains at night, and it is slow going. It is also cold out and Miss Talbot can be in little more than a nightgown. I do not think that is the plan. Is there another way he could make his way into the valley without going through the gates? It may be that Bevis is waiting in his carriage somewhere on the road."

"Yes," Lady Wirksworth said. "He can take a track behind the house up into the mountain, but it is not a direct route, and it will take him some time to get down into the valley again."

"Good," he said, rising to his feet. "As he cannot go more than a slow walk and will have to lead the horse down any steep slopes, that gives us a chance." He glanced at Lord Kirkby. "We need your curricle."

"Certainly."

"I took the liberty of informing your groom you might need your curricle, Lord Kirkby," Tinsley said. "I also had a carriage prepared to bring the young lady home."

"Freddie," Lord Kirkby said. "If you come with us, you must take the groom's seat."

"I shall," he said.

"And Drucilla and I shall go in the carriage," Lady Frampton said.

Lady Wirksworth went to Freddie and briefly hugged him, murmuring in his ear, "Remember, my dear, Bevis is only guilty of this crime."

Freddie's expression hardened. "It is enough."

CHAPTER 25

They saw no carriage in the valley and turned onto the hill. It had stopped raining hours ago, and although the road was not a quagmire, the rain having the valley to run into, it was muddy in places. As they turned the bend, they saw a horseless carriage tilted at an angle ahead. There was a flat grassy area on the opposite side of the road and the curricle pulled up on it. Freddie jumped down and ran across to the vehicle. After a brief inspection of the carriage, he returned.

"It looks like it slewed off the road a little and the back wheel was smashed by a rock."

Sir Anthony was examining the ground around the curricle. He straightened and pointed towards a stand of trees. "There are hoof marks going in that direction."

The carriage containing Lady Frampton and Drucilla pulled up behind the curricle and Freddie went to it. Drucilla pulled down the window, her face pale but composed.

"We have found a trail and shall follow it. Wait here. Under no circumstances follow us; there will be some rough work tonight and it may be dangerous."

He heard her soft gasp and briefly cupped her cheek in his hand. "Do not worry, my darling. I will bring your sister to you."

"I know," she said. "But, Freddie, be careful."

He nodded, ordered the coachman to turn the carriage so that no time would be lost when they returned and joined the others. They sprinted to the copse but lost the trail there, the moonlight barely filtering through the boughs. An owl hooted, and as if in response, the sound of a neigh carried on the breeze. It seemed to come from somewhere above them and to their left. There was no clear path, but they weaved through the trees in that direction, uttering muffled exclamations as they tripped on tree roots or stubbed their toes on concealed rocks.

"Over here," Sir Anthony called softly. "I have found an animal trail of some sort."

When they emerged from the trees the hill rose steeply for fifty yards before the track turned to their left. They followed it around a bend and saw the dark outline of a squat building a few hundred yards ahead. The glow of a candle illuminated a window. Soft whinnies carried clearly to them now.

"A shepherd's hut, I presume," Freddie said.

"There will be at least three men," Sir Anthony said softly. "The coachman, Samuel, and Bevis. I imagine the first two will be with the horses, and Bevis inside with Miss Talbot. Leave him to me."

"She is my responsibility," Freddie protested.

"No," he said sharply. "She is mine. I have been

betrothed to her for years, or at least she thought so. Have your pistols in easy reach but try to subdue them as bloodlessly as possible. Do not be restricted by any principles of honour, however; anyone involved in this nefarious business can have none."

Another whinny floated towards them.

"It sounds as if the horses are grazing somewhere on the far side of the hut. We will creep up to it and listen for voices to ascertain my theory is correct. When you act, it must be swiftly, but you need to know where to strike. You will have the advantage of surprise, use it well."

"Yes, Captain," Lord Kirkby said dryly. "I do not know where I'd be without such clear orders."

Sir Anthony flashed him a quick grin, but his eyes were glacial. "Old habits, Robert. Now, let us go."

When they reached the hut, they took up position to either side of the window, listening. They heard footsteps and then an irritable voice. Bevis's voice.

"I told you not to harm her, you idiot."

"An' I told you, sir. She woke as I was tying the gag and fought like a vixen. She tried to gouge my eyes out with her fingers, and I had no choice but to thump her. She should have woken up by now. I only hit her hard enough to stun her."

"Clearly you knocked her senseless, you dimwit."

A white-hot rage fired through Freddie's veins, and he began to move. He found his arm taken in a vice-like grip. Sir Anthony put his lips to his ear.

"Not yet. Wait until the footman leaves and you may deal with him then. And calm down; your anger needs to be ice not fire, or you will make a mistake. At least we know he has had no opportunity to violate her."

Freddie nodded and subsided against the wall of the cabin, sucking in a deep breath. He tensed as he heard a groan.

"Ah, she is coming to," Bevis said.

There was the sound of footsteps. "Here, drink this. It will clear your head."

Sir Anthony leant towards Lord Kirkby. "I do not think the coachman is there; look for him."

The viscount nodded and moved away into the darkness.

Silence, and then a small shriek. "Get away from me."

"Do not be afraid, Drucilla. I am your betrothed, after all. Anything that happens between us this night will merely cement that promise."

"Promise!" she spat out. "I made no promise."

"But your father did, and you must honour it," he said, his silky tone menacing.

"You are mad!" she said. "And I am not D… I am damned if I will have anything to do with you!"

Freddie's eyebrows rose. She had been about to inform him she was not Drucilla. Why hadn't she?

"I am afraid you will not have any choice in the matter. I will make you mine."

Freddie pushed away from the wall, but Sir Anthony held up his hand, mouthing the words *not yet*. He had expected Bevis's words to strike terror into Miss Talbot, but she gave a hard, mocking laugh.

"You are too late. Did you know your father insisted that I was examined to ensure I was chaste?"

"I did," he said. "But your father suffered his stroke and all that was put off."

"It was not put off!" she said fiercely. "My sister and I were forced to suffer the indignity of the doctor's examination. He failed to find proof that I was chaste because I am not. I have been defiled once before, sir, and I will not be again."

The gentlemen outside looked at each other, their eyes registering shock. Either she was a very good actress, or she spoke the truth.

"You lie!" Bevis said, his voice rising.

"I do not lie, and you forcing yourself on me will not ensure I marry you. I am already ruined." A half sob escaped her. "I can marry no one, for I will not tie anyone to me without telling them the truth, and who would have me then?"

"I will have you anyway," Bevis growled. "Get out, Samuel."

A door creaked. Sir Anthony grabbed Freddie's arm. "Go now, and do not fear. I will not be gentle with Bevis."

They ran. Sir Anthony to the door at the end of the hut, and Freddie into the darkness beyond. He saw Samuel a few feet in front of him. The footman turned just before he came upon him. Freddie threw a punch at his face, but Samuel blocked it with his arm.

"I shall look forward to watching you hang," Freddie bit out, aiming his next punch at his midriff.

The man grunted and retreated a few steps. He said nothing, his expression ugly, and Freddie understood his mistake. If he had not realised it before, Samuel now knew he was fighting for his life. Even as the thought crossed Freddie's mind, Samuel charged him, grabbing him around the waist and taking him to the ground. The breath was knocked from him, and the footman straddled him. He raised his arms as Samuel began raining punches about his head. Then he remembered his gun. His hand reached into his coat, and he felt the smooth, hard handle of the weapon. He realised it was too late, for even as he tugged at it, he saw the moonlight glint off the blade of a knife as it descended towards him.

There was a flash in the darkness and the sharp report of a gunshot. Instead of entering his chest, the blade sliced into the fabric of his coat at the shoulder as Samuel slid from him. Freddie rolled away.

"Thank you, Rob…"

He blinked, for it was not his brother-in-law who had saved him, but Drucilla. Her eyes were wide, and her arms still outstretched, one shaking hand holding a small pistol and the other supporting her wrist. Her dress was wet at the hem and torn in several places. As he rose, she ran towards him, burying her face in his shoulder.

"Oh, Freddie. I am sorry I went against your wishes but…"

His arms tightened about her, and a shaky chuckle escaped him. "I am rather glad you did, my avenging angel."

She pulled back and put her hand to her cheek, wiping at a smear of blood. She regarded her fingers and gasped. "You are injured."

"A veritable scratch thanks to you, my love. Your sister is in the hut and Sir Anthony has gone to rescue her. Stay here whilst I see if he needs any help."

But even as he turned towards it, Sir Anthony

strode out of the door, Abby in his arms wrapped in a blanket. They hurried over to them. Abby's eye was puffy, and a livid red mark stained the side of her face.

"Abby, oh, my dearest Abby," Drucilla said on a sob.

She managed a small smile. "I am not hurt, Cilla, or at least not very much." Her eyes dropped to the small pistol Drucilla still clutched in her hand. "You found my pistol. How I wished I had had it with me tonight. I carry it everywhere in my reticule."

"I dressed hastily in your room and took your reticule as I could not immediately find mine. I thought it a little heavy, but it was only when Lady Wirksworth gave me some smelling salts to put in it that I discovered its contents." She frowned. "Abby, I shot Samuel and think I have killed him. Not that I meant to of course, indeed, I had my eyes fast shut when I pulled the trigger."

"You have undoubtedly killed him," Lord Kirkby said, leading three horses towards them. "But he no doubt deserved it."

Lady Frampton came out of the darkness, her hand clutched to her side. "Oh, thank heavens, you have found her."

"I am quite all right, Aunt," Abby said.

"It is very brave of you to say so, but also foolish," Sir Anthony said. "I shall take you up before me on one of the horses, and we will get you to the carriage immediately."

"No," she said quickly. "I hate the smell of horses."

He glanced down at her intently. "Very well, then I shall carry you."

"What has happened to Bevis?" Freddie said, walking to the door. He turned back. "You have killed him." There was a certain grim satisfaction in his voice.

"He did," Abby said, glancing up at her rescuer, a grateful smile on her lips. "One punch was all it took."

Sir Anthony's smile was a little grim. "He hit his head on the corner of a table as he went down."

"How will we explain this?" Lord Kirkby said.

Sir Anthony frowned. "What happened to the coachman?"

"I found no one," Lord Kirkby said. "It appears Bevis drove the carriage himself which perhaps explains why he suffered an accident. I expect Samuel was to drive it back."

"Then we will do nothing. Release Bevis's horses; they must be found nearby. We were never here."

"Do you think you could stay on the horse if I put you on it and lead it, Lady Frampton?" Freddie said. "You look exhausted."

"Of course I can stay on the horse," she said tartly. "I was riding before you were born." She sighed. "Forgive me, Frederick. If I had not heard that shot, I would probably still be stumbling about in the dark. I am exhausted, and it is very thoughtful of you to realise it."

They had just reached the carriage when Freddie said, "Miss Talbot, why did you change your mind about revealing that you were not Drucilla?"

Her eyes widened. "You heard that?"

"Yes, we were outside waiting for Samuel to leave."

"What use would it have done?" she said. "Either

he would not have believed me, or he would have tried to take Cilla at another time." She licked her lips as if they were dry. "Mr Ashton, about the other thing that you heard. It was true, but it was another instance of us being in each other's rooms. Everything was just as it should have been with my sister."

"Miss Talbot, I do not doubt it, but it would not have mattered either way. Any man worth his salt would not blame a woman for what she could not help."

Abby smiled wanly. "You are a unique individual, sir."

Sir Anthony glanced down at her. "I beg to differ, Miss Talbot," he said, his voice gentle. "For I am in complete agreement with Ashton."

⁓

Drucilla sat next to her sister and found one of her hands beneath the blanket. "You are cold," she said.

"A little." Abby stroked her thumb over Drucilla's hand. "Dearest, I know that by allowing Lord Bevis to think I was you, I once again risked ruining your reputation, but I thought it would not matter. As you are to marry Mr Ashton, I thought any malicious rumour he might spread would be put down to sour grapes."

"And you were right," Drucilla said. "Do not give it a thought. But, Abby, I gained the impression that when Freddie said any man worth his salt would not blame a woman for what she could not help, he was talking of something other than—"

"You are correct," Abby said, leaning her head against the squabs and briefly closing her eyes.

"Leave any further explanations until later, Abigail," Lady Frampton said. "You must have a headache."

"I do," she acknowledged, "but I would rather talk about it. I already feel lighter now that my secret is out."

"Your secret?" Drucilla said.

Abby grimaced. "It seems that every time we swap bedchambers something untoward occurs. Do you remember that about a week before we left Glasbury Heights I asked you to sleep in my room and pretend to be me if Mrs Wardle came in?"

"Yes," Drucilla said.

Their governess had always checked on Abby before she retired for the evening, but rarely had she looked in on Drucilla, knowing that it was highly unlikely that the mouse-like girl who trembled when chastised would dare do anything to invite her wrath.

"I pretended to be asleep when she came, but I was quaking beneath the covers."

"But why did you ask it of her?" Lady Frampton said.

"Because I wished to have some fun. Milly, one of our maids, was going to a dance in a farmer's barn nearby. I persuaded her to lend me some of her clothes and take me with her."

"Abigail!" Lady Frampton gasped. "It was very wrong of you, and of Drucilla to play her part."

"Do not blame my sister," Abby said. "I could always make her do my bidding."

"That is true," Drucilla said. "But I did know it was wrong, perhaps even dangerous, and I should have had the resolution to refuse." She sighed. "But you were so miserable, and I disliked Mrs Wardle so much, that I went along with it anyway. You were sick for several days afterwards."

"Yes, sick in body and mind. I had a merry time of it, at first. The dances were so fast that by the time each one ended I was hot and thirsty. There was no lemonade but only cider, which I gulped down to quench my thirst. After an hour or two, I began to feel dizzy and was sure I was going to be sick. I went outside to get some air. I had danced with a groom earlier, and he followed me out. He grabbed me and started kissing me, and he only laughed when I tried to push him away. He pulled me into the field." She squeezed her eyes shut. "I felt far too ill to be able to offer any serious resistance, and he forced himself on me. He smelt of sweat and horse."

"Oh, my darling girl," Lady Frampton said, her voice tight with unshed tears.

"It was my own fault, I suppose," Abby said. "I should never have gone. I remember looking up at the stars. The sky seemed to be spinning, and then I was sick. Milly found me and took me home."

"Abby," Drucilla said fiercely, "it was not your fault. Your actions may have been unwise, but the groom's were unconscionable, despicable, and unforgivable."

"That is true," Lady Frampton said.

"Is that why you set your sights on Freddie?" Drucilla asked.

"Yes. I would not have married any man without telling the truth, and I thought he just might be able to forgive my not being pure."

"And you have now discovered that he would have

but, Abby, you have discovered that Sir Anthony is also capable of such kindness."

Abby smiled wryly. "So I have, but he does not wish to marry me either."

Lady Frampton snorted. "I would not be quite so sure of that, my girl. If he does not yet, he might discover before too long that he does. The way he cradled you in his arms and looked at you when he told you it did not weigh with him, were not the actions of a disinterested man. He might be the very one for you. He will not allow you to ride roughshod over him, but he will stimulate you, spar with you, and protect you."

~

A week later.

Freddie had come to a decision. He walked beside Drucilla in the garden. He had told her everything. Although Aunt Seraphina and he had agreed that there was nothing to be gained by informing Lucinda of the truth of the night their parents had died, he would not hide anything from his future wife. All their joys and sadnesses would be shared. They would be true companions.

"Would you mind very much if I sold Ashton Manor?" he said.

She smiled up at him. "I would not mind in the least. Indeed, I think you very wise. The happy memories you have recovered will always be with you wherever you are, and I hope that the horrid ones will fade in time. But I think you will always be reminded of that night when you are here."

"Yes," he said. "So do I. And I think being here would always remind you of what happened to your sister and—"

"I know what you mean. I killed a man, Freddie, and I cannot be sorry for it because if I had not, he would have killed you. But when I close my eyes, I do sometimes see that knife coming towards you."

They stopped before the archway into the rose garden and he took her hands.

"Dearest Drucilla, we will make so many happy memories together that the bad ones will be driven out."

She smiled. "Do you know my brother said something very similar. I never wished to go back to Talbot Hall, but now you are to come with me, I find I do not mind so very much after all. He will be so happy for us."

"Not as happy as I am," Freddie said, leaning down and touching his lips to hers.

When she sighed and leant into him, he deepened the kiss, breaking away some minutes later, light-headed and giddy.

"Drucilla," he said, his voice a little hoarse, "I cannot wait to make you my wife."

She stood on tiptoe and kissed him lightly. "And I cannot—"

She broke off abruptly as voices came from the other side of the hedge. She giggled. "Freddie," she whispered, "we very nearly got caught kissing again. It will not do. It would be the fifth time this week."

He leant down and murmured in her ear. "I do not care in the least."

The voices came again, louder this time.

"It is Abby," Drucilla said softly. "She is alone with Sir Anthony *again*. And they are arguing *again*."

"I am not being contrary!"

Freddie chuckled. "Shall we break up their tête-à-tête?"

She shook her head.

"You say you would like the freedom that men have, and whilst you *cannot* and will *never* be admitted into gentlemen's clubs or be able to directly affect any of the laws of this country, you can learn to ride! Abby, you would so enjoy the feeling of freedom galloping over the countryside gives you."

Drucilla's eyebrows rose. "He called her Abby," she whispered.

Freddie grinned.

"You are being unreasonable, Anthony," she grumbled. "You know why I am afraid of horses."

"Fears must be faced and conquered," he said. "I did not think you so cow-hearted."

"Oh, you… you beast. You know that I am not."

"Perhaps we should return to the house," Lucy whispered. "It is not polite to eavesdrop."

But Sir Anthony's next words stilled her.

"Are you afraid then to be kissed?"

There was a moment's silence, and Abby's answer when it came was uncertain.

"I do not know."

Sir Anthony's voice gentled. "Would you like to find out?"

Another silence.

"I thought so," he said. "Utterly cow-hearted."

"Very well," she snapped. "But if you make me gag, do not blame me."

"I will not," he said softly.

A much longer silence.

"Oh," Abby sighed.

"Well? Give me your verdict."

"Why?" she said breathlessly. "Do you need your prowess to be trumpeted?"

He laughed. "My prowess? How flattering."

"I did not mean to flatter you. I am sure if one does something often enough, one must become accomplished at it."

"How true," he said. "And you, Mistress Prickles, are definitely in need of some practise."

There was a gasp and another silence.

Freddie looked down at Drucilla. "Fairbrass has some dashed good ideas," he murmured, pulling her into his arms.

Sir Anthony's deep, husky voice recalled them to themselves.

"Abby, my contrary, brave, sharp-tongued thorn in my side. You have my heart in the palm of your hand. You have since the moment I saw you standing so proudly before me. Will you do me the honour of becoming my wife? Will you walk through life by my side, not as my possession but as my true companion?"

Freddie put an arm about his betrothed and offered her his handkerchief. Drucilla's sob was drowned out by Abby's.

"Oh, Anthony. Anthony!"

As another silence ensued, Freddie took his love's hand and led her back towards the house.

ALSO BY JENNY HAMBLY

Thank you for your support! I do hope you enjoyed True Companions. If you would consider leaving a short review on Amazon, I would be very grateful. I love to hear from my readers and can be contacted at: jenny@jennyhambly.com

Other books by Jenny Hambly

Belle – Bachelor Brides 0

Rosalind – Bachelor Brides 1

Sophie – Bachelor Brides 2

Katherine – Bachelor Brides 3

Bachelor Brides Collection

Marianne - Miss Wolfraston's Ladies Book 1

Miss Hayes - Miss Wolfraston's Ladies Book 2

Georgianna - Miss Wolfraston's Ladies Book 3

Miss Wolfraston's Ladies Collection

Allerdale - Confirmed Bachelors Book 1

Bassington - Confirmed Bachelors Book 2

Carteret - Confirmed Bachelors Book 3

Confirmed Bachelors Books 1-3

Ormsley - Confirmed Bachelors Book 4

Derriford - Confirmed Bachelors Book 5

Eagleton - Confirmed Bachelors Book 6

Confirmed Bachelors Books 4-6

What's in a Name? - Residents of Ashwick Hall Book 1

ABOUT THE AUTHOR

I love history and the Regency period in particular. I grew up on a diet of Jane Austen and Georgette Heyer.

I like to think my characters though flawed, are likeable, strong and true to the period.

I live by the sea in Plymouth, England, with my partner, Dave. I like reading, sailing, wine, getting up early to watch the sunrise in summer, and long quiet evenings by the wood burner in our cabin on the cliffs in Cornwall in winter.

Printed in Great Britain
by Amazon